THUSS, L

GOING LOCO

GOING LOCO

Lynne Truss

review

Copyright © 1999 Lynne Truss

The right of Lynne Truss to be identified as the Author of
the Work has been asserted by her in accordance with the
Copyright, Designs and Patents Act 1988.

First published in 1999
by REVIEW

An imprint of Headline Book Publishing

10 9 8 7 6 5 4 3 2 1

British Library Cataloguing in Publication Data

Truss, Lynne
Going loco
I.Title
823.9'14 [F]

ISBN 0 7472 2157 X (hardback edition)
ISBN 0 7472 7374 X (printed papercase edition)

Printed and bound in Great Britain by
Clays Ltd, St Ives plc.

Set in Centaur 11.5/14
by Palimpsest Book Production Limited,
Polmont, Stirlingshire

Headline Book Publishing
A division of Hodder Headline PLC
338 Euston Road
London NW1 3BH

To Mum, who never had the choice

Part One

Chapter One

Since being the heroine of her own life was never quite to be Belinda's fate, we may as well begin with Neville. Belinda was a real person, while Neville was an imaginary rat with acrobatic skills; but since he inhabited the pit of her stomach, their destinies were inextricable. Since Christmas, at least, they had started each day together, and if either performed an action independently – well, neither knew nor cared. Belinda would wake, and at the first choke of anxiety concerning the day to come, Neville commenced preliminary tumbling. Belinda clutched her throat; Neville donned a body stocking and tested his trampoline. It was pretty alarming sometimes, a bit too vivid, especially for someone who had never been particularly drawn to the romance of the Big Top. But she had no control over it. By the time Belinda was dressed and committed to the beat-the-clock panic that seemed to have become her waking life, Neville was juggling flaming brands on a unicycle and calling authentic acrobat noises such as 'Hup!' and 'Hip!' and 'Hi-yup!'

Belinda did once mention Neville to Stefan, but since her husband's own alimentary canal had never been domicile to a rat in spangles, he didn't know how to react. Being a clever Swedish person, he was eager to learn new idioms, new English phrases, which was why Belinda sometimes gambled that he

3

might understand something emotionally foreign to him as well. But when Belinda complained, 'And now I've got a rat in my stomach,' he had merely looked up from his book, sighed a bit, and turned down the volume on *Abba: Gold*.

'A rat?' he queried. 'This is a turned-up book.'

'Mm,' she agreed.

They listened to Abba for a bit. Stefan mouthed the words. Perhaps under the influence of the song, Belinda found herself staring at the ceiling, wishing she were somewhere else instead.

His scientific mind slid into gear. 'What sort of rat? *Rattus norwegicus?*'

'I don't think so,' she said. No, the name Neville had no ring of Scandinavia. 'He's more of an acrobatic rat. In tights. With a high wire and parasol.'

Stefan gave her one of his steady, serious smiles; she broke the gaze, as always, by pulling a silly face, because its intensity scared her.

'You're working too hard,' he said, quietly. 'Jack is a dull boy, I think.'

'I know, I know. *Of course I am.* That's what I'm trying to tell you.'

'So why do you invent a rat? Why not say, "Stefan, my old Dutch, help. I'm working my trousers to the bone, but I just can't beat the clock"?'

Belinda pouted. 'I don't think I did invent him. I can feel him doing back-flips.'

Abba started singing 'The Name of the Game'. Stefan turned up the volume again.

At which point Neville walked on his front paws through her intestinal tract, gripping a beach-ball between his back feet.

'Ta-da!' he cried.

A couple of things need to be made clear about Belinda Johansson. First, she was not Swedish (obviously). Second, she was under the rather hilarious illusion that she had a hard life, when in fact she had an enviable existence as a freelance literary critic and creative writer in some demand, living in one of the better bits of South London. And third, if she saw an abandoned sock on the bathroom floor, she would glare at it defensively rather than pick it up and sling it into a laundry bag.

This last tendency may not sound too bad, but as any slattern can attest, neglected balled-up socks have a talent for embodying reproach. 'I'm still here,' the sock will tell you, in an irritating sing-song tone, on your next five visits to the bathroom. 'I'm going crusty now. And I believe I missed the wash on Sunday morning.' Belinda's healthy intelligence would not allow her to be browbeaten by mouldy hosiery, which was why she wouldn't stoop to silencing its reproaches by simply tidying it up. But add this insinuating sock to the pile of attention-seeking newspapers in the kitchen ('We're still here too, lady!'), the ancient wine corks accumulating fluff and grease ('Remember us?'), and the deadline for her latest potboiler ('Tuesday, or else'), plus the pressure on her long-term book on literary doubles ('You bitch! I can't do it on my own!') and you begin to understand why Belinda was giving house room to the rat. The deadlines alone she might have managed. It was the cacophony of reproach from all fucking directions in this fucking, fucking house that she couldn't tolerate much longer. It's sad but true that, had Belinda's DNA not tragically lacked the genetic code for basic household organization, none of the following story need have taken place.

You couldn't feel sorry for her, and nobody did. Many women had more responsibilities than Belinda, with considerably fewer advantages. At the nice age of thirty-six, she lived in a nice, large Victorian villa in Armadale Road, Battersea, with a nice, rather entertaining Swedish husband she'd met well into her thirties. Her work was nice, too — compiling a serious literary book alongside more lucrative horsy stuff for girls. On this Monday morning in February she was about to deliver *A Rosette for Verity* and collect three thousand pounds. The Swede was a senior scientist, so the Johanssons had money. Only Stefan's habit of perusing *Over-reach Your English for Foreigners* on the toilet each morning could be seen as a cause of strain.

Unfortunately, however, the justice of Belinda's complaints was not the point. The point was, her body was a twenty-four-hour adrenaline pumping station. And at the time this story starts, Belinda's behaviour was deteriorating badly. She had caught herself waving two fingers at the postman from behind the curtains, just because he innocently delivered more post. 'Take it away,' she yelled. 'Don't bring it, take it away!' A magazine editor had rung up with the offer of a laughably easy horse-tackle column (she'd coveted it for years), and instead of saying, 'That's great!', she'd barked, 'Do you think I just sit here with my thumb up my bum waiting for you to ring? Get a life, for God's sake.' At the supermarket, she had rammed her trolley into that of a dithering pensioner, saying, 'Look, have you got a job?' In short, the flight-or-fight mechanism Nature gave Belinda for emergencies had gone horribly haywire, as if someone had removed the knob, and lost it.

Stefan would tell her to take off the weight, or hang loose. Stefan was one of those people who has a regular job – or even, in recidivist lapses, a 'yob' – who attends college in office hours, and comes home in the evening to relax. In about fifteen years, he would retire. True, a certain amount of research was required of him, but it was no skin off his nose, as he was proud of remarking. Why Belinda made such a meal of things, he didn't know.

So things came to a head in that pleasant suicide month of February, on a Monday morning. Belinda was racing out of her agreeable house at nine thirty-five for a ten a.m. train from Clapham Junction, and there was (for once) the faintest chance she would make it. She felt terrible, afflicted by a painful and humiliating dream in which she had punched Madonna on the nose for hijacking her car, only to discover that the passengers were all disabled children. This was not the sort of dream to be dislodged easily. The children had waved accusing crutches at her through the car windows, and though she'd grovelled to Madonna, she'd woken unforgiven and felt like a murderer.

Meanwhile, the manuscript of *A Rosette for Verity* had done its usual job of transmogrifying into a bowling ball in her shoulder-bag. She was brushing her hair with one hand and fumbling for bus-fare with the other, and Neville was helpfully practising trapeze. 'Steady on, Neville,' she muttered absently. And then the telephone rang in the hall.

'Oh bugger,' she said, as the phone trilled. Oh no. She flailed about, as if caught in quicksand. Here she was, late already, hair not dry, feeling sick with guilt about the poor crippled kiddies, and wearing a strange fashionable black slidy nylon coat she'd allowed her mother to buy her, which made her feel like an impostor.

'Ring-ring,' it said, as she passed.

'Nope,' she told it.

'Ring-ring,' it persisted. *'Remember me?'*

So she snatched up the receiver and answered the phone. Why? Because life's like that. It's a rule. The later you are, the less time you can give to it, the more vulnerable you are to far-fetched misgivings. What if it's the publisher phoning to cancel? Or Stefan with his head caught in some railings? All her life, Belinda's idea of an emergency was someone with their head caught in some railings.

'Hello?'

A high-pitched male voice with an Ulster accent. A friendly voice, but nobody she knew.

'May I speak with Mrs Johnson, please?'

'Johansson,' she corrected him automatically, shooting a despairing glance at the hall clock. Why did cold-callers always waste time assuming you aren't the person they've phoned? She gritted her teeth. Before catching the train she needed to buy some stamps, renew her road tax, phone a radio producer and touch up chapter three, because she'd just remembered the bay gelding of Verity's chief rival Camilla had emerged from a three-day event as a chestnut mare. Perhaps he had got something caught in some railings. Dramatically (and distractingly) Neville swung back and forth in a spotlight, with no safety-net, accompanied by a drum-roll. Meanwhile her bag slid off her shoulder with a great *whump*, as if to say, 'Well, if we're not going out, I'll stop here.'

'Hello Mrs Johnson, my name is Graham, and I work for British Telecom. We recently sent you some details of new services. I wonder, is this a good time to talk?'

'Hah!'

Belinda gave a hollow laugh and started to fill this annoying wasted time by hoisting her bag from under the hall table – the area Stefan cheerfully called the Land That Time Forgot About. Heaps of stuff made a big tangly nest under here, even though Belinda had frequently begged Mrs Holdsworth just to chuck it all out. She looked at it now, and it said, 'Ooh, hello, remember us?' rather excitedly, because it didn't get the chance as often as the socks in the bathroom or the newspapers in the kitchen. Weekly free news-sheets and fluff in lumps mingled with Stefan's favourite moose-hat, and some spare coat buttons. Three empty Jiffy-bags bled grey lunar dust over a novelty egg-timer, a bottle of Finnish vodka, a CD of the 1970s Malmö pop sensation the Hoola Bandoola Band, and an ice-hockey puck. And there among it was a single white envelope bearing the symbol of registered post. 'Sod it,' she said, as she stretched to reach it.

'This is Graham from BT,' the man reminded her. 'Is this a good time to talk?'

She looked at the clock again: ten forty-three. This envelope clearly contained the cash-card she'd argued about with the bank. 'You never sent it!' she'd said. 'But you signed for it!' they replied. And here it was, saying, 'Remember me?' In her stomach, Neville started calling other rats for an acrobatic display – 'Yip!' 'Hoopla!' 'Hi-yip!' From the way their weight was shifting around, they had started to form the rodent equivalent of the human pyramid. She felt compelled to admire their ingenuity. It felt as though they'd acquired a springboard.

'Look, I've got to go. This isn't convenient.'

Graham made a sympathetic noise, but did not say goodbye. Instead, he asked, 'Perhaps you could suggest a more convenient time in the next few days?' It was a routine phone-sales question, but it unleashed something. Because suddenly Belinda lost control.

It was because he had asked her to think ahead, perhaps. That's what did it. Normally she went through life as if driving in the country in the dark, just peering to the end of the headlights and keeping her nerve. But daylight revealed the total landscape. 'A more convenient time in the next few days'? Her lip quivered. She considered the next few days, a vision of the M25 choked with cones and honking, with nee-naws – of appointments and deadlines and VAT return and, and – and started to sniff uncontrollably.

Damn this bloody rushing about. *Sniff.* Damn this fucking life. *Sniff, sniff.* She'd had a big argument about this letter, and why had it been unnoticed on the floor? Why? Because there was no time to Hoover this fluff or to clear these papers. Because there was no time to sack Mrs Holdsworth for her incompetence. No time to sew buttons on, or build a nice display cabinet for moose-hats, listen with full attention to Hoola Bandoola with a Swedish dictionary, or get to the bottom of the ice-hockey puck once and for all.

There was never any time, and it wasn't fair. She glanced

into the kitchen, where the table was heaped with unpaid bills, diaries. On each of the stairs behind her was a little pile of misplaced items tumbled together (foreign money with holes in, nail scissors, receipts). If items had human rights, the UNHCR would be down on Belinda like a ton of bricks. On the wall above the phone was a handsome blue-tinted postcard of the Sussex Downs with a serene quotation from Virginia Woolf: 'I have three entire days alone – three pure and rounded pearls.' Stefan had given it to her 'as a yoke'. She saw it now, and in an access of Bloomsbury envy familiar to every other working female writer of the twentieth century, Belinda simply broke down and sobbed.

'Mrs Johnson?'

Belinda made a wah-wah sound so loud it shocked her. She wiped her nose with the back of her hand, and then, at a loss, wiped the back of her hand on mother's glossy coat – which was of a material, alas, designed specifically not to absorb mucal waste.

No one would understand what a bad moment this was. Belinda was not the sort of person who bursts into tears. In times of stress, she simply increased adrenaline production while Neville ran a three-ring circus. She didn't cry. Stefan hated cry-babies. His imitation of his first wife's cry-baby mode ('Wah, wah! I'm so unhappy, Stefan!') was quite enough to put anybody off.

'Perhaps you would like some time?' Graham persisted. 'I can tell you don't have time right now.'

'No, I don't have any time,' whimpered Belinda.

'Shall I give you a couple of days?'

Silence. A sniffle.

'Mrs Johnson, would you like a couple of days?'

At which point, Belinda sank to the floor again, to sit flat on her bum and sob. 'Would I like [sniff] a couple of—?' A loud, helpless wah-wah was coming down the phone.

'Have you got a tissue, Mrs Johnson?' Graham asked, gently.

'Jo-hansson!' she sobbed.

'I'll give you a couple of days.'

Belinda struggled to her feet, dragging her bowling ball towards her.

'Give me three pure and rounded pearls, Graham. What I want' – she sniffed noisily – 'is three pure and rounded pearls.'

You shouldn't dislike Belinda. She had a great many redeeming features. She knew lots of jokes about animals going into bars, for example. But clearly she had a big problem negotiating the routine pitfalls of everyday existence.

'It's a control thing,' her friend Maggie said (Maggie, an actress, had done therapy for thirteen years). 'You want total control. You somehow think an empty life is the ideal life, and a full life means it's been stolen by other people. You think deep down that everything in the universe – including your friends, actually – exists with the sole malevolent purpose of stealing your time.'

'Oh, I see,' said Belinda. 'And is this the five-minute insult or the full half-hour?' But secretly she was aghast. The description was spot-on. Mags was right: even this short conversation now required to be added to the day's total of sadly unavoided interruptions.

The first thing she'd noticed about Stefan was that he smiled a lot, especially for a Scandinavian. He was solemn, and said rather peculiar things, like 'A nod is as good as a wink' and 'That's all my eye and Betty Martin', when first introduced, but he smiled even at jokes about animals in bars, which was encouraging. They had met three years ago in Putney at her friend Viv's, at a Sunday lunch, where they had been seated adjacently by their hostess, with an obvious match-making intent. Belinda resented this at first, and almost changed places. Viv had an intolerable weakness for match-making. In a world ruled by Vivs, happy single people would be rounded up and shot.

But she took to Stefan. He was recently divorced, and recently arrived in London to teach genetics at Imperial College. He was solvent, which counted for a lot more than it ought to. Tall, blond, slender and a bit vain, he wore surprisingly fashionable spectacles for a man of his age (forty-eight at the time). Of course, he wasn't perfect. For a start, middle-of-the-road music was a passion of his life, and he would not hear a word spoken against Abba. He idolized *Monty Python*, played golf as if it were a respectable thing to talk about, and was proud of driving a fast car. A couple of times he told stories about his mentally ill first wife, which struck Belinda as cruel. Also, he was condescending when he explained his work on pseudogenes. Like most specialists, she decided, he muddled reasonable ignorance with stupidity.

But basically, Belinda fancied him straight away, and had an unprecedented urge to get him outside and push him against a wall. In the one truly Lawrentian moment of her life, she felt her bowel leap, her thighs sing and her bra-straps strain to snapping. Having been single for seven years at this point, she knew all too well that she must act quickly – a specimen of unattached manhood as exotic and presentable as Stefan Johansson would have an availability period in 1990s SW15 of just under two and a half weeks. Her biological clock, long reduced to a muffled tick, started making urgent 'Parp! Parp!' noises, so loud and insistent that she had to resist the impulse to evacuate the building.

The lunch was half bliss, half agony, with Stefan dividing his attention between Maggie and Belinda, and finding out whose biological clock could 'Parp' the loudest. Perhaps his understanding of natural selection contributed to this ploy. Either way, Belinda – who had never competed for a man

– was so overwhelmed by the physical attraction that she contrived to get drunk, make eyes at him, and (the clincher) ruthlessly outdo Maggie at remembering every single word of 'Thank You for the Music' and the Pet Shop Sketch.

'Lift home, Miss Patch?' he'd asked her breezily, when this long repast finally ended at four thirty. She'd known him only four hours, and already he'd given her a nickname – something no one had done before. True, he called her 'Patch' for the unromantic reason of her nicotine plasters; and true, it made her sound like a collie. But she loved it. 'Miss Patch' made her feel young and adorable, like Audrey Hepburn; it made her feel (even more unaccountably) like she'd never heard of sexual politics. 'Lift home, Miss Patch?' was, to Belinda, the most exciting question in the language. Soon after it, she'd had her tongue down his throat, and his hands up her jumper, with her nipples strenuously erect precisely in the manner of chapel hat-pegs – as Stefan had whispered in her ear so astonishingly at the time.

And now here they were, married, and Belinda was having this silly problem with the El Ratto indoor circus; and Maggie could decipher plainly all the selfish secrets of her soul, and she'd burst into tears like a madwoman talking to a complete stranger on the phone because he offered her big fat pearls but didn't mean it. However, Stefan was still smiling because (as she had soon discovered) he always smiled, whatever his mood. He had told her that he was known in academic circles as the Genial Geneticist from Gothenburg.

'So what did your masters think of *Verity's Rosette*?' he asked. It was Monday evening, and they were loading the dishwasher to the accompaniment of 'Voulez Vous'.

'*A Rosette for Verity*? They'll let me know. We discussed the idea that she might break her neck in the next book and be all brave about it, but I said, "No, let's do that to Camilla." *Six Months in Traction for Camilla* – what do you think?'

13

He smiled uncertainly. 'You are yoking?'

'A bit, yes.'

'You remember we visit Viv and Yago tomorrow?'

'We do?' she said. 'Damn. I mean, great.'

'Maggie will be there, too. Maggie is a good egg, for sure. I want to tell her she was de luxe in the play by Harold Pinter. Mind you, no one could ever accuse Pinter of gilding the lily, I think.'

'Shall we watch telly tonight? *The Invasion of the Body Snatchers* is on.'

Although she was really desperate to get on with some work, she felt guilty about Stefan, and regularly made pretences of this sort. Hey, let's just curl up on the sofa and watch TV like normal people! She fooled nobody, but felt better for the attempt. The trouble was, whenever she felt under pressure, she had the awful sensation that Stefan was turning into a species of accusatory sock. Besides which, it was nice watching television with him, and cuddling. She always enjoyed those interludes with Stefan when they didn't feel the need to speak.

'Don't you want to work?'

'Well, I—'

He smiled.

'You have been Patsy Sullivan today, all day?' (Patsy Sullivan was her horsy pseudonym.) 'Then you must work yourself tonight.'

'Are you sure? It's just, you know, it's February, and the book is due in October. And I feel this terrible pressure of *time*, Stefan. And I've got fifty-three *Verity* fan letters in big handwriting to answer. I have to pretend to the poor saps that I live on a farm with dogs and stuff. And I've got to go and see saddles tomorrow in Barnet. Do you know the line of Keats — "When I have fears that I may cease to be, before my pen has glean'd my teeming brain"?'

Stefan thought about it. 'No, I don't know that. But it sounds like you.' He turned to go, then stopped. 'So I shall look forward to tomorrow night. Now just tell me about Yago and Viv. Why is it that whenever I perorate in their company, they react as though I have dropped a fart?'

This was difficult to answer, but she managed it.

'They're scared of you, Stefan. It's scary, genetics. There you sit, knowing all about the Great Code of Life, and all Viv and Jago know about is Street of Shame gossip and the *Superwoman Cook Book*. It's a powerful thing, knowing science in such company.'

'In the land of the blind, the one-eyed man is king?'

'Exactly.'

'I have got bigger fish to fry?'

'That's it.'

Belinda was glad she'd reassured him. She decided not to mention the fart. 'Even I'm scared of you, a bit,' she said, squeezing his arm and looking into his lovely eyes. They were like chips of ice, she thought.

'Oh, Belinda—' he objected.

'No, it's true. I sometimes think you could unravel my DNA just by looking at me. And then, of course, you could knit me up again, as someone else with different sleeves and a V neck.'

Belinda envied the way Stefan's work fitted so neatly into the time he spent at college. She imagined him now with enormous knitting needles, muttering, 'Knit one, purl one, knit one, purl one,' in a loud, clacky room full of brainy blokes in lab coats all doing the same, trying to finish a complicated bit (turning a heel, perhaps) before the bell rang at five thirty.

People were always telling Belinda that genetics was a sexy science, but Stefan said it was harmless drudgery – and she was happy to believe him. Clueless about the nitty-gritty, she just knew that his research involved things called dominant and recessive genes. 'So some genes are pushy and others are pushovers, and the combination always causes trouble?' she'd once summed it up. And he'd coughed and said gnomically, 'Up to a point, Lord Copper.'

At that momentous Sunday lunch, she had not told him much about her own work. As she discovered later, Swedes don't ask personal questions; they consider it ill-mannered. But she had told him about Patsy Sullivan, and made him laugh describing the horsy adventures. However, the time she regarded as daily stolen from her had nothing to do with her desire to write about red rosettes for handy-pony. It wasn't time she wanted for 'herself', either. Magazines sometimes referred to women making time for 'themselves', but driven by her Keatsian gleaning imperative, Belinda had absolutely no idea what it meant. 'Make time for yourself.' Weird. Chintzy wallpaper probably had something to do with it. Long hot baths. Or chocolates in a heart-shaped box.

Thus, if well-intentioned people chose to flatter Belinda in a feminine way, it just confused her. 'Buy yourself a lipstick,' Viv's mother had said during her university finals, giving her a five-pound note. But the commission had made her miserable. She'd hated hanging around cosmetics counters with this albatross of a fiver when she could have been revising the Gothic novel in the library. Belinda's revision timetable had been incredibly impressive, and very, very tight. Only when Viv absolved her with 'Buy some pens, for God's sake,' did she race off happily and spend it.

Yes, for someone who lived so much in her head, it was an alien world, that feminine malarkey. Luckily the other-worldly Stefan didn't mind too much, but Belinda's well-coiffed mother despaired of her, and left copies of books with titles like *Femininity for Dummies* lying around in her daughter's house. Yet even as a teenager Belinda had flipped through all women's magazines in lofty, anthropological astonishment, amazed at the ways contrived by modern women to occupy their time non-productively. Facials, for heaven's sake. Leg-waxing. Fashionable hats. Stencils.

16

From this you might deduce that Belinda's secret personal work was of global importance. But she was just writing a book called *The Dualists*, a grand overview of literary doubles through the ages. Being Patsy half the time had given her the idea. 'Like Dr Jekyll and Mr Hyde,' she explained, when people looked blank. 'Or like me and Patsy Sullivan.' But if she implied that she took the subject lightly, she certainly didn't.

In fact, like most areas of study, the closer you got to the literary double, the more importantly it loomed; the more it demonstrated links with life, the universe, everything, even genetics and photocopying. Abba impersonators, Siamese twins, *Face/Off* – the world was full of replicas. And why was the genre so popular? Because everyone believes they've got an alternative, parallel life – in Belinda's case, perhaps, the ideal existence of that unregenerate toff Virginia Woolf, with her pure and rounded pearls. This parallel life was just waiting for you to join it, to stop fannying about. Every time you made a choice in life, another parallel existence was created to demonstrate how your own life could have been. Surely everybody felt that? Surely everybody looked in the mirror and thought, That's not the real me. It used to be, but it's not now. Surely everyone measured themselves against their friends? Especially these days, when everyone was so *busy*?

Either way, for the past three years, between all the demands of Patsy and socks (and Stefan), Belinda had left unturned not a single existential book in which a malevolent lookalike turned up to say, 'I'm the real you. And hey, you're not going to like what I've been doing!' Her office, formerly the dining room, was heaped with books and notes. She had become an expert on the dark world of Gogol and Dostoevsky, Nabokov, Stevenson and Hogg. Name any writer who shrieked on passing a reflective shop window, and Belinda was guaranteed to have a convincing theory about the personal crisis that conjured up his story, and summoned his double to life.

Oh yes, the nearer you stood to the literary double, the more (spookily) it told you universal truths of existence. Unfortunately for Belinda, she could never quite appreciate that the further you stood back from the literary double (as all her friends effortlessly did), the more it resembled leg-waxing by other means.

The phone rang at ten o'clock and Stefan answered it.

'It was a man from British Telecom, seemed a bit rum,' he reported to Belinda, who was curled up with a book in her study, Neville snoozing contentedly save for the occasional twitch of his little pink tail. 'His name was Graham.'

Belinda bit her lip. 'Oh yes?'

'He was ringing from home, to check you were recovered. I told him, "This is ten o'clock at night, were you born in a barn?"'

Belinda looked amazed. Neville stirred.

'You *are* all right, aren't you, Miss Patch? He said he only mentioned his money-off Friends and Family scheme and you wept, like cats and dogs.'

She nodded. She felt cornered. When women had breakdowns, their husbands left them. It was a well-known fact. When Stefan's former wife Ingrid had a breakdown, he left her good and proper, in an institution in Malmö.

'You try to do too much,' he said.

'I know.'

'It's not my fault, is it?'

Belinda gasped. *His* fault?

He searched her face, which crumpled under the strain of his kindness.

'Of course it's not,' she snuffled.

'Come to bed,' he said, reaching to touch her.

'All right,' she said.

'You must not forget, Belinda. No man is an island.'

'No.'

She put down her book, and got up.

He smiled. 'The thing about you, Belinda, is you need two lives.'

'Well, three or four would be nice,' she agreed, switching off the light. 'Why don't you make some clones for me? You know perfectly well you could knock up a couple at work.'

Chapter Two

It was eleven thirty on Tuesday night in Putney, the candles were guttering, and Jago was telling a joke over coffee. It was one of the smart showbiz ones he'd picked up on a trip home to New York several years ago.

'So the neighbour in Santa Monica says, "I tell ya, it was terrible. Your agent was here and he raped your wife and slaughtered your children and then he just upped and burned your damn house down." And the writer says, "Hold on a minute! ..."' Here Jago paused for a well-practised effect. His guests looked up.

'"Did you say my *agent* came to my *house?*"'

Belinda laughed with all the others, although she'd heard Jago tell this joke before. Oh, understanding jokes about agents, didn't it make you feel grown-up and important? She remembered the first time she'd managed to mention her agent as a mere matter of fact, without prefacing it with 'Oh listen to me!' It had been one of those Rubicon moments. No going back now, Mother. No going back now.

To be honest, Belinda's grand-sounding agent – A. P. Jorkin of Jorkin Spenlow – was a dusty man she'd met only once. But he was adequate to her meagre purposes, being well connected as well as reassuringly bookish, though alas, a sexist. 'Let's keep this

relationship professional, shall we?' she'd said to him brightly in the taxi, when he put his hand on her leg and squeezed it. 'All right,' he agreed, with a chalky wheeze, pressing harder. 'How much do you charge?'

Ah yes, she'd certainly made a disastrous choice with Jorkin, but changing your agent sounded like one of those endlessly difficult, escalatory things, like treating a house for dry rot. For a woman who can't be arsed to pick up a sock, it was a project she would, self-evidently, never undertake. 'Perhaps he'll die soon,' she thought, hopefully. Random facial hair sprouted from Jorkin's cheek and nose, she remembered dimly. She really hated that.

Jago's agent, of course, was quite another matter. Not that Jago ever wrote books, but having a big-time agent was an essential fashion accoutrement once you reached a certain level in Fleet Street: the modern-day equivalent of a food-taster or a leopard on a chain. Dermot, who often appeared on television, was famously associated with those other busy scribblers, the Prime Minister and the Archbishop of Canterbury. Complete with his too-tight-fitting ski tan, he was tonight's guest of honour, amiably telling Stefan about rugby union in South Africa, fiddling with a silver bracelet, and recounting jaw-dropping stories about being backstage at Clive Anderson. No random facial hair on this one. No hair at all, actually. When she'd told him in confidence about her book on literary doubles, he'd laughed out loud at the sheer, profitless folly of it. 'Here,' he'd said, taking off his belt with a flourish. 'Hang yourself with that, it's quicker.'

Tonight he was feeling more generous, so he gave her a tip. 'Belinda, why don't you write a bittersweet novel about being single in the city with a cat?'

'Perhaps because I hate cats and I'm not single, and I don't write grown-up fiction.'

'OK, but single people sell.'

'Which is why I'm writing about double people, no doubt.'

'Well,' he sighed, leaning towards her and picking imaginary fluff from her shoulder, 'you said it.'

Belinda wondered now whether she should have taken his advice. Was her literary work above fashion? Or just so far beyond it that it had dropped off the edge? She poured herself some more wine and took a small handful of chocolates. Relaxation on this scale was a rare and marvellous thing. Neville had given the other rats the night off, evidently, and was spending the evening quietly oiling his whip. Stefan was now teasing Dermot about the real-life chances of an attack of killer tomatoes (for some reason, Dermot was rather exercised on this point); Jago was arguing good-naturedly with Dermot's assistant about modern operatic stage design. Maggie (bless her) seemed to be adequately hitting it off with the spare man Viv always thoughtfully provided – this time a long-haired, big-boned sports reporter plucked without sufficient research from Jago's office. And, with all the dinner finished, it now befell Belinda to adopt her perennial role at dinner parties – i.e. pointlessly sucking up to Viv.

'That was such a good meal,' she began. 'I don't know how you do it. I feel like I've eaten the British Library. I can't even buy ready-cook stuff from Marks and Spencer's any more, did I tell you? Every time I go in, I see all the prepared veg and I get upset and have to come out again. Even though I haven't got time to prepare veg myself, I'm so depressed by bags of sprouts with the outer leaves peeled off that I have to crouch on the floor while my head swims. Has that ever happened to you?'

Viv shrugged. She refused to be drawn into Belinda's domestic inadequacies. After all, they'd been having the same conversation for eighteen years. Also, praise always made her hostile – a fact Belinda could never quite accept, and therefore never quite allowed for.

'I like your top,' Belinda said.

'Harvey Nicks. I went back to get another one, actually, but they only had brown. Nobody looks good in brown. I don't know why they make it.'

Belinda wondered vaguely whether her own top-to-toe chocolate was exempt from this generalization. She didn't like to ask.

'What do you think about Leon for Maggie?' Viv demanded.

'The petrolhead?'

'Yes.'

'Well, I can't say he's perfect. So far his only conversation is pit-stop records. He just told Maggie that Rembrandt wasn't a household name.'

'Yes, but Maggie is so lonely and desperate, she might not mind a diversity of interests.'

They paused to hear what was happening between Maggie and Leon.

'Villeneuve's a *person*?' Maggie was saying. 'Good heavens! So what's the name of that bridge in Paris?'

Belinda raised an eyebrow, while Viv pretended not to hear. What a terrible life Maggie had. She looked pityingly at Maggie and saw how her own life might have turned out, if only she hadn't responded so well to the nickname Patch. In her spare time, Maggie did therapy. When she got work, it was underpaid. It was common knowledge that she slept with totally unsuitable people. And when she went out to her friends' house for a pleasant evening, looking more glamorous than the rest of them put together, they thoughtlessly paired her with a talking ape.

Sitting here, Belinda was caught in a common dilemma of women who compare themselves with others. With whom should she compare herself tonight? Beside Maggie, she looked rather accomplished. Whereas beside Viv, she looked like a road accident. Viv did dinner parties for eight without breaking stride. She had three sons with long limbs and clean hair who said, 'Hello, Auntie Belinda, do you want to see my prize for

24

geography?' and 'Guess what, I've got another part in a radio play.' Viv dressed beautifully in navy. She attended a gym and went swimming. She canvassed for the Labour Party. And, just to give her life a bit of interest, she was the youngest ever female consultant anaesthetist of a major London private hospital.

Belinda took another reckless swig of wine. She used to say she had only two modes when it came to drinking: abstinence and abandonment. Looking at her fifth glass, she realized this system had recently simplified.

'Jago got made executive features editor at the *Effort*.'

Belinda put down her glass with a clunk. 'I didn't know that.'

'Last week. Bunter Paxton was kicked upstairs.'

'Fuck.'

'Dermot says it's all part of his plan. I'm warming to Dermot. Are you?'

Belinda struggled to find the right thing to say. She was impressed, upset, mortified. Comparisons might be odious, but Viv and Jago were her own age. Identically her own age. She and Viv had started adult life with almost identical opportunities, from exactly the same spot, in fact: queuing for DramSoc at University College London, where they were subsequently cast as Helena and Hermia in *A Midsummer Night's Dream* alongside Jago as Bottom. Viv was in medicine; she and Jago were in English. She had rather fancied Jago in those days. Hard to imagine now. Stefan was so good, so *dear*, the way he just fitted in. What a shame his first wife, the loony one in Malmö, had got custody of all their Swedish friends.

Viv nudged her to look at Maggie and Leon again. They had their heads together. 'Anal?' Leon was querying, his body language expressive of severe discomfort. He ran his hand through his long, greasy hair. 'Are you sure?'

Belinda wrestled briefly with self-pity, and lost. *Just look at what Viv had made of her life. I could have had that.* She was beginning to remember why she didn't enjoy going out.

'And yet you go to all this trouble,' she marvelled, waving a hand.

Viv sighed. Not this again. Not that Superwoman crap.

'I'm not getting into this again, Belinda, I warn you. As I've told you a million times, my cleaning lady does everything in this house, and I don't lift a finger. In fact, I'm sorry to say this,' Viv's voice rose, 'but I wish you'd just shut up about it.'

Even in her drunken state, Belinda was startled by Viv's high-handed, imperious tone. Just because you abjectly deferred to someone year after year, paying them superlative compliments, that surely didn't give them the right to assume some sort of superiority, did it?

'All right, keep your hair on,' slurred Belinda, 'I only said—'

'Listen, I'm just going to say this to you, Belinda. Just this. Sack Jorkin. Lose Patsy. Boot Mrs Holdsworth.'

'Is that all?'

'That about covers it, yes.'

'Should I move to Botswana as well?'

'I'm just telling you how it looks from where I'm standing. And where lots of other people are standing too.'

'Mrs H washes her hair with Daz, Viv. She lives on water boiled up from old sprout peelings. She hasn't had a new scarf for ten years.'

Other chatter stopped abruptly as Belinda's voice rose. Only Leon could be heard, saying, 'Penile? In what way?'

Stefan intervened. 'I agree with Viv you should award Mrs Holdsworth the Order of the Boot,' he offered, with a smile. 'Viv is right, as always. Mrs Holdsworth takes the piss and cooks her own goose long enough. Tell her to up stumps. A good wine needs no bush.'

Belinda was confused, and a bit resentful. She didn't understand how sacking the cleaning lady would in any way improve
her ability to give dinner parties. And she disliked it, naturally
enough, when pleasant evenings with chums and husband turned
Stalinist all of a sudden. She couldn't remember the last time
she saw it on a menu. Dessert followed by show trials; then
coffee and mints.

'You need people with a bit of initiative around you,' said
Viv. 'There's nothing supernatural about what I do. I just hive
off bits of my life I don't want. You could do that. I give mine
to Linda. The cleaning lady. She does everything. She's doing
the washing-up right now. She did all the shopping and most
of the cooking.'

Belinda nodded. 'Linda,' she repeated, dumbly. So deeply
did Belinda believe in Viv's domestic powers, she had always
suspected Linda was an invention.

'I've got no sympathy for you, Belinda. None whatever.'

'Thanks.'

'You know what I mean.'

Belinda sniffed loudly, and started to fish under her chair
for her handbag. 'Stefan, shall we go home soon?'

'Oh for God's sake, don't take offence,' snapped Viv. 'I'm
only thinking of you, as usual.'

Belinda noticed that the others had stopped talking, in
order to listen better. She was not unaware that tiffs with
Viv were becoming a regular feature of fun nights out. She
tried a last-ditch compliment, to deflect attention. It didn't
work. 'You've redecorated this room,' said Belinda. 'It's lovely.
All this white is very attractive.'

'Well, we got sick to death of sea green. No one has that
any more.'

Belinda experienced a familiar sensation, remembering her own
sea-green bedroom, bathroom, kitchen, hall and array of fitted
carpets. 'All right,' she said, seeing that flattery was getting her

nowhere. 'Assuming I can get someone brilliant like your Linda, how do I choose which bits of my life to give her? I wouldn't know where to stop, I mean start.' Belinda thought about it, and felt a bit sick. 'No, I was right the first time. I wouldn't know where to stop.'

Viv arranged some wine bottles in a line. She was resisting the urge to hit Belinda. 'Belinda, just imagine you had the choice. Would you rather sit in your study reading about – what is it you want to read about all the time?'

'Doubles. Like Dr Jekyll and Mr—'

'OK. Would you rather sit in your study reading that ridiculous old nonsense, or – I don't know – keep the loo seat free from nasty curly pubes?'

Belinda masticated a truffle. It tasted wonderful, like violets. It took her mind off the hurtful implication that her curly pubes were nasty. 'All right,' she said warily, 'I'll replace Mrs Holdsworth. But I'm keeping Jorkin and Patsy.'

'It's your funeral,' said Viv, and getting up, she started to clear dessert plates.

Stefan leaned across. 'How about we ask this Linda if she can work for us too? She doesn't work for you every God's hour, I think?'

It was the most innocent of questions. But had they heard a suicidal gunshot from the downstairs cloakroom the effect could not have been more Ibsenesque. Viv stood up and knocked over her chair; Jago shot her a meaningful glance; Viv's eyes widened in anger as she turned to face Belinda.

'If you do that,' she said, 'I warn you, I'll never speak to you again.'

Belinda laughed. They all did. Maggie even clapped. But Viv was serious. 'Take my cleaning lady, you ungrateful bitch—'

'Viv, we're only talking about a cleaning lady! This is ridiculous.'

Jago chipped in. 'I know it sounds crazy. Linda's more than

a cleaning lady, that's all. She has a way of making herself indispensable. And let's just say—'

'That's enough, Jago.'

Belinda fell back in her chair, exhausted. 'I don't get it,' she confessed. 'I'm sorry, but I don't get it.'

'Coffee?' said Viv.

'I'll help,' offered Dermot.

Belinda and Stefan pulled faces at one another.

At the other side of the table, Leon presented Maggie with a perfect, tiny origami racing car, folded out of a napkin. 'All right,' he said. 'Tell me what's anal about *that*.'

Belinda woke up suddenly. How long she'd been nodding at the table she didn't know. Noticing Viv was missing from her side, however, she stood up to find her but lurched unexpectedly and almost sat down again. She must be drunk. Jago was now telling Leon a familiar joke about a Jewish widow addressing her husband's ashes in her hand. '"Remember the blow-job you always wanted, Solly?"'

Trying for a second time, she got up successfully and propelled herself towards the door – at which point, she heard Viv on a darkened landing, whispering angrily to Dermot.

'I wouldn't mind but she owes everything to me,' Viv was saying.

'Belinda's a real nobody,' Dermot agreed. 'A nothing of a nobody.'

Belinda leaned against a wall and listened.

'I introduced her to Stefan. It was all me. But she's never content.'

'Some people suck the blood out of you. They're vampires. I see it every day, people taking the credit when everything they do is my idea. You have to tell them how great they are all the time. Belinda just takes and takes.'

'You're right. People only ever want to talk about themselves.

We're just mirrors they see themselves in. Mirrors in which they flatter themselves.'

Dermot's voice became tender. 'You shouldn't be bothering with vampires, Viv. You should think only of your lovely, lovely self. I know I shouldn't say it, but Viv, I mean this, you're such a good person.'

Belinda held her breath and grimaced. Dermot clearly didn't understand that flattering Viv made her vicious – sometimes to the point of violence. But something else happened. Because Viv evidently caught a sight of herself in Dermot's flattering mirror.

'Am I?' said Viv.

'You're so good, so fine. In fact, I admire you very much.'

'You do?'

'I've got no reason to say this, incidentally.'

'I know.'

There was a pause while the loathsome Dermot thought of some more sugary things to say. Belinda was astonished.

'You're fantastic,' he continued.

'Thank you.'

'And, you know, I love just talking about you freely like this, without you feeling you have to say anything reciprocal about me.'

'Wow.'

Belinda backed away to the kitchen, fearful of overhearing the inevitable culminating squelch of a kiss in the dark. Her emotions were mixed, and her demeanour unsteady, but her intention was perfectly clear. As she made her way to the kitchen, she had one single thought. She would hire Linda. Ungrateful vampire bitch that she was, she was determined to take, take, take. Petulance was an emotion that held no fears for Belinda. If Viv thought so badly of her already, then stealing her cleaning lady was obviously the very least she owed her reputation.

*   *   *

None of Viv's friends had come face to face with Linda, so it was quite a surprise that she looked like Kylie Minogue. Belinda had imagined a composite of stereotypes. Lumpen librarian in a thick skirt and frilly blouse. Rubber gloves in primrose yellow. Intimidating. Carrying a bucket. A Cordon Bleu, perhaps, pinned to her sensible apron.

But the woman reading the magazine in the kitchen was in her early thirties and pretty. She wore fitted jeans and a spotless white T-shirt, with strappy shoes. Her auburn hair was thick and long, and when Belinda noticed her hands – small and clean, with nails beautifully polished, like mother-of-pearl – she felt an unaccustomed jolt of envy.

Hearing Belinda in the doorway, this youthful vision of unlikely cleaning lady assumed it was Viv. 'I wish you'd let me do the rest of it, Viv,' she said, indicating rather a lot of washing-up on the kitchen surfaces, 'but I have to say I'm enjoying this *Lancet*. Oh, hello.'

Something about this greeting puzzled Belinda but, on the other hand, she was so fuddled by drink she could barely remember her mission.

'Psst. Are you Linda?' she hissed.

Linda was evidently amused. 'Yes,' she hissed back, exaggeratedly.

'Shh,' said Belinda. 'I'm Mrs Johansson, but you can call me Belinda.'

'All right, Mrs Johansson.'

'Listen, Linda. I've got something to ask you.' Belinda staggered slightly. 'I want to ask you to work for me.'

'That's nice,' said Linda. 'I wondered when you would. That's a lovely top.'

Belinda looked down at it, but couldn't focus. 'Are you sure? It's not black, you know. It's brown.'

Linda smiled.

'Shall I come tomorrow?'

'Wow, yes. If you're sure. Blimey, that was easy.'

Belinda turned, and steadied herself in the doorway. 'Dr Ripley may not be happy about this,' she added, over her shoulder. She felt she ought to mention it.

'That's OK,' said Linda.

'Really?'

'Leave it to me. Are you all right?'

'I'm OK,' said Belinda. 'Thanks.'

Stefan tried never to argue with his second wife. Things had gone badly enough with the first one. But that night, as he drove home late through South London, he was impatient. Because for some mad reason Belinda had gone behind Viv's back and attempted to steal her cleaning lady. Moreover, she'd informed him as if he would be pleased.

'This underhandedness is a rum go, Belinda,' he said. 'Honest to goodness, I feel I may blow my top.'

'I'm sorry,' she said. Stefan drove too fast when he was angry. She'd only said Viv was a cow who regularly pierced her heart with a hundred poison quills, and now they were going to get killed jumping traffic-lights.

'Listen. Viv is a lovely person. Your behaviour beggars description.'

'No, Stefan. You're wrong. There's a subtext. Underneath all Viv's loveliness towards me she actually hates me and she wants me dead. It's a sibling-y kind of thing.'

'You hate *her*, more likely. Because you make a meal of everything and to her it's a doodle.'

'Doddle.'

They stopped too late at some traffic-lights, and the car slewed with the braking force, jolting both of them forward. Belinda judged that this was not the right moment to mention how much she disliked Stefan's driving.

'Tell me you won't hire this Linda.'

'I can't. Besides, Stefan, it was your idea. You can't make an omelette without breaking eggs.'

He put the car in gear, revved high, and let out the clutch so that they shot forward at forty miles an hour.

'Belinda, I tell you straight. It is not just the Linda thing. I am fed up to the back teeth, you are coming a cropper and I will not fiddle while Rome burns. Maggie says to me tonight, "Belinda is wedded to her work, not to you, Stefan." You cry on the telephone to the man. I don't want you going loco, Belinda. It happened to me before.'

Belinda frowned. What did he mean, it happened to *him*?

They cornered with a squeal of rubber.

'Let's leave Maggie out of it. She's got her own agenda.'

Stefan slowed for some lights, and Belinda took a deep breath. 'Look, I'm not going loco, as you put it. It's just that nobody understands me except Neville.'

Stefan swung the car into Armadale Road, spotted a parking space and braked abruptly. It was an excellent spot, twenty yards from the house. He reversed the car into the space, turned off the engine, extinguished the lights. And putting his hand on Belinda's arm, he pulled a solemn face.

'Belinda, this isn't like you. You are breaking up.'

'For heaven's sake, she's only a cleaning lady.'

She kissed him hard, running a hand round his collar, smelling his hair. She'd never been addicted to a person before Stefan.

'You'll like her,' she said. 'Once you've met her, I promise you. You won't be able to help it. And Viv will get over it. The cow.'

Back at Jago's, at three a.m., Viv crept downstairs to check the burglar alarm and found Linda sitting in the dining room in the dark, a book of Viv's old photos in front of her on the table.

'Linda?' But Linda did not look up.

Viv switched on a table lamp and coughed.

'Viv!' Linda said pleasantly. 'What a nice evening. Your friends are so interesting.'

'Well, Leon was dreadful. Honestly, Jago is such a desperate judge of character. Do you know, after all that boring Brands Hatch nonsense, it turned out he doesn't drive? Maggie had to give him a lift to Wandsworth Town. I don't know why I try so hard for people, they never co-operate.'

Viv tidied a few things while Linda watched. The light-bulbs hummed. She smoothed a curtain. She had something important to ask. Talking to the cleaning lady, she had none of the commanding manner she adopted with Belinda. She seemed almost deferential.

'Linda?'

'Mm?'

'You know how I depend on you?' Viv laughed nervously. 'I had a scare this evening. Did Belinda speak to you? You wouldn't leave us, not after everything?'

But, as Linda turned a page and studied the pictures, Viv's heart sank. She had hoped Linda would do the cleaning-lady equivalent of running into her arms. Instead, it was like asking, 'You do love me, don't you?' and knowing after a few, short, vertiginous seconds that an affair was all over. The longer you have to wait for an answer to that sort of question, the more certain you can be that the answer is not the one you want.

'How old is Stefan?' asked Linda.

'What? Oh, fifty-one.'

'And you introduced him to Belinda.'

'Yes. My sister met him at Imperial.'

Viv joined Linda to look at the album. It included fuzzy colour pictures from the old DramSoc days. Viv perused the page. Their faces were almost unrecognizable, but nothing had changed, really. At college, Maggie was disastrously involved with a succession of goaty lecturers. Belinda complained all the time about the timetable. And Viv organized an excellent summer outing, to which Jago brought along some useless dickhead they never saw again.

'Are you going to Belinda?'

'I thought I would, yes. Oh, Viv, don't look like that. I'm so sorry. But at the end of the day, I'm only your cleaning lady!'

'How can you say that?' Viv gasped.

Linda took Viv's hand and squeezed it. It would have been clear to any onlooker that the usual relationship between employer and cleaning lady ('How are the feet?' 'We need more Jif') had been long since outgrown.

'It's gone a bit mad here,' said Linda.

Viv laughed. 'You can say that again.'

She thought about it, took a deep breath, and resolved to be brave. 'So. How are we off for J-cloths?' she asked.

Linda smiled at her gratefully. 'How the hell should I know?' she retorted.

At which the two of them laughed and laughed in the small hours until they had to hold each other up.

At three a.m., Belinda woke Stefan by turning the light on. She'd had a dream she needed to write down. And since he was now awake, she was quite keen to tell him about it, too. And also to treat him to an instant analysis, as she always did. In this dream, she said, she'd been bundled up in the bedclothes and placed in the washing-machine by an unseen hand. 'It was an unseen hand,' she said, significantly. 'But I think we know whose it was. She was singing "I Should Be So Lucky".'

Stefan shrugged.

'Kylie Minogue,' she explained. Belinda popped to the loo, and came back, over-confident that she had captured her husband's attention. She shook him awake to continue.

Belinda often had premature burial dreams, but this one was

different. No shovel, no grit. No bone-white fingers poking through the black earth. No, this was the opposite of the Gothic nightmare. Instead of feeling frightened and stifled in this one, she'd had rather a wonderful time. The water was warm and sudsy, something like amniotic fluid but with bright blue enzymes for a whiter white. And the rhythm was very comforting. 'Slosh-to-the-right, two, three, slosh-to-the-left, two, three. Over, over, over, over, slosh, slosh, slosh.' It reminded her of perhaps the greatest joy of her infancy – the bathtime game her father had played with her, safely cradling her in strong arms, then gently drawing her the length of the bath while singing the old music-hall song, 'Floating down the river, on a Sunday afternoon'.

Stefan closed his eyes. As a scientist, he was more interested in the physiology of dreams than their nostalgic evocations.

'No chance of you drowning, my dear? I say it helpfully, you understand.'

'No, no. I didn't even struggle. It was so cosy. Sloshing about. I just tapped on the milky glass from time to time – "Hello? Excuse me! Hello?" – because life was going on outside, and you were out there, Stefan, eating a bagel. You didn't even seem to notice I'd gone.'

'Which cycle were you on?'

'Special treatments.'

'Oh, good. I have always wondered what that was for.'

Belinda happily snapped shut her dreams notebook and turned the light off. 'You know what this means?'

'Something about the womb?'

'No, it means Accept the Cleaning Lady. That's good, isn't it? Even my subconscious says it's a good idea.'

'Well, I'm going up,' said Viv. 'Thanks again for everything tonight. It will be odd not to make a list for you.'

'It was all a sham, Viv. It's time for you to admit it.

You are Superwoman. We talked about this. We knew it couldn't go on.'

Viv's chin wobbled. 'I'm not Superwoman,' she said.

Linda put her hands on Viv's shoulders. 'Yes you are.'

And Viv jumped, as if she had been stung.

'And what was the spin like?' said Stefan.

'Oh, that's a point.'

Belinda turned on the light again as Stefan groaned.

'What is it now?'

'I woke up before the spin.' She made a note. 'Perhaps I'll have to have the spin another time.'

When the lamps were finally out, they lay quietly in the dark for a minute. Stefan's pre-sleep breathing had a little rhythmic squeak in it, a whistle in his nose. Belinda listened to it comfortably, happy. The room was otherwise perfectly still, perfectly quiet.

Hiring a new cleaning lady had been such a small decision, yet it had changed everything. On her way to the bathroom she had spotted a heap of laundry at the top of the stairs but it had not said, 'Remember me?' Instead it had asked rather excitedly, 'When does she start? When does she start?'

Something else had changed, too, although at first she couldn't put her finger on it.

'Neville?' she whispered, at last. In her abdomen, a spotlight swivelled around a deserted Big Top, finding only sand and sawdust, and bits of torn paper streamer. 'Neville, are you there?'

Chapter Three

Belinda was right to say that Maggie had her own agenda. In fact, Maggie's agenda was about as well disguised as a Centurion tank in a hairnet. Thus, when she told her oldest friend Belinda, 'You work too hard', what she really meant was 'You don't spend enough time listening to my problems'. When she said to Stefan, 'Belinda cares only about her work', what was clearly imported by this treachery was 'I'll always love you, Stefan, I want to have your babies, and it's not too late'. Telling Leon she thought Villeneuve was a bridge in Paris translated as 'You're a dreadful motor-racing bore and I can't believe I'm listening to this.' Indeed, the paradox of Maggie's life was that the more rudely she semaphored her real message, the more her friends felt it polite to take her words at face value.

When she woke on Wednesday in her Clapham flat, the morning after the dinner party, it surprised her to find that Leon was still there. She assumed it was Leon, anyway. An enormous naked male body was sleeping face down diagonally in her four-foot bed, which was as unprecedented as it was uncomfortable. Blokes who went to bed with Maggie were, of course, not literally 'all the same', as she would sometimes complain, but they certainly shared many tendencies, and one of these was the quite strenuous avoidance of sleep. As if obeying house rules pinned to the door, they would resolutely roll out of Maggie's bed and breast the cold night air without so much as a cup of tea or a post-coital cuddle. It was a strange, inexplicable nocturnal-urgency syndrome she had often remarked on.

'Gotta go,' they'd say, hopping about zipping their trousers and cleaning their teeth at the same time, like characters in a bedroom farce. 'Unfortunately, I've got a very, very early appointment in the morning. Is this soap scented? It's not bluebell or something?'

'All my conquests are either undead or office cleaners,' she would tell her mates, by way of brave humour. But in fact her conquests were fathers of small children, of course; fulfilling some sort of universal genetic imperative to cheat on the wife during the first year of parenthood. Maggie made a point of meeting the wives of her Undead Office Cleaners as soon as possible – not to cause trouble but simply to prevent her from becoming 'the other woman'. Meeting the wife had this curious way of dispelling any self-deluding fantasies about adultery. Before you met the wife in the living flesh, you could imagine you were the real person and the wife was the anonymous incorporeal phantom. Whereas after you met her, the mirror swivelled to offer a truer perspective, in which the wife was the real person and you were the lump of garbage.

Anyway, ask any of her friends, and they could tell you Maggie's exact emotional pattern on these wham-bam occasions, because she'd described them often. As the taxi roared off at two a.m., she would wave gaily from the doorway in her dressing-gown, feeling all jelly-legged and warm. Then she'd go back to her tousled bed with Ariel and Miranda (the cats), *Hello!* magazine and a hot cup of something brown and chocolatey called Options (nice touch), and as she brushed the condom wrapper from the sheet, she'd tell herself that no scene could better sum up the freedom of modern womanhood.

Oh yes, Simone de Beauvoir would be so proud. Look, all that money, yet Barbra Streisand still had a hideous home! On the verge of sleep, she might decide it was high time a sexy woman of her calibre had her navel pierced. And then, seemingly a minute later, she woke alone in broad daylight. The room looked dusty; her pillow was caked in dribble and cat hair; she felt ravaged and cheap. The man in question was by now several miles away playing with baby in the bath, and would doubtless ignore her the next time they met, making her feel she'd been punched in the stomach. 'What have I done?' she would wail, then burst into tears and phone Belinda.

'Shouldn't you be getting home?' (translation: 'Get out of my house') she asked Leon. She kicked his bum, which wobbled. Although she couldn't now remember all the details, it had not been a terribly successful night, and it was annoying to find him still here. Evidently in Formula One they can refuel a car in under seven seconds – a statistic that was now proving hard to dislodge from her memory. Good grief, she still had her bra on.

Quite rightly it offended Maggie that while she was fit, pretty, clever, a bit famous and had screen-tested for *Titanic*, she'd still allowed herself to go to bed with Leon. It was so obvious she was too good for her sexual partners, yet strangely, there was no system of justice governing such matters, no god of eugenics who intervened on her behalf. 'Stop!' a voice should have said, as Leon gently placed his big paw on her neck in the car. 'This coupling goes against nature, and must not proceed. This woman is reserved for clever, attractive males who write poetry and stuff. Kenneth Branagh, at least.'

But Maggie knew that the voice saying, 'Stop!' would never be hers. While she waited for Stefan to stop loving Belinda, she made the best of things; responded to advances from all directions; made quite a few advances of her own. Not that she was blind to male imperfections; far from it. But in sexual matters, you are often obliged to take your partner at his own

41

estimation, and it's a sad fact of life that many ugly, bald men look in the mirror and see Kevin Costner. Consequently, Maggie's romantic career had encompassed sexual partners who, in former, more brutal, God-fearing eras, would have been stoned to death by mobs.

Leon snored and flapped a big white arm, but otherwise showed no sign of life, so she got up. She could have snuggled down, growled an erotic Murray Walker impersonation to rouse his ardour (she was good at accents). But on second thoughts, a bacon sandwich was more appealing. It was nearly lunch-time. So instead she made unrestrained noise having a shower, getting dressed, playing an oldies programme on Radio Two, and singing. She switched off half-way through Abba's 'Take A Chance On Me' – it reminded her too painfully of her first-in-line feelings for Stefan.

She checked Leon wasn't dead, of course. Remembering her duty as a hostess, she held a mirror to his lips until she saw vapour. But he wasn't dead, and he wouldn't wake up. So, humming 'Gimme, Gimme, Gimme (A Man After Midnight)', she left him a note with directions to the Gemini corner café, and went out.

At college, Stefan was having coffee with Jago in the library canteen. They had arranged it the night before, when Jago overheard Stefan on the subject of killer tomatoes. 'We'll do a genetics supplement and you can be consultant editor,' he'd told Stefan. 'I'll see you at eleven.' The trouble with journalists (as Stefan had often said to Belinda) was that they couldn't help regarding you not as a person but as a *source*.

'I need some Swedes quick,' Jago might ring up to ask, mid-thought in his scurrilous weekly column in the *Effort*. No preamble, of course. Busy man, Jago. Part of his charm.

'For sure. Ingmar Bergman, August Strindberg, Björn Borg.'

Jago could be heard tapping his keyboard in the background. 'B-U-R-G?'

'Well, B-E – which one?'

'All of them. You tell me.'

'Ingmar is B-E-R-G, August is B-E-R-G, and Björn is B-O-R-G. The reason for such a high incidence of the name Berg and its variants, of course—'

'Great. You sure?'

'Yes.'

'One more Swede who isn't a Berg, in case the subs don't take my word for it?'

'Abba?'

Four more emphatic taps.

'Good man, gotta go.'

'That was Yago,' Stefan would tell Belinda, still holding the dead receiver in his hand.

'How did I guess?'

The phrase 'need-to-know basis' had been invented for Jago. He was only interested in anything when he needed to know. Tell him a fact at an inappropriate moment (when he wasn't writing an article, or commissioning one) and he literally screwed up his face to prevent it getting in. He was a *tabula rasa* with a straining Filofax, and other people were the fools who stored primary material until he came along to nick it. Not that your help would earn you any loyalty from him, let alone thanks. You could help him a hundred times, and he'd stitch you up on the hundred and first. The curious thing was, when Jago looked in a mirror he saw George Washington.

'So how big is this supplement in the *Effort*?' Stefan sighed, playing with his specs in a professorial manner.

'Twelve pages. Minus ads. That leaves room for about three articles and a dozen pics.'

'Why do you think I'll contribute to it?'

'Um, because if you don't, I'll go straight to Laurie Spink?'

Stefan smiled but didn't reply. Laurie Spink made television programmes about genetics. He had a column in *The Times*.

'OK, forget that Spink blackmail thing, that was tacky. If you do this for me, Stefan, I promise never to tell Belinda how I know you're not a natural blond. What more can I say? Copy is by next Friday. A thousand words on anything. Is there a gene for monstrous boobs? Could you look for it between now and next Friday? I'm only thinking of the picture desk.'

'Do people actually read these supplements, Yago? I'm afraid I am a doubting Thomas.'

'Well, I'm glad you asked that. Research shows that, yes,' he screwed up his face, as if trying to remember the exact figure, 'one million, two hundred and twelve people read these supplements.'

'But really they're thrown in the bin?'

'In a New York second.'

Stefan checked his watch and stood up. Jago took the hint. Besides, he'd arranged to call Laurie Spink in five minutes' time. 'I'll be off,' he offered. 'So you'll do it?'

Stefan shrugged. 'No. It's not really me, I think.'

'Of course it's you!'

'I'm not a writer, Yago.'

'No problem, big guy. We'll write it for you in the office. I'll ghost you. Happens all the time.'

'Monstrous boobs may be for some the cat's pyjamas, but – no.'

'Stefan, why are you doing this to me?'

'Because it's a free country.' Stefan shrugged. 'East is east and west is west. Genetics is not all beer and skittles.'

Jago was confused, but more than that, he was hurt. Journalists always pout if you puncture their plan, even if they've only had the plan for the last ninety seconds.

'Why do you call it copy?' Stefan asked.

Jago looked puzzled.

'Call what copy?'

'*Copy*. I mean, the writing is supposed to be one-off, I think?'

'Well, I wouldn't go that far. This is journalism we're talking about.'

'I mean, would you ever say, "Gosh, hey, this is very original one-off copy"?'

Jago had had enough. 'If I ever said, "Gosh, hey," at all, I'd lose my job, Stefan. As should you, I might add.'

He strode out of the canteen, and extracted his mobile phone from an inside pocket. Stefan had just completely wasted his time. What a two-face! 'Gosh, hey, this is very original one-off copy!' he said, with Stefan's careful accent. He couldn't wait to get back to the office to try that one on the guys.

Belinda spent the morning writing an imaginary riding-in-Ireland piece for Jago's paper, and wondering what had happened to Neville. He was not his usual bouncy self. Even when the phone rang and it was her mother (eek!) there was only a twitch or scuttle from Los Rodentos. Someone phoned up to ask Belinda to appear on radio (she declined, but felt agitated); she remembered Stefan's birthday was next week; the usual pressures most certainly applied. But no trampolining by small furry bodies. The rats were on a go-slow. Ever since she'd decided to hire Linda, she'd felt like the proverbial sinking ship. 'Psst, Neville,' she whispered. 'Are you all right?' Not a scuttle; not a squeak. Life was odd without his wheeling and bouncing. She pictured him with little round spectacles, like John Lennon. But no matter how much she hummed 'Imagine' to encourage him, he simply wasn't interested.

Belinda always had a marvellous time alone with her imagination. Having invented quite a good travel piece, if she said so herself ('Wind and soft rain whipped the ponies' fetlocks; my hat was too tight, like an iron band') she was now plotting the next

45

Verity novel, *Atta Girl, Verity!*, in which Verity's impoverished mum would break the terrible news that she couldn't afford to stable Goldenboy at the Manor House any more – or not unless Verity took a backbreaking after-school job pulling weeds in Camilla's mummy's seven-acre garden.

How she enjoyed visiting pain and anguish on Verity, these days. She beamed as she considered Verity's fate. Ho hum. By the rules of such fiction, Verity must, of course, come back from a perfect hack on Goldenboy, and be rubbing him down with fresh-smelling straw when in the distance, eek! splash!, Camilla falls into the ornamental fishpond! Run to the rescue, Verity! Don't care if your plaits get wet! Recover Camilla unconscious, apply life-saving techniques, and after a feverish period awaiting Camilla's recovery, receive as reward (wait for it) free stabling for the rest of your life! And not forgetting double oats for good old Goldenboy!

The children's book world was mainly supplied these days with grim stuff about discarded hypodermics, but Belinda knew her own smug little readers would lap up the free stabling plot all right, mainly because they had already proved themselves stupid with no imagination. How easy they were to manipulate, these little princesses. Psychoanalysis might never have been invented. 'Camilla cuts off Verity's plaits,' she wrote now, mischievously. 'Verity caught cheating in the handy-pony. Shame increases when V investigated by RSPCA; maltreatment of G Boy exposed on national TV by Rolf H. V's mother seeks consolation in lethal cocktail of booze and horse pills, and is shot by vet. Camilla wins Hickstead.'

Just then a key turned in the front door. Mrs Holdsworth? Belinda felt stricken. She'd been so busy torturing Verity! What was the etiquette for sacking a cleaning lady? Did you let her do the cleaning first, or what?

'Only me,' called Mrs H, coughing as she slammed the front door, and struggled out of wellingtons.

Belinda stayed paralysed at her desk, panicking. 'Hello!' she called, and waited.

'"Come into the garden, Maud,"' sang Mrs H, coughing between words. '"For the black bat night has——"' Here a great explosion of phlegm-shifting, culminating in 'God almighty, Jesus wept.'

She popped her grey head round the study door, fag in mouth. Here goes, thought Belinda, then noticed that Mrs H's left arm was suspended in a rather grubby sling.

'Don't fucking ask,' said Mrs Holdsworth gloomily. 'Doctor says six months. I tell you what for nothing. My fucking brass-polishing days are over.'

'That's awful,' sympathized Belinda. 'And when they'd hardly begun. What a shame. I'm sorry.'

'So am I. No grip, you see.'

'I've been thinking——' Belinda began.

'Fucking stairs are the worst, of course.'

Mrs H scratched her knee through her overall, using her one good arm. Recollecting that there were three floors to her house (plus attic), Belinda didn't see how an injured wrist stopped you from going upstairs, but she said nothing. Asking Mrs Holdsworth to elaborate on an intriguing statement was a mistake she'd regretted on too many occasions, and she now had a policy of restricting herself to a non-committal 'Mm' wherever possible.

'Mm,' she said now, with as much of a funny-old-world tone as she could manage.

Mrs H continued to stand in the doorway. It always grieved her to spend less than half of her allotted three hours telling people how long it was since she bought a scarf. She tried again. 'Bleeding great 'urricane on the way, apparently.'

'Mm.'

'That Salman Rushdie was in the butcher's again. I said to

47

him, "Very good, mate. Disguising yourself as a pork chop, are you? That's fucking original."'

'Mm.' Belinda pretended to be deeply engrossed in her notes.

'My boy says he's written a new book called *Buddha Was a Cunt*. Is that true?'

In the café, Maggie read last week's *Stage* from cover to cover, filling time before her therapy appointment at two p.m. Maggie had run the gamut of therapy over the years. She'd done Freudian twice and Jungian three times, but had so far avoided Kleinian because Belinda had once said, 'What, like Patsy Cline?' which had somehow ruined it. Belinda had an awful way of belittling things that were important to you, by saying the first thing that came into her head. Kleinian therapy would now only involve singing maudlin I-fall-to-pieces country songs, which was what Maggie did at home anyway without paying.

Nowadays Maggie was working with a new therapist, Julia, who was the best she'd ever had. The idea was to work on isolated problems, and correct the thinking that led to inappropriate behaviour or beliefs. For example, Maggie had a problem about other people being late. 'So does everyone,' pooh-poohed Belinda. 'Not like me,' said Maggie. And it was true. Maggie not only got angry and worried as the minutes ticked by, but after a while she started to imagine that the other person was not late at all. He had actually arrived on time, and was standing at the bar or something — *but that she had completely forgotten what he looked like.*

'But he'd recognize you?' Belinda objected. 'So you'd still meet up.'

No, said Maggie. Because it was worse than that. *He'd forgotten what she looked like, too.*

'That's mad,' Belinda had said, helpfully. 'You should never have become an actress if you can't handle the odd identity shift, Mags.'

Luckily, the therapist took a more constructive approach.

'Now, since this non-recognition event has never occurred in reality,' said Julia, 'we must uncover the roots of your irrational anxiety, which I'm afraid to say, Margaret, is your sense of total unlovability. It's not your fault. Not at all. Your needs were never met by your parents, you see.'

'You're right.'

'You were made to feel invisible by those terrible selfish people, who should never have had children.'

Maggie sniffed. 'I was.'

'They looked right through you.'

Tears pricked Maggie's eyes. 'They did.'

'Did they tell you to stop dancing in front of the television, perhaps?'

It was a lucky guess.

'Yes!'

And so Maggie had wept and signed up for six months, figuring that she had very little else to do, and Julia was local (in Tooting). Besides which, she couldn't keep sitting stock-still with panic in theatre foyers with a sign pinned on her chest: 'It's really me! Is that really you?'

Professionally, things were a bit bleak for Maggie, and this didn't help matters. Her total unlovability was being confirmed in all quarters. The Pinter had been good experience, though incredibly badly paid. She'd had a job on *Casualty*, classified in the script as 'Bus crash scene – a woman moans'. But all the while her ambition to rejoin the Royal Shakespeare Company was coming to nothing. For the time being she must comfort herself with memories of two years ago, when she'd peaked in Stratford as the lady Olivia in Shakespeare's *Twelfth Night*, getting a review that singled her out as 'quite extraordinary' and 'probably quite good-looking'.

She had really loved that production, which was very loyal of her because it was generally reviled. Playing to paltry houses who sometimes booed, it did not transfer to London. But Maggie loved her Olivia. Never one to argue with a director's concept, she even loved her Olivia's Mongolian peasant costume and comical clog dancing. ('Nobility is relative,' their director Jeff told them.) Jeff, whom the *Financial Times* described as 'an idiot', had bucketfuls of bold ideas, including the unprecedented notion of casting as Viola and Sebastian (identical twins) two actors who looked absolutely nothing like each other. 'Most wonderful!' Olivia would say each night in the last scene, doing a hilarious double-take through bottle-glass specs. Even the critics liked that bit. She wished now she hadn't slept with Jeff, especially as he was married to the famous TV actress who had played Viola. But he'd done her a great service with that casting of asymmetricals. No one usually finds Olivia's final-act confusion the least bit funny.

Leon pushed open the steamy door, and wiped his shoes. Oh God. He looked slightly less enormous than she'd remembered, and had washed his hair. Maggie fiddled with her teaspoon in the sugar, glancing up occasionally. But though he looked round carefully, he evidently failed to spot her, so she carried on reading the *Stage* – or pretended to, having read it all already.

She heard Leon order a cup of herbal tea and braced herself. He brushed past her ('Sorry'), and sat at a nearby table with *Time Out*, studying the ballet listings. She stared at him until finally he looked up. 'Well, hello,' she said pointedly.

He frowned.

'It's me,' she said. 'Penelope Pitstop. You must be Muttley.'

He took a sip of tea, and looked behind him. 'Sorry, were you sitting here?' he suggested, at last.

'What?'

'Were you sitting here?'

His voice sounded funny. But it was definitely him.

'No.'

50

He tried to look away again, but couldn't. She was staring at him, and clearly getting angry with him, too.

'Sorry,' he said. 'Do I know you? I'm afraid I'm terrible at forgetting people. I meet such a lot of people in my work, you see.'

At which point, the door opened again, and a blonde woman came in, smiling directly at Leon. It was Julia, Maggie's therapist.

'Ah, there you are, Julia,' said Leon, with relief. 'Perhaps ...' and he gestured awkwardly towards Maggie, evidently hoping his wife could identify her.

'Margaret?' she began, but in a second Maggie had pushed past her, left the café and was outside.

Verity, high on crack cocaine, was just being bundled into a police van (they were manhandling her plaits) when Belinda wondered whether it might be time to ease up a bit.

'Phew,' she said, shaking her head proudly as she perused the last two pages of notes, and wishing she smoked cheroots. 'What a scorcher.'

The phone rang. It was Viv. 'Am I interrupting something?'

'Only a drug bust. So I see you're still talking to me? She's only a cleaning lady, Viv.'

'It's about you and me,' Viv said. 'I was wrong, you were right.'

Belinda paused to take this in. 'And who is this impersonating Viv, please?'

'Belinda, listen. I was wrong to interfere in your life. If you want to be bad at things and disorganized and never tidy up, you can do that. You're nearly forty, after all.'

'I'm thirty-six, the same as you.'

'You see, Linda isn't what you think. I know I've always said she was Mary Poppins and all that, but the truth is I've been covering up for her.'

'Viv!'

'No, it's true. She's got a terrible self-esteem problem. You have to bolster her all the time. And you end up—'

'Viv, I can't believe you'd stoop so low.'

'You haven't sacked Mrs Holdsworth?'

'That's a point. Hang on.'

Alerted to the telltale sound of vacuum cleaning in the hall, Belinda popped her head round the door and found Mrs H pushing the Hoover back and forth on the same spot, apparently lost in thought. 'Fucking disgusting!' she yelled to Belinda, over the din of the Hoover.

Belinda gave her a thumbs-up and went back to the phone.

'Not yet. I thought if I gave her a month's money—'

'Leave things as they are, Bea.'

Belinda harumphed grandly. Nobody harumphed as grandly as Belinda.

The doorbell rang.

'I've got to go.'

'If it's Linda—'

'I'll ring you later. God, you're so *interfering*. Why do you always think you're responsible for other people's lives?'

'Perhaps because I'm a bloody anaesthetist, in case you've forgotten!'

Belinda pursed her lips.

The doorbell rang again.

'If it's Linda—' Viv began.

'I've got to go.'

Belinda felt rather good about standing up to Viv. Letting Verity's behaviour go haywire had obviously given her a boost.

'Atta girl, Belinda,' she said to herself on the way to the door, stepping over Mrs H's wellingtons – and opening it found, in a pool of afternoon light, carrying a very thoughtful bunch of chrysanthemums, the woman who was going to change her life.

*   *   *

Mid-afternoon, Jago rang Laurie Spink again. Spink was now body and soul the property of the *Effort*, because it was easier to give him an extremely well-paid regular column than think of someone else to write for the supplement. And now that Jago had his number, he could expect the usual Jago call.

'I need some geneticists.'

'I've got a tutorial.'

'I need them this minute.'

So Spink had reeled off a few names, some of them with phone numbers. 'I've got to go now,' he added. 'Copy by Friday, yes?'

'Just one more thing. What do you know about Stefan Johansson's work? He hasn't done anything on monstrous boobs that he's keeping quiet about?'

'Oh, a lot of his notes were lost, unfortunately.'

Jago had been doodling. He stopped. 'Lost when?'

'When he died.'

'Stefan Johansson *died*? Since this morning?'

'No, no. Three or four years ago. Tragic. A fire. Best cloning brain outside the US. I suppose most people don't know about it. He used his own genetic material for research – ghastly end. Led to all sorts of enquiries and bans, but it was mostly hushed up. Wife went mad, terrible stories.'

'But he's teaching at Imperial.'

'Can't be.'

Jago blinked hard. In a second he had cut off Spink and phoned Imperial. They had no Johansson. He phoned the cuttings library; they promised to e-mail an obituary from an obscure science journal. He cast his mind back (a manoeuvre that did not come easily to him). How much had Viv known about Stefan when they introduced him to Belinda? Nothing. Viv's sister met him in the canteen, that's all. He was an impostor! A cheating, clever impostor! Like, like—

'Get me the names of some impostors quick!' he ordered his secretary.

Jago was nearly hyperventilating. What a great story! What a madly dangerous scheme to take the identity of a famous dead scientist and, moreover, pretend to be Swedish. Jago's mind raced, as he scanned the obituary that had just arrived on his screen. Key words leapt out at him. 'Cloning ... brilliant ... Swede ... pseudogenes ... Sweden ... reckless ... only in the mind of Robert Louis Stevenson ... Human Genome Project ... very, very mysterious ... Malmö.'

Jago couldn't read it properly, because he never did read anything properly. But he got the idea. The man they knew as Stefan — who was he? 'Unless, unless—' he muttered. He scrolled to the end, scrolled to the top again. More key words leapt out. 'Gene sharing ... Malmö ... foolhardy experiment ... replica ... Frankenstein ... condemned by scientific fraternity ... Church ... offence against God ... mutation ... Abba ... Malmö.'

But then he looked at the picture, and everything changed. It was Stefan. Stefan was dead, yet alive. A great shiver of excitement went up his spine. He heard again Stefan saying, 'Gosh, hey, this is very original one-off copy!'

The conclusion was staring him in the face.

'Oh my God. The man we know as Stefan Johansson ... is a clone.'

Running from the Gemini café, Maggie choked on tears of humiliation. Good grief, if this was what happened when you just popped out for a bacon sandwich she'd become a vegetarian immediately. For someone with Maggie's particular invisibility complexes, here was a triple calamity: (a) the man she'd condescended to sleep with had entirely failed to recognize her the next lunch-time; (b) he was a bastard and was the partner of her therapist, to whom she now couldn't talk about it; and

(c) after all that Michael Schumacher nonsense, it turns out he's really interested in classical dance! 'They're all the same,' she sobbed openly, as she ran home. 'All the bloody same.'

'Margaret?' Leon was now calling after her and, from the sound of it, running. His feet were slapping the pavement, and he was gaining on her. Why was he calling her Margaret? 'Bastard, bastard, bastard,' she muttered as she ran.

'Margaret, could you stop, please?'

She turned into her own street. Nearly home. Her heart was pounding as she picked up speed to escape him, and saw — emerging sheepishly from her flat, with hair slightly dirtier than it had been last night — Leon. He stopped and lit a cigarette, then started ambling in the opposite direction.

'Aieee!' she cried. 'Stop, stop, stop!'

Looking back, she saw Leon running towards her; looking forward, she saw him walking away. What an irony, she thought, as she staggered against the wall, clutching her chest. To spend all your professional life practising double-takes. And then, when a double-take would really come in handy, just fainting away on the spot.

Chapter Four

'Well,' said Linda, 'I had no idea doubles could be so interesting!'

As Linda boiled the kettle and opened some biscuits she'd thoughtfully brought, Belinda found herself feeling spectacularly happy. What an intelligent and intuitive woman Linda was. Everyone else scanned the ceiling for flies when she talked about *The Dualists*, or fiddled with a dinner napkin. It had the same turn-off effect as Stefan telling people he came from Malmö or, indeed, from Scandinavia. In both situations, her mother would say, 'That's nice,' then steer the conversation to the new range from Dolce and Gabbana. Linda, however, was of finer empathetic stuff. She had seen instantly not only that Belinda's book urgently needed writing but that it needed writing well.

'So do people meet their doubles in real life?' Linda asked.

'No. Not that I know of.'

'Shame. Because, as you say, most of us are leading double lives, aren't we?'

'At least double, yes. Or we wish we had two lives, just to deal with everything.'

It felt odd to talk about it. Could Linda truly be interested?

'So is it that one person is really two people? Or two people are really only one person?'

'Both. The main thing in most doubles stories is that the hero has his life taken over by a dark, malevolent force that shares his identity and implicates him in misdeed. Or sometimes the double just gobbles him up. I've got lots of theories about it. That's why I'm writing the book.'

Linda made the tea, as if it were perfectly normal to potter in Belinda's kitchen. With airy confidence, she gave Belinda Stefan's favourite mug, and opened a new packet of tea-bags because she didn't know the system with the old brown jar.

'Well, I think you're right,' Linda decided, putting the milk away in the fridge in the wrong place. 'You mustn't feel guilty about making time to write your special book. Our special work is what we're put on earth to do. I firmly believe that.'

Belinda nodded. Should she ask what Linda's special work was?

'And, as you said before,' Linda continued, 'men have always shut themselves away to write books, without anyone accusing them of neglecting the household chores. I mean, Tolstoy didn't write *Crime and Punishment* in between trips to Asda.'

'You say the best things, Linda.'

'Thank goodness you don't have any children.'

'Mm.'

Linda reopened the fridge and ran a professional eye over its contents. She took a deep breath. 'I feel very good about this,' she said, folding her arms. 'I am absolutely sure that, between us, we're going to write that book.'

Belinda looked at the new cleaning lady and marvelled. What a formidable ally to have. She had a silly schoolgirl urge to tell Linda she was lovely. She had such a fruity firmness about her, plus the easy elegance that is often found in people who, at a crucial moment in their teenage development, chose hockey club over Georgette Heyer. Paths divide at every moment of the day, of course. But Belinda believed in the universal hockey-Heyer divide most strongly. In her experience, those who at puberty chose solitary reading over group exertion may (oh, yes) have grown up to be brainboxes earning more money, but they could never quite catch up again in self-confidence with those hearty, practical girls, despite all their well-meant gym subscriptions in later years.

Outside in the hall, Mrs Holdsworth ran her Hoover into a coat-stand, and said, 'Shit,' as it crashed to the floor.

'I can't sack Mrs Holdsworth,' Belinda said.

Linda shrugged. 'I can leave her a patch of hall carpet. Where are the phones, by the way?'

'What?'

'The phones.'

'One in my study, one in the hall.'

'When I'm here, I'll field your calls. Completely uninterrupted time is what you want, isn't it? Shall I throw those newspapers away?'

Belinda nodded. It was like a dream.

'Okey-dokey.' Linda smiled. 'Well, the best thing I can do this afternoon is get some shopping and prepare the dinner. I'll give you a bill at the end of each week. You're in tonight? What time does Mrs Holdsworth finish?'

'Four.'

'I'll return at four ten. And I'll finish at six thirty. What are you working on this afternoon?'

'Oh, hack work. It has to be done. I write for money as Patsy Sullivan. Horsy stories. Patsy subsidizes us all. She'll be paying you too.'

'So you've got a double life yourself, Mrs Johansson!'

'I ought to ditch Patsy, really. Now I'm on the same footing as Tolstoy it doesn't seem right.'

'Well, one thing at a time. Perhaps you're fond of her.'

'Oh, I am. Tell me about yourself, though, Linda.'

But just at that moment the phone rang, and Linda lifted down her coat (a neat ivory mac) from the kitchen door, where she had hung it on a little collapsible hanger. She folded the hanger and put it in her bag. 'I'll answer that on the way out,' she said.

Belinda was startled. 'What? I mean, you can't—'

Mrs H yelled, 'It's your fucking phone, Belinda!' above the din of the machine.

Linda gave her a funny look. 'Trust me,' she said.

Belinda's mother regarded herself in her pocket mirror as the taxi bounced along the north side of Clapham Common. With effort and concentration, she twitched the corners of her mouth to form a ghostly smile. She would never actually regret the face-lift, but she had to admit that the general reaction was not what she had hoped for. Instead of her best friends saying, 'Virginia, you look so good today, so *young*, but somehow I can't put my finger on it,' they walked right past her, even in Harrods Food Hall. To make matters worse, meanwhile, complete strangers were jabbing her in the chest, saying, 'Do you mind me asking? How much it cost?'

It had cost thousands, of course. Cheekbone enhancement, lips like sofa cushions, realigned eyebrows, and a revolutionary polymer skin treatment guaranteed to keep the whole lot immovable for at least five years, as long as she took certain precautions. She could go swimming, she could be kissed on both cheeks, and she could sunbathe as long as she wore an enormous hat. 'But if you feel at all tempted to peek inside a blast furnace,' her surgeon told her darkly, 'don't.'

Lucky, then, that there were so few steel mills still under commission in Knightsbridge. Nevertheless she had taken this alarming advice very much to heart. At home, in her Primrose Hill flat, she'd stopped using the oven, and turned all the radiators down. The iron was permanently set to one-dot, and was used at arm's length. Selling chestnuts on street corners was now totally ruled out as a profession. On the plus side, however, she had given up smoking. After decades of fruitless begging from Belinda, Mother had now kicked the habit overnight, and had even started decrying it in others. In fact, along with rabid jealousy of her facial upholstering, this was the main reason her old friends were dropping her. It gets on your nerves if every time you light up a Benson and Hedges, your companion shrieks, 'No!' and shades her face like Nosferatu. Auntie Vanessa, her identical twin sister (though not as identical as she used to be), was a champion smoker and now flatly refused to see her.

'Hello?'

'Belinda, darling! What a terrible line!'

'This is the Johansson residence. Who is this speaking, please?'

Mother regarded her mobile phone with a puzzled expression, and knocked it against the car door a couple of times. 'Belinda?'

'I'm afraid Mrs Johansson is working at the moment. May I pass on a message?'

'It's her mother, for heaven's sake. And I'm just on my way to see her.' The taxi purred at traffic-lights. 'Right here, then Armadale Road,' she yelled, pointing.

Linda effortlessly took an executive decision. In fact she took two, because she bobbed down and unplugged Mrs H's Hoover at the same time, leaving the old woman open-mouthed.

'Oh, I've heard so much about you!' she lied. 'Mrs Johansson was just saying how much she'd like to see you. But she is so terribly busy today. I'll ask her either to call you later or to give me a message for you. Did you have a nice day shopping?'

'What?'

'I very much look forward to meeting you. I'm Linda.'

She plugged the Hoover back in, and replaced the receiver.

'You must be Mrs Holdsworth,' she smiled, extending her manicured hand. 'What a lovely scarf. Is it new?'

Jago spent his afternoon making secret calls to Dermot on his mobile from the gents'. He had no idea that the vile Dermot had been smooching with his wife the night before – or, indeed, that as he spoke to Dermot, mobile-to-mobile, he was in bed with her, showing her the extremely out-of-the-way places where his tan stopped.

Dermot, it has to be said, was more excited by the human clone in their midst than he'd been about making love to Viv – and, to Viv's chagrin, did not try hard to disguise it. In fact he waved her away rather nastily, and she retreated to the *en suite* while he offered Jago his professional opinion – viz., that if Stefan were really a clone in our midst, Jago could get half a million for a book, plus serialization fees. However, if it turned out that Stefan was merely in our midst (and not a clone), he'd be lucky to get a poke in the eye with a sharp stick.

'You're not an investigative reporter, Jago. Did you ever do anything like this before? What's the nearest you've been to cutting-edge stuff?'

'I interviewed Tom Stoppard when his marriage was breaking up.'

'What did he say about it?'

'About what?'

'His love life.'

Jago's voice rose. 'You saying I should have asked him? Jesus, can you imagine how awkward that would be?'

Dermot didn't have time for this. He sat up in bed and tucked a pillow behind him.

'See what you can get, Jago. But you know how it is. You'll need patience and perseverance and tact to get this story.'

Jago winced three times. He hated all those words.

'My suggestion is, hire someone to watch him. Find out

what happened in Sweden. And don't get obsessed with the clone thing. Do you think Belinda knows she might be married to a clone?'

'No.'

Dermot looked up at Viv, who was suddenly standing next to him. If she had overheard, there was nothing he could do about it.

'Don't tell her.'

'You're right. I mean, for one thing I don't want to alarm my oldest friend unnecessarily. And on top of that—'

Dermot was there already. 'She might get in first with a book deal?'

'Exactly.'

Mrs Holdsworth finished Hoovering her little patch of hall and tottered to the kitchen for her coat. She pocketed the money Belinda had left her with an aggressive swipe, as if she would just as happily trample it underfoot. It had been an unsettling afternoon. Three times she had tried Belinda with conversational gambits of such outstanding ingenuity that she'd had to have a sit-down afterwards. But even 'Do you think Richard Branson is really the Antichrist?' and 'Whatever made anyone invent the scone?' failed to find their mark. And then, to top it all, this woman in the light mac had unplugged her Hoover. In cleaning-lady terms, this was a direct challenge that cannot be overstated. It is the equivalent of the glove smacked across your face from right to left, and then from left to right.

From her ground-floor office, Belinda listened as Mrs Holdsworth left. She felt half guilty and half excited by the idea of hurting her feelings. She loved the sense of danger. What if Mrs Holdsworth told her off?

'I'll be off, then, Belinda,' the old woman called. 'We're out of Jif.'

'Right. Many thanks.'

'Back next week.'

'Mm.'

'Did you know the other woman took a key?'

'That's OK.'

She heard the front door opened; felt the draught; heard traffic noise. Mrs H was evidently taking her time, deciding whether to pursue it. Then, with a muttered 'Fuck it,' the door was slammed, and Mrs H could faintly be heard coughing ('God Almighty, Jesus wept') at the garden gate.

Stefan was not expecting to meet his mother-in-law Virginia lurking behind a denuded London plane tree as he walked from the bus along Armadale Road. It was six thirty and dark, which didn't help. And since she no longer looked remotely like the woman he knew as Mother, he walked straight past her, consulting a little book and talking to himself. 'Make it snappy or make tracks,' she heard him saying. 'You have made a hole in my pocket but I won't make a song and dance. How do you make that out exactly? Ha! That makes you sit up, for sure.'

'Stefan!' she called. She had always liked Stefan, because he was big and handsome; and he had always liked her, too. The reason they saw Mother so infrequently was only that Belinda was discouraged by criticism, and Mother, unfortunately, had no other mode of communication.

He turned. 'Let's make a night of it, baby,' he said. 'Oh, hello, Virginia. Didn't recognize you. Something up?'

Mother's permanently fixed expression of wide-eyed alarm often gave rise to this question. But on this occasion at least the context made it the right thing to say.

'I had to see you,' she said. 'Who's Linda? What's going on?'

Stefan's eyes swivelled. 'I don't understand. Why are you out here in the street? Has there been dirty work at the crossroads?'

Mother pursed her lips. Or, more accurately, she attempted to purse her lips but gave up.

'Yes, I rather think there has,' she said at last. 'I wanted to invite Belinda to the opera tonight. This Linda refused to let me.'

'Really? She sent you away from the door, like a dog in the night?'

'I phoned. They wouldn't let me in, Stefan.' She pouted. 'I've been out here in the cold. It was someone called Linda and she was very rude. Typical of Belinda to hire somebody who'd be rude to her mother.'

At which point, as they approached the front door, Linda opened it and smiled at them both. She was evidently just leaving, but when she saw them she ushered them inside, gesturing at them to keep the noise down.

'Mrs Johansson is working until seven,' she whispered. 'The dinner will be ready at seven thirty. I've rigged up a temporary answering-machine, made a list of the more urgent bills, filed the letters, cleaned the kitchen windows, sprayed the cat for fleas and changed all the beds.'

'Linda is our new Mrs Mop,' Stefan explained, somewhat redundantly.

'The newspapers I took to the dump,' Linda continued, 'but I've rung the recycling people and they'll start coming next Tuesday. Um, what else? Your dressing-gown is warming in the airing cupboard, Mr Johansson. I didn't know what to do with this ice-hockey puck, but I can ask Mrs Johansson at our three o'clock meeting tomorrow. Normally our meeting will be at one o'clock, when I'll provide soup and a hot dish, but tomorrow I'll be a little late, as I'll be having lunch with Mrs Johansson's agent on her behalf.'

A number of objections raised themselves in the minds of Stefan and Mother, but under this barrage all they could do was laugh nervously.

'Does Belinda know all this?'

Linda was surprised. 'Of course not. That's the idea.'

Stefan ran through the list again in his mind. He frowned. 'I think the cat was not ours, Linda. We do not own a cat. I fear you have de-fleaed the cat of another.'

Mother made a strangled noise. 'The cat of another?' she exploded. 'Who cares about the cat of another? I've never heard anything like it. This is so typical of Belinda. Having lunch with Jorkin? How dare you?'

Linda looked puzzled. 'I am thinking only of what's best for Mrs Johansson, and for everybody. Truly, I'm very good at this sort of thing. One of my previous employers said I was like Nature. I abhor a vacuum. Meanwhile, as I'm sure you're aware, Mrs Johansson has fears that she will cease to be before her pen has gleaned her teeming brain.'

Mother tried to look aghast, but (of course) continued only to look mildly surprised. In any case, it was hard to have a proper scene huddled by the front door, talking in hushed tones for fear of interrupting the sacred work of Belinda.

'I don't believe it,' she hissed. 'This house! This is so typical! You waltz in here. You just waltz—'

Mother, breathless with exasperation, seemed to be getting stuck on the insufferable image of Linda waltzing. 'I mean, here's an idea, Linda, whoever you are,' she spat. 'If you're doing everything for my daughter, why don't you just come to see *Così Fan Tutte* with me tonight, then sleep with Stefan afterwards?'

'Virginia!' exclaimed Stefan. English sarcasm always outraged him.

But Linda had her head on one side, as if making her mind up. 'Would you stay there, please?' she said, and disappeared in the direction of Belinda's study. They waited awkwardly by the front door, like neighbourhood children waiting for a friend to come out to play.

Linda returned. 'I'd love to,' she said. 'I mean, I'd love to come to the opera in Belinda's place. She's happy to carry on working, and she said it would be a good opportunity for me to get to know you. She also said you know perfectly well she hates poncy opera. So thank you, thank you very much. Is that a Prada coat? I thought so. Look at the tailoring.'

She attempted to give Mother a kiss on the cheek, but was almost shoved away. 'Poncy?' Mother queried, obviously hurt. 'Belinda!' she called.

Stefan intervened. 'If the ticket is spare, Virginia, why not take Linda? She takes us by surprise, yet it is a swell idea. Here is a vacuum for her to fill, I think. Surely we should give her the glad hand for the kitchen windows and such. Only the cat of another has the right to bad feeling.'

'May I call you Virginia?' asked Linda, with a smile.

'Of course not.'

Mother was beginning to feel dizzy.

'You must come to dinner tomorrow night, mustn't she, Mr Johansson? I happen to know Belinda's aiming to finish her chapter on Dostoevsky this week, and she'll be so relieved to know she needn't do anything.'

'Poncy?' Mother repeated. '*Così* isn't poncy.'

Linda waved it away. 'May I call you Mother?'

'No.'

'Well, this is very exciting. Do I need to change first, do you think? Or shall I come as I am?'

Back in her flat, Maggie stroked Ariel and Miranda in the dark, and tried to imagine how she would tell Belinda what had happened. Belinda ought to be informed about a real-life case of doubles, surely? But, on the other hand, the vocabulary was so difficult. 'I met a double' would sound like she'd met her own double; 'I met two doubles' sounded like she'd met four people, possibly dressed in tennis whites, which was in no way a reflection of what had happened.

If only she had a contact number for Leon! If only she had listened more carefully when he told her the details of his next indie-car yawnfest assignment in Oshbosh, Oklahoma. 'Off to Oshbosh,' said his note. 'You were lovely. I want to see you again. Yours anally, L.' She couldn't possibly ask Jago about him: it was imperative that her friends never find out the calibre of person she allowed herself to sleep with. But, there again, Leon's presence was desperately required, simply to prove to her bloody therapist that she hadn't made him up.

Olivia in *Twelfth Night*, she reflected, had had such an easy time of it by comparison. 'Honestly, you look *exactly* like him,' she had lamely told Noel, Julia's husband, in the café, when he'd revived her. But he only nodded solemnly and exchanged professional tut-tut glances with Julia. He was a therapist too, naturally. Neither of them believed her. It was a nightmare. They wanted to know why she'd identified herself as Penelope Pitstop, but since neither of them had a sense of humour or had watched children's television, it had been necessary to abandon the explanation.

'Margaret won't mind me telling you,' Julia was informing Noel now. 'We've been working for several months on a specific complex, relating to her feelings of invisibility. Her greatest fear – I think this is true, Margaret? – is of being publicly ignored and rejected by people who've been intimate with her. I think we agreed that of all humiliations this one utterly annihilates you, doesn't it, Margaret?'

Maggie nodded reluctantly, horrified that Julia should discuss this with somebody else. Julia lowered her voice. 'We think it's probably to do with her father.'

Noel looked impressed by this discovery. 'The father is so often the cause,' he agreed. 'And today that fear was projected on to me? Tch, I'm so sorry I hurt you that way, Margaret.'

'It wasn't your fault,' insisted Maggie. 'And it wasn't anything to do with projecting. It's just that you look *exactly* like the man I slept with last night. It was a case of mistaken identity, that's all.'

'I know,' said Noel.

'I know,' echoed Julia, and automatically offered Maggie a packet of tissues from her bag. Likewise automatically, Maggie took one. She shoved it up the sleeve of her jumper.

'You *do*,' she insisted, and waggled her hands.

'Yes, yes,' said Noel, thoughtfully. 'I'll tell you what, Margaret. Can I call you Margaret?'

'You already have.'

'Well, Margaret.' Noel rested his chin in his hands. 'I'm struck by an idea here. It's pretty revolutionary, I warn you. But why don't we all work together on this? I happen to be an expert on therapeutic role-playing. For therapeutic purposes, and under the strictest ethical controls, I could take the role of this man, this – Leon?'

'Yes, Leon.'

'And – well, I'm just feeling my way here, of course – but I could be Leon and, um, well, recognize you. Why not take advantage of the fact that you see a resemblance? I could recognize you and respond to you, and make you feel better. Sometimes I wouldn't recognize you, and you could hit me. Although only under the strictest ethical doo-dahs and whatsits, et cetera. What do you think?'

'I don't know. To be honest, I was thinking of leaving therapy altogether.'

Noel and Julia both gasped.

'The thing is,' she continued, 'I spend so much time talking about my life, I feel I'm not actually living it.'

The therapists swapped glances.

'All the more reason to continue with therapy, but step it up, add another dimension,' Julia advised, quickly.

'Really?'

'Oh, yes.'

They watched her as she wavered. Noel coughed. 'I'll come clean with you, Margaret. I think you have a very serious problem.'

'Really?'

'Yes. Ignoring this problem is simply not a choice you have. No, you can either solve this problem through years of analysing it, or you can confront it and blow it out of the water. Tease it out slowly, or blitz it. Well, I think I know you well enough to know which course you'd prefer.'

'You don't know me at all,' Maggie pointed out, reasonably.

'Margaret, your hostility and defensiveness are all part of your problem.'

'That's true,' said Julia. 'You resist intimacy, even with me.'

Maggie wanted to hit her. She wanted to hit him, too. The café would be closing at half past two, and she still hadn't had her bacon sandwich.

'Look. I'm sorry. But the point is, you're the lady I pay to help me sort out a problem, and you're a man who just happens to look exactly like the man I slept with last night. I didn't like him, and to be honest, I'm not warming much to you, either.'

Julia shook her head and sighed.

'No, it's OK,' Noel told her. 'I can work with that. Let's say I'm the man you slept with last night, Margaret. See? I'm Leon. *Nyow-nyow*, and here comes Michael Schumacher in the Renault. First things first. Was I any good in bed?'

'You were terrible.'

'OK,' he said again, with slightly less enthusiasm. 'I can work with that, too.'

'No,' she relented. 'You were nice. I'm a bitch. I mean, *he* was nice. What am I saying?'

A man came to collect their cups. 'Michael Schumacher drives a Ferrari,' he observed. 'As a point of fact.'

'I didn't say this was going to be easy,' snapped Noel. 'I just said it was the best way to stop this lovely young woman spiralling into madness.'

At which the man pronounced the Gemini closed.

Sitting here in the dark now, Maggie realized Miranda and Ariel were practising that special cat alarmed expression, which says, 'Who the hell are you? Am I in the wrong house? My God, I'm getting out of here.' It didn't help. She got up and brushed them off her lap.

This is all bloody Leon's fault, she thought. Bloody, bloody Leon.

When Jago returned from the office at nine that evening, he said nothing about Stefan being a clone. He just brought home with him five books by Laurie Spink, four by Steve Jones and two by Richard Dawkins. It was clear that his efforts to absorb and enjoy these books had defeated him. He looked tired and miserable, as though he'd been wrestling feebly with a muscular opponent who'd not only held him by the wrists but had laughed at him. The minute he was indoors he made a tall pile of the books in the hall and kicked them against a door. Viv heard the noise and rushed in. 'Special supplement on genetics,' he explained, waving a hand at the scattered, broken-backed volumes. He wore a wounded expression. 'Do you think Melvyn Bragg really understands any of this?' he cried. 'Because I'm fucked if I do.'

Viv watched sympathetically as he retrieved the books and showed them to her, one by one. He was almost in tears. 'Look at this. "Winner of the Easy-peasy Book Prize",' he pretended to read from the cover of one. '"Best popular science book of 1995, a million copies sold to babes in arms",' he snarled. 'Pah! Look. "I couldn't put it down – Sooty".'

Viv wondered whether he was going to confide his theory about Stefan, but it looked as if he wasn't. Since she could hardly explain how she happened to know already, she would just have to wait until he told her, and then act surprised.

'Why don't you phone Stefan if you want to know about genetics?' she said, therefore. 'He knows all about it.'

'Oh yeah, very funny,' snapped Jago.

'Why?'

Caught out, Jago bit his lip and thought fast. 'Someone from the letters desk said Richard Branson is the Antichrist today. Can you believe that? The things people will say.'

'Mm,' said Viv. As they made their way to the kitchen, she hoped she was better at lying than her husband was. Jago was not only sweaty and jumpy but an obituary of Stefan was sticking out of his pocket, and he'd brought home a copy of a sensational American weekly paper, opened at the page 'Ten Ways to Tell if Your Grandparent is a Clone'.

'I think Linda's defected,' said Viv.

'Shame,' said Jago, who didn't care. He had poured himself a drink. 'Listen to this,' he said. '"Ten ways to tell if your grandparent is a clone. One. Sleeps fewer hours than you do. Two. Sometimes gets confused about things that happened relatively recently, yet claims to have personal memories of the Second World War. Three—" Do you think this is on the level?'

'I was talking about Linda,' insisted Viv. 'She said she'd still come on Thursday, but I feel she's gone. So you need to know the consequences.'

Jago nodded. He wasn't listening.

'Ten ways to tell that your wife is inconsolably upset,' Viv persisted. 'One. She doesn't speak to her oldest friend Belinda ever again. Two. She resigns her job at the hospital.'

'Three?' he said automatically, then looked up. 'What?' he said. 'You resigned your *job*?'

72

'I rang them today. I've resigned. I'm not going back.'

'Don't you think that's a little extreme? We could replace Linda, for heaven's sake.'

Viv laughed. 'I doubt it.'

Jago put down his weekly paper and coughed. 'Viv, I've got something to tell you,' he said. 'I came home one day when Linda was supposed to be here, and I saw you putting the washing out when you should have been at work.'

'So?'

'So, I never thought Linda really did much, and I'm glad she's gone. I think she had some kind of a hold over you.'

Viv was stricken. It was true. Life had been much simpler before Linda came along and streamlined it. But she felt no duty to tell Jago the full story, because Jago had cheerfully never absorbed a full story in his life. Even at undergraduate level, he was only really interested in headlines. 'Blind Puritan Pens Mega Poem' was his level, mostly. 'Queen Is Faerie Shock.' When she'd first needed to tell him she was pregnant, she'd left him a note with 'Wife Up Duff Blunder' on it. And when Stefan announced his engagement to Belinda, she'd wrestled for hours with variants of 'Norwegian Wooed' before admitting to herself it would never quite come right.

' "Char In Mystery Job Whammy",' she said, for his benefit, now. ' " 'I Never Knew,' Says Husband'." '

At ten thirty, as Belinda and Stefan snuggled on the sofa, the phone rang. It was Virginia. Stefan answered it and came back.

'Your mother wanted to let us know she'd had a rattling good time at the opera with Linda,' he reported, pouring his wife the last of the wine. 'She said Linda was very appreciative and attentive and didn't keep telling her what to think of it, like some people she could mention.'

'Oh,' said Belinda. 'Well, that's good.'

'She also said it was nice to go out with someone who didn't keep squirming in their seat.'

'That's my mother.'

Stefan looked at her. 'You don't mind?'

Belinda laughed. 'Mind what?'

'Being compared like that? Are you sure? As sure as eggs is eggs?'

'Why would I want to spend an evening with Mother when I could be here with you? Thank you very much, Linda. That's what I say. What a star.'

They snuggled together again.

'Some people would be jealous, that's all. Ingrid was a jealous person. And you are jealous of Viv sometimes, I think.'

'I'll tell you the only time I feel really jealous,' said Belinda, putting her hand under Stefan's shirt and stroking his skin. 'It's when I think of Ingrid. Or when you look at Maggie, or Maggie looks at you. I saw her whisper to you last night and I got hot and raw and murderous, and I felt sick. That's when I feel jealous.'

Like most people, Stefan was both pleased and apprehensive at the idea that his loving partner would kill to keep him true.

'That was a dandy meal Linda made. Sea bass. It's a crying shame you couldn't have it. You will have to tell her you think fish is strictly for the birds.'

'Yes. But anyone who does what she does – well, you've got to make a few allowances. Did you hear about next door's cat?'

'I did.'

'She's going to be amazing. She's having lunch with Jorkin for me tomorrow.'

'You know about that?'

'I overheard.'

'You don't mind about that either?'

'Oh, Stefan, why should I mind? I loathe Jorkin, he never has any decent ideas, and the extra time not having lunch

74

with him means I can get on with the masterwork. I think it's marvellous.'

'I would lay down the law, if it were me. And stop the rot.'

'Mm.' Belinda shrugged.

'I mean, who is this Linda? Was she born under a gooseberry bush? You entrust her to run our lives, and bake my dressing-gown in the airing cupboard, and question me about my moose-hat, and make sea bass without asking – and all I know is that she tell me she's like Nature, she abhors a vacuum.'

'Is that what she said?' said Belinda, evidently pleased by the idea. 'Honestly, Stefan, don't take it so seriously. It's all in a good cause. The way I see it, if she really does abhor a vacuum, that's marvellous news.'

'And she can always use a dustpan and brush,' said Stefan, solemnly, before breaking into a proud grin. 'Which is a good yoke, I think.'

Belinda kissed him. 'What is it you used to call me?' she asked, teasingly.

'I used to call you, um, "Come to bed, Miss Patch".'

'I can't believe I let you get away with that.'

'No. Sometimes neither can I.'

Chapter Five

Life without Neville turned out to be exhilarating for Belinda. For yes, as she soon recognized with a pang, the rats had taken one look at Linda, packed their trapeze equipment and gone. Only a whiff of sawdust remained, and the echo of a drum-rolled 'Hup!' Belinda wondered whether she should break the good news to Stefan; but since he'd never subscribed to the Flying Vermin Brothers in the first place, decided to let this important Linda achievement pass unmarked.

Besides, banishing imaginary rats from her employer's alimentary canal was only one of Linda's more rudimentary accomplishments. For, returning next day from lunch with Jorkin, she bit her lip for a minute and then admitted that she'd sacked him.

'I'm so sorry, but the thing is, he had no ideas and no belief,' she told an astonished Belinda, as she tied an apron over a rather smart, pale pink skirt she'd worn for the meeting. She climbed a little set of steps and started methodically sorting a kitchen cupboard and, without the least fuss or bother, slipping most of its appalling contents into an open bin-liner.

'You don't mind, do you?' she asked, disposing of an ancient lolly-making set. 'Sacking your agent?'

'Not at all,' said Belinda, almost choking with bewildered

excitement. Linda had worked here for less than twenty-four hours and had already jettisoned Jorkin!

'I just felt that the book should come first. I mean, that's right, isn't it? So all I said to him was that we needed an income from the Patsy Sullivan stories that wasn't dependent on so many new titles. In other words, a push on merchandising, serialization and foreign sales. I thought that's what you'd have said if you'd been there. I mean, it's obvious to anybody.'

Belinda, who had never had such a smart idea in her life, agreed readily. 'Merchandising. Obvious. Anybody.'

'Well, that's what I thought you'd think.' Linda tossed a bag of old paper napkins, a cracked wooden tray and some baby-blue birthday candles into the sack. A lot of this stuff had come with the house, and Belinda had never even looked at it.

'So you don't mind?'

'Far from it. I just—'

'He didn't see it at all. He was very obstructive. But it seems obvious to me. Verity dolls, Verity bedspreads, tiny mucking-out sets, little bales of straw at ten pounds each, curry-combs the size of your fingernail. I read a couple of the Verity books last night, just to get the feel of them, and I have to say, I think they're very good.'

'Do you?' Belinda, who loved praise, wanted to ask which ones her new friend had read, but stopped herself. Despite her high-flown literary pretensions, she was exceptionally proud of the second book, *A Big Day for Verity*.

'It just makes me mad that your agent can't see we're sitting on a gold mine.'

'He's quite literary,' Belinda apologized. 'More of a Faber poets kind of chap. There's not much call for Christopher Isherwood mucking-out sets. I don't suppose Jorkin has ever met anyone like you before. Who did you tell him you were, by the way?'

'Oh, well, I hope you don't mind,' Linda said, 'I sort of implied I was you.'

The shock made Belinda blink and swallow for a couple of seconds, but she managed to keep smiling. A silver cake-stand she'd received as a wedding present was tipped into the bag.

'Didn't Jorkin remember what I looked like?' she ventured, at last.

'I suppose he can't have done.' Linda was now mopping and dusting in the empty cupboard, turning her back. 'Although he did say he was expecting someone in blue stockings, and was pleasantly surprised. You don't wear blue stockings, surely, Mrs Johansson?'

'I expect he was being unpleasantly metaphorical.'

'Oh, I see. Anyway, what do you think?'

Belinda looked up to see the effect of Linda's work. She felt gooey with admiration.

'Actually, there's something else,' Linda continued. 'On the subject of real stockings, he tried to put his hand on my knee, so I'm afraid to say I struck him.'

Belinda yelped. 'You struck him?'

'Just on the head. Only enough to knock him down. He was able to get up again and finish his spotted dick.'

'Where were you?'

'The club he belongs to. Begins with a G.'

'The Garrick?'

'That's it.'

'Jesus,' said Belinda, with feeling. 'Any people around?'

'Yes. The place was quite full.'

'And you said you were me?'

'Yes.'

'Oh my God.'

Neatly, Linda stepped off her little ladder, which Belinda now realized she'd never seen before. More of a surprise, however, was that the cleaning lady appeared to have tears in her eyes. What was happening?

'I only did what I thought you'd do, Mrs Johansson,' she protested. 'It was all for you. But if I was wrong—' She dabbed her eyes with a tissue, and gave Belinda a soulful look reminiscent of a chastened puppy on a biscuit-tin lid. She slumped as if her backbone had been removed.

Belinda felt stricken. Had she really sounded so disapproving? She'd only said, 'Oh my God,' and suddenly Linda had turned from a white tornado into a tepid drizzle.

'You've already been so nice to me,' Linda faltered. 'So have your husband and your mother. If you want me to leave—'

As Linda sank to a chair, Belinda suddenly remembered in a wave of panic what Viv had told her: that Linda needed reassurance. Was this what she meant?

'Don't upset yourself, please,' interrupted Belinda. 'I think you're wonderful. I've been thinking about how to put this without sounding drippy, but I can't. Basically, if you were a girl at school and I were a girl at school, I'd worship you.'

'You're not just saying that?' Linda's eyes, sparkling with tears, were of the purest indigo.

'No. Absolutely not. The fact is, I wish more than anything that I'd struck Jorkin in the Garrick. Absolutely the next best thing is you doing it for me without asking.'

'I know I get carried away a bit,' Linda sniffed. 'But what sometimes people don't realize is that I'm—' She struggled now against her feelings, fielding the tears that suddenly rolled down her cheeks. 'I'm completely on their side.' She wiped her eyes and adjusted her apron. 'So you will tell me if I do anything you're not happy about, won't you? Because I'll just go. I won't make a fuss.'

Belinda smiled reassuringly and patted Linda's hand. She wanted to mention the expensive cake-stand; she wanted to mention that she really, really didn't like fish. But now she knew how feeble Linda's confidence was, now she knew how easy it was to hurt her feelings, she simply couldn't bear to do it.

Over the next few days Jago's genetics research led him nowhere, especially after Laurie Spink assured him personally that despite the journalistic dash and verve of the article 'Ten Ways to Tell if Your Grandparent is a Clone', scientifically it was less than watertight. Thus, even if Stefan exhibited all ten of the detailed tendencies, such as incontinence, deafness and a greedy appetite for cakes and puddings, the signs could not be wholly relied on.

But if the muddied waters of clone technology might take a while to clear, Jago was sure at least that Stefan was not teaching at Imperial. That lie at least was uncovered. For, over a period of three days, Stefan was observed to board a bus each morning, cross the river in approximately the right spot, but then hide away in Habitat in the King's Road, drinking coffee and reading English-language reference books, whose pages he would mark with sticky tabs. Sometimes he had a cookie; sometimes a Danish pastry. Then he would stroll to the college in the afternoon to do part-time work as a lab assistant. And that was it, save for the bus home, and more reading. The dossier presented after a week by young Tanner, a rather supercilious graduate trainee in Features, was depressingly slim. Double-spaced, and on one side of the paper only, it still amounted to just one page.

Jago waved it irritably. 'So what happens after six thirty?' he demanded. They were alone in his office, and he had shut the door.

'At home, of course,' Tanner scoffed, and ran a hand over his fashionably shaven pate. He couldn't think of much else to say. His ambition was to make his name one day in investigative reporting, and he couldn't see how tracking harmless Swedes for maniac executives fitted in. Tanner's father, chairman of the board of the *Effort*'s parent company, expected more for him than this.

'All right, tell me. Did you notice anything odd about him?'

'Mm, one thing.'

'What?' Jago was breathless.

'Kept turning round. Seemed to think he was being followed.'

Jago rolled his eyes. You couldn't bawl out Tanner, he knew that. He was too well connected. This useless boy could get him sacked. 'All right,' he said. 'You've done all you can here, Tanner. Now I want you to go to Sweden.'

'Whatever for?'

'I want you to dig some dirt in Malmö.'

The boy sighed. 'Do I have to? Oh, what a bore.'

'You don't seem hungry for this job, Tanner. I have to say that. This could be an enormous story. Impostors, cloning, Sweden, what more could you ask?'

Tanner shrugged. 'Been offered a stint on Fashion, actually. The editor rang Daddy. It's just that my sister is the youngest designer ever at Christian Dior, and he wants a piece on it.'

'How old is she?'

'Five.'

'Damn. That's a fucking good story! Damn.'

Tanner smirked. 'I'll come back to the clone, though.'

'You will?'

It was hard for Jago to be patient with this irritating upstart, but at the same time utterly necessary.

'Why not?' said Tanner. 'Where is Malmö, anyway? Sounds ghastly.'

'No idea. Get an atlas.'

'An atlas,' repeated the boy. 'Any atlas?' He surveyed Jago's office with the curled lip of someone who would certainly redecorate before he moved in.

'Any atlas with Sweden in it.'

Tanner didn't move.

'Try the library.'

'Right.'

He started to leave, but Jago pulled him back. 'You haven't breathed a word of this to anyone?'

'Of course not.'

Tanner sighed deeply, but only when fully out of earshot. 'What a stupid, stupid man,' he said to himself. 'I wonder if Daddy could do something about him?'

When Maggie finally phoned Belinda, ten days after the encounter with Noel, she interrupted a pleasant Sunday morning scene. Mother, Stefan and Linda were finishing a large, lazy breakfast while Belinda had slipped away to her study to make notes. Linda and Mother were admiring the style supplements together; Stefan basked in a dressing-gown that had been thoughtfully warmed in the airing cupboard. Occasionally, however, he popped to the window to check for lurkers with notepads.

'What's wrong, Stefan?' asked Mother. 'That's the third time you've looked outside.'

'Oh, nothing,' he said airily. 'There's not a soul out there, no one to hear my prayer. Ha ha.'

Should he mention the youth who had followed him home three nights this week? Once, in the Habitat café, the strange, bald-headed boy had actually approached him and asked whether he'd just eaten a cookie or a pastry. 'A cookie,' he'd told him, watching the boy write it down in large fledgling shorthand. 'With nuts.' Since Friday, thank goodness, the boy had desisted. But when the phone rang, Stefan was still glad to see Linda answer it. It was astonishing how quickly they had all come to rely on her.

'I'm afraid she's working at the moment,' she said to Maggie.

'But I'll be glad to help if I can. No, I'm afraid Mr Johansson is busy too.'

She replaced the receiver. 'It was Belinda's friend Maggie,' she explained. 'She rang off.'

'Hooray,' said the others, callously.

Any observer of this scene would have noticed that it took place in a spacious new dining room, painted a fashionable ochre, but formerly the dark, dusty book-dump that had served as Belinda's office. For Linda had not been idle in the intervening week. Spotting that one of Belinda's spare bedrooms was well suited for a study, she had promptly disposed of its furniture, removed its threadbare carpet, brought in a carpenter and a couple of strong lads, and gently transplanted Belinda to the first floor, where she had the benefit of better light and excellent shelves, and was permanently removed from the annoyance of the telephone. Thoughtfully, Linda installed for her a coffee-machine and a couch, and a cunning two-way baby-listening device so that Belinda could call for attention downstairs without all the bother of rising from her desk.

'What are you working on?' Linda asked her, every day. And Belinda would excitedly read her a bit from her analysis of Nabokov's *Despair*, and Linda would marvel at Belinda's brilliance and then bring a plate of thickly buttered muffins. No bill had been presented as yet, except for the amounts expended on equipment. Linda had decided to move in, however – an arrangement that suited everybody, especially with Mother suddenly moving in as well.

'Look what your mother bought me!' Linda said on the second Saturday, holding up a navy suit from Betty Jackson. 'I've never had anything so beautiful! You don't mind, Belinda? I mean, she'd have bought one for you if you'd been there. She got me this Estée Lauder foundation as well.'

'Of course I don't mind,' Belinda replied. In fact, she considered it miraculous that Linda shared Mother's interest in expensive tortured cloth and coloured, perfumed grease. It removed from herself the unbearable pressure to look smart and fashionable; it liberated a very needy (and misunderstood) aspect of her nature that hankered for elasticated waists and roomy cardigans. Here was a consequence of hiring a new cleaning lady she had certainly never anticipated when she formerly argued the cause of Mrs Holdsworth. She looked at Linda's tight little suit and shuddered. Tight little suits induced claustrophobia in her. She wanted to rip constricting garments with gardening shears while screaming, 'Let me out of here.'

It was now too late to tell Linda about the fish, unfortunately. But aside from the nice little trays of cod, prawns, *bouillabaisse* and *goujons* Belinda was silently tipping down the loo in between indulging in the ample and enjoyable snacks, she felt no praise was high enough for Linda. It was quite true. Wherever she had a vacuum, Linda went right ahead and abhorred it. Just like a force of nature. Linda really was, as she had said at the outset, completely on her side.

Thrown entirely into her work, moreover, Belinda was serenely happy. She had yearned all her life for such a release from daily cares, for hours on end to read and write, uninterrupted by the requirement to do anything manual, social, culinary or selfless. Ahead of her stretched an endless string of Virginia Woolf's pure and rounded pearls. Viv phoned; she was told nothing about it. Maggie phoned; ditto. Belinda honestly didn't care. Linda took care of breakfast, dinner, tea and sympathy. And what a bonus that she seemed to enjoy it! Belinda had always felt guilty at making Mrs Holdsworth do the housework; with Linda, she felt she was doing her a favour; she was helping Linda to be fulfilled simply by accepting everything she did.

Meanwhile, Linda also continued to show astonishing initiative. For example, after a week, a woman from the *Today* programme on Radio 4 phoned, asking Belinda to take part in a short discussion about making scenes in public places (the Garrick story had spread). But, blissfully secluded upstairs, Belinda knew nothing whatever about it.

'What shall I do?' Linda whispered to Mother, with the receiver pressed against her chest. 'Exposure is useful to a writer, isn't it?'

Mother made a noise. A sort of 'tch'. 'Belinda always says no to that sort of thing. She won't even do book signings. If you ask me, she has a horror of the mob.'

'No,' agreed Linda, 'I don't suppose she'd do it.'

She pulled a face at Mother, who suddenly had an idea. 'You do it, Linda.'

'Me?'

'In my opinion, you'll do it better than she would. Besides, it was you who hit Jorkin.'

So Linda agreed. And the next morning, without mentioning it to Belinda, went by BBC car to Broadcasting House and by general consent acquitted herself magnificently.

Not expecting visitors, since none had come in fifteen years, Mrs Holdsworth was surprised when Viv Ripley came to see her on the second Friday. Viv had heard Linda on the *Today* programme and been outraged. She had tried to phone Belinda six times. 'They said she was Belinda on the radio!' she explained to Jago. 'She's impersonating Belinda on the public airwaves! She's only been working there a week and look what she's done!'

'You're obsessed,' said Jago.

'No, I'm not. I care about my friend.'

'You're not just sore Linda left?'

'No, I'm not.'

'Yes, you are. You're jealous as hell. Giving up your job was insane.'

So she had sought out Mrs Holdsworth, and was now taking tea with that lady in her council flat in Battersea, where the smell of boiled sprouts filled the room to a height of five feet.

Viv discovered that if you stood up and tipped your head back you could, in fact, inhale air smelling of something else. But unfortunately you couldn't spend a whole visit pretending to admire the Artex swirls on the ceiling.

'So, if you still have access to the house, Mrs Holdsworth,' she said, 'you could see what Linda is getting up to. I would pay you handsomely.'

'How handsomely's that, then?' Mrs H, sitting down, lit a Dunhill menthol from a flat green box, an accessory curiously out of keeping with her general eschewal of all things debonair.

'Fifty pounds now, and fifty more when you've reported back. Just think. You could buy a new scarf straight away.'

Mrs Holdsworth looked offended. 'What's wrong with my fucking scarf?'

'Nothing at all. I just meant you might like another one.' Viv felt she wasn't getting anywhere. She tried a new tack. 'I'll come clean with you, Mrs Holdsworth. I am not only Belinda's concerned friend, I am also Linda's probation officer.'

The old woman took a deep drag on the cigarette, and narrowed her eyes. Viv was indeed a much better liar than Jago. The woman was wavering.

'Bleeding probation officers don't give you fifty quid.'

'Linda is a dangerous woman, Mrs Holdsworth. Surely you noticed?'

'I'll tell you what, she unplugged my Hoover.'

'Exactly.'

And so it was Sunday morning now. The Johanssons were happy in their well-organized new home; Jago and Viv were scarcely speaking; Mrs Holdsworth was boiling sprouts; and in Malmö, Ingrid Johansson watched the horizon through a barred window, and hummed tunelessly. Meanwhile Maggie was sitting grimly in her flat with the curtains closed while Noel rang her doorbell and rapped at the letterbox. The fateful role-playing moment had clearly arrived.

Rap, rap. Ring, ring. Rap. Ring.

'It's me,' he called. *Rap, rap.* 'It's Leon!'

Maggie curled her feet under her, and tried to concentrate on *Bridget Jones's Diary*. She grimaced and put it down. It was a book she never could get on with somehow. She'd had it open at the same page for three solid years.

'Open up,' continued Noel, cheerfully. 'I know you're in there. Nyow, nyow!'

'Piss off!' she shouted.

She had decided to have nothing to do with this experiment of Noel's. Let her problem take twenty years to sort out; Noel's short-sharp-shock technique was all too clearly a smokescreen for base motives. 'Full transference' was what he wanted from Margaret, he said. It was an ominous phrase. Call her a weary old cynic who'd been sleeping around too long, but she felt sure the energetic exchange of body fluids would be bound to come into the full-transference process somewhere.

'Go away, I'm reading *Bridget Jones's Diary*,' she called. 'I happen to have located a very funny bit, actually.'

But he knocked and rang until her patience ran out and she opened the door – only to be flattened by the full whirlwind force of Noel's impersonation. Despite herself, Maggie was impressed. The only time she'd seen anything like it was at a Stanislavsky summer school, when the group had been advised to imagine themselves as experiencing nuclear fission while at the same time taking barbiturates.

'Did you miss me?' he said, bursting through the door in a cataract of luggage. Kicking a suitcase across the room, he plonked down a flight bag, a duty-free carrier, a lap-top briefcase and a large fluffy toy in the shape of a red racing car. 'Present from Oshbosh. Do you like it?'

He sat down, ran a hand through his hair, and gave her a wide grin. She had to hand it to Noel. As an act, it was terrifyingly good. The toy had a price in dollars on it, and there were old, dog-eared Grand Prix stickers on the suitcase. Stanislavsky would have wept with joy. She suddenly remembered how huge Leon was — the man now perched awkwardly on her sofa was, like Leon himself, constructed on far too big a physical scale for her flat. His legs were twin telegraph poles. His shoulders under his leather jacket were like beach balls. She expected her furniture to crumple under his weight, like a child's chair under a gorilla. She eyed a bowl of fruit on the coffee table, and prayed he wouldn't peel himself a miniature banana.

'Look, I know I wasn't great,' he said. 'I'm sorry. I've come to make it up to you. The truth is, I've been thinking about you all week long at Oshbosh, I couldn't get you out of my mind.'

Maggie pursed her lips. Yes, it was a good act. He looked like Leon and sounded like Leon, and even dressed like Leon. There was just one problem: this speech of devotion wasn't remotely reminiscent of Leon's personality.

'Why don't you say something?' he asked. He grabbed the duty-free bag and produced a bottle of Cognac. 'For you,' he said.

Maggie frowned as she took the bottle. When did she tell Noel about the Cognac? Leon had finished it off without asking, and said, 'I'll buy you another one.' But she hadn't remembered it until now.

'Tell you what,' she said at last, hardly able to look at him, 'how about you go away and leave me alone?'

He looked wounded. 'Oh, come on, Maggie. I said I was sorry.' He crossed his enormous legs and hugged his arms across his enormous chest. Was he wearing padding?

'Hey, I can't have been that bad.'

'I mean *you*,' she said firmly.

'What?'

'Just go,' she said. Her histrionic gesture towards the door was somewhat undermined by the big red fluffy racing car she clutched to her chest, but she still meant it. 'I'm flattered you should go to all this bother. But honestly, just go.'

He gathered his things sullenly, hunching his shoulders protectively, like a bear who'd been smacked on the nose. He had to stay true to character, she supposed. She felt quite sorry for him.

'Look, I'm off for a month of stuff,' he said, as he gathered his things. 'Boxing in Las Vegas, tennis in Germany, basketball in Sweden. Can I call you sometime? Or when I'm back? I'd really like to.'

'I can't stop you,' said Maggie. Noel was a very cruel person, she was realizing. When you know how needy for affection a person is, you shouldn't tease them this way.

'Look, I really like you,' he blurted. 'I think I love you.' He touched her arm.

'Don't.'

He cupped his hand and moved it to her shoulder. Then he stroked her face. 'You're lovely,' he said. 'I never met anyone like you.'

'Don't,' she whimpered.

'Why?'

'Because you don't mean it.'

'You're very hard, Maggie. Come to Malmö in March.'

'Oh please, stop it. How can they play basketball in Malmö in March? They'd slip over on the ice.'

'Basketball is indoors, Maggie.'

'Is it?'

'Yes.'

He left at last, and she watched him hail a taxi. 'Wandsworth, the Arndale Centre,' he told the driver, even though she knew Noel and Julia lived in the opposite direction, in Kennington. She admired his thoroughness, but was so pleased to see the back of him that when she returned indoors she fell straight asleep.

*   *   *

'You're putting on weight,' observed Mother, that Sunday afternoon. 'That's no way to keep a husband, if you don't mind me saying so. Don't you want to watch *The Clothes Show* with us?'

'No thanks,' said Belinda. She'd been lying on her new couch reading a biography of Hans Christian Andersen and eating a Mars bar. A bag of mini Twixes was at her side. From outside, she could feel the reassuring tremble of the commuter trains as they thundered through the cutting at the end of the road. Her blanket was warm, and she was horizontal in the middle of the afternoon. She had never been happier in her life.

'Doesn't Linda do a lovely shark with peppercorns?' Mother asked. She looked mildly alarmed at the memory of it, but then she always did.

'Mm.'

'What was it you cooked for me the last time I was here? Baked beans on something?'

'Baked beans on cream crackers. You know very well.'

'That's right. You'd run out of bread!'

Belinda tried to keep reading, but Mother hadn't finished with her yet. 'Linda's cleaned the bathroom floor. Did you know it was green under all that?'

'No. Look, is there something in particular?'

'No, no. Just to say brill with kumquats tomorrow.'

'Great.'

'Brill,' Mother repeated. 'Whoever would have thought it in your house?'

She went away, and Belinda rearranged herself under the blanket. Hans Christian Andersen's story 'The Shadow' had been the original inspiration for her book – a story so troubling that she had never been able to forget it. It concerned a scholar from a grey north European country who took a holiday in Italy and discovered for the first time that his shadow had a personality. At midday it crouched near his feet; in the evening it stretched and lengthened and enjoyed itself. Then, one night, the scholar stood on his balcony and saw the shadow projected against the shutters of the house opposite. What if my shadow could go inside? he thought. Go on, shadow!

Of course, the shadow detaches itself, and the scholar goes home without it. But years later the shadow returns – now accomplished and worldly, standing upright, with its own clothes and jewellery, but unable to put on much weight. The scholar is helpless as the shadow takes over his life, forcibly swaps identities with him, and finally orders his execution. Belinda's theory was that the story fell into a parental pattern – it was about the essential shock of parenthood. You give children your blessing to go off and leave you, to learn more than you ever did, and the next thing you know, they're telling you what to do. Power abruptly transfers to the child. Or doesn't, of course, if you've got a mother like Virginia, who remembers an innocent baked-bean supper catastrophe for the rest of her natural life.

Linda brought her a sticky toffee pudding, and some home-made biscuits for later. She also topped up Belinda's coffee machine.

'Thank you, Linda,' she said, without moving. 'You're a marvel. Mother says the bathroom floor is green. They should give you an archaeology award. You should also get a medal for being the first person of my acquaintance that my mother approves of.'

Linda smiled weakly, but merely gathered some crockery and turned to go. At which point, with a shock like a punch to the stomach, Belinda noticed there were tears in her eyes again.

'Oh no,' she said. 'What's happened?' She could scarcely breathe. The effect of these tiny drops of moisture was devastating. 'Is there something wrong, Linda?'

'I'm afraid I've discovered something so upsetting about you that I'll have to leave.'

'No,' Belinda gasped. 'About me?'

All the guilty secrets she'd ever had whirled into her mind. The sin of stopping an ice-cream van once in childhood, when not wanting an ice-cream, had given her sleepless nights until she was thirty years old, but she'd always known that, crime-wise, this incident was rather small potatoes to anybody with an ounce of mature perspective.

'When I think of all the things I was preparing to do for you,' Linda said, 'it makes me feel like a fool. Did you know I'd agreed to do the *Late Review* for you on Thursday? No, I thought not. I've been reading an Updike novel and I've seen a play with lots of swearing in it at the Royal Court, and – and – and now this.'

'Now what?'

Linda's chin was wobbling again.

Belinda put an arm around her shoulder. 'Please, tell me. What have I done?'

'Mr Johansson just told me—' She sniffed. 'He told me—'

'What?'

'That you don't like fish.'

Belinda yelped with laughter.

'It's not funny,' Linda snapped.

'Yes it is. Oh Linda—' She reached to touch her, but Linda stiffened. Her jaw jutted out. 'The point is, you lied to me, Belinda. I've given you lots of fish because it's good for the brain, and you didn't tell me that you didn't like it, and you swore you'd tell me if I did anything you didn't like. You *swore*. But now I find this out, and I know you must have been laughing at me, and now you're laughing at me again. I'm just so disappointed in you, I feel as if you've stuck a dagger in a baby's heart.'

'I'm sorry.'

'Well, so am I.'

'Don't go.'

'How can I trust you now? You might say you're pleased I've

set up a deal with a toy company, but really you disapprove. I couldn't bear that.'

'Have you set up a deal with a toy company?'

'Not yet. I've got a meeting on Wednesday. But what's the use in me carrying on if you can let us both down like this?'

Belinda made a decision. Being browbeaten by your cleaning lady on such a trivial matter was ridiculous. 'Listen,' she said, 'I do like fish.'

'What?'

'Stefan was mistaken. I told him about a nightmare I had once, which did put me off for a while because I was wading through a pond with fish nibbling my legs. But in fact I adore fish and could eat it every day.'

Linda melted. Such a simple lie, but completely effective. 'You're not just saying that?'

'As if.'

'I couldn't bear it if you were just saying it to appease me.'

'No, no. Brill and kumquats, yum-yum. That's what I say.'

'Do you swear that you like fish? There must be something you don't like? You can tell me.'

Belinda knew this was her last chance to mention shellfish, the mere sight of which set her stomach in a spasm, but she didn't believe Linda's assurances any more. She could not tell Linda that she abhorred langoustine, or that crab claws made her vomit. The woman might threaten to walk out again, calling her a Judas. 'No, I love it all,' she pronounced.

'Octopus?'

'Yep.'

'Eels?'

'Fab.'

Linda visibly relaxed. She had forced Belinda to lie extravagantly about a love of seafood. And, for some reason that Belinda could not fathom, this evidently counted as a triumph.

*　　*　　*

Fifteen minutes after Noel left Maggie's, the doorbell rang.

'Oh God, he's come back,' said Maggie, as she went to answer it.

'It's me again, Leon,' said the man outside, holding a very small bunch of daffodils. 'I wondered if you'd like to come out for a drink.'

'Oh my God,' she said. It was indeed Leon again. But the trouble was, it wasn't the Leon who had called earlier. He was smaller and brainy-looking.

'Where did you get that dreadful phallus?' he asked her.

Looking down, she realized she'd been absently hugging the Oshbosh car. 'Didn't you just give it to me?' she queried. But she knew he hadn't. This was quite obviously Noel, and his impersonation was terrible.

'What on earth are you talking about?' he said. 'Really, Margaret, if you don't go along with this, how's it ever going to work?'

Chapter Six

Stefan Johansson was not a clone, but he had a secret. And his secret was considerably larger than the petty ice-cream-van offence that had, on and off since childhood, murdered the sleep of his innocent wife. The truth was, he wasn't Swedish. Nor was he a geneticist. He was in fact an apple-farmer from Kent. And his real first name was George.

Linda had guessed something of this right away, even before she found albums of photographs showing his family on long-ago outings to Canterbury and Rye. She thought it suspicious that you could never help him out with a word. Normally, with any foreigner, you can supply 'wasp' or 'jamboree', and feel incredibly clever. But with Stefan you couldn't. And now, to confirm her misgivings, here was little Stefan in a big sun-hat, dappled at a typically English model village, and little Stefan on a donkey on the beach at Camber Sands, with Union Jacks fluttering in the background. Lots of childish wasps, probably. And a sense of childish jamboree. Both these pictures, moreover, were clearly marked. 'Me, George,' said one. 'George – Me,' said the other.

To give Linda her due, once she had the evidence she produced it. One stormy evening, after a splendid supper of halibut steamed in seaweed with lugworm Hollandaise, she placed the albums gently on the table, then sat down beside Stefan on the sofa in front of the fire. Belinda was working; Mother had gone to bed; Stefan was thinking likewise of climbing up the wooden hill to Bedfordshire. When he saw the albums, however, he stiffened. Then he smiled at Linda a little uncertainly.

'They were under the bathroom floor,' said Linda, simply. 'I can imagine why you thought they were safe.'

'Oh my God,' said Stefan.

'I won't tell anybody.'

'You won't?'

'No.'

'My real name is George, you see.'

'Yes.'

'I'm not Swedish.'

'No.'

Stefan went to the kitchen to recover himself. He came back with a bottle of red wine and two glasses. He poured it unsteadily and took a long drink.

'It all began in Malmö,' he said.

'Yes?'

'I went to Sweden for a holiday in 1971, and I found myself there.'

'Is it a particularly lovely place, this Malmö?'

'Lovely?' he repeated, surprised. 'No. Although it was quite prosperous, in those days, with the shipyard.'

He went to the door and shut it, poured some more wine, and sat down beside Linda again. And then, as the fire burned brightly in the grate and the wind blew interestingly outside in the naked branches, he told the story of what happened to him in Malmö.

'It was the early seventies, as I think I said,' he began. 'I was young, I had just left agricultural college. I was good-looking, I had a bit of money, and Sweden being well known for its permissiveness at that time, I was optimistic of having a very happy summer of love. Knowing nobody didn't matter. There was to be a folk festival in the Slottsparken, featuring the radical Hoola Bandoola Band – a group sinfully overlooked by the other countries of Europe, in my opinion, but that's another story.

'Malmö is just a short ferry-ride from Copenhagen, you know. For centuries the whole of the south of Sweden was Danish, and a certain identity crisis persists in the region to this day. Anyway, the ferry from Copenhagen dropped me on the dock on a pretty pink summer evening, and I followed the little crowd towards the lights at the station, where I bought my first drink at the Bar Central. I felt gloriously free. People looked at me, wondering if I was Terence Stamp – a lot of people thought that in those days. The sabre-flashing scene from *Far From the Madding Crowd* was one I was often called upon to reproduce. I have to admit it was a peerless seduction technique. Although, for reasons that will become apparent, the idea of all but slicing bits off your girlfriend has rather lost its appeal to me, as the years have gone by.

'Anyway, Swedish pop music was playing in the Bar Central, and it was heady and foreign, backward and progressive, all at the same time. I was dizzy from the drink and the sun, and the promise of all life held ahead of me.

'I don't remember how I got involved in the game of blackjack, or how I managed to win fifty kronor. I knew the game only as "pontoon", which I'd played for pennies at my prep school in Tenterden. But I seemed to be good at it. Stakes were low, but it was fun. Someone bought me a drink, and then another. I played some more, and won even more money, which was a surprise. I noticed one man, about my own age, who couldn't take his eyes off me. And when the time came to leave, I staggered outside into the strange summer dusk, and came face to face with Stefan Johansson.'

He paused for a reaction, so Linda nodded. Her attention

had certainly been caught by the story, but there was something else. 'I've just noticed,' she said. 'I hope you don't mind. You're talking normal English.'

'Yes, of course. I think I've explained by now. I'm not Swedish.'

'It's a relief,' she said.

He laughed, mirthlessly. 'You're telling me.'

'So who was Stefan Johansson?'

'Oh, yes. Who was he? What can I tell you of Stefan Johansson? At this time, he was a stringy young human-chemistry student at the nearby university at Lund, rather charming, blond, in a ragged beige suit, who had just completed eighteen months cleaning toilets as a penance for refusing to undertake military service, and had no money to play blackjack. That's what he told me. He pulled his pockets out to prove it. "But I've got a system," he said, in good English. "And because I'm a mathematical genius, I can memorize the cards. How much money do you have?" I told him the truth: I had five thousand kronor, or about five hundred pounds. I had cashed all my savings at home, and sold the car I'd had at seventeen. "Then I'll show you what I can do in this dump," he said, indicating the bar. "And then I'll take you to a club I know. We'll split everything fifty-fifty. Agreed?" And heaven help me, I agreed.

'So I led him back to the card table, where Carl, the dealer, greeted us. And I gave Stefan fifty kronor, and over the next two hours I won steadily with small amounts while he bet boldly and quadrupled his stake. For a student, he was an excellent gambler. I had always thought the art of the card table was concealing how little confidence you have in your hand, disguising your dismay. But with Stefan the art was to conceal his certain knowledge of every card on the table. He bet just the right amount not to draw attention to himself, and quit with perfect timing. He gave me half the winnings, and then we went outside.

'Where are we going?' I asked. He was leading me through

grand squares southwards, across canals, away from the sea. The buildings were closing in, and it was late.

'The Möllevångstorget,' he said.

'Easy for you to say,' I quipped, little thinking how the name would in time be impressed on my memory.

'But when we got there, on this occasion – to the Möllevångstorget, or the Möllevången Square – I remember only a blur of impressions. An unsavoury neighbourhood, scary, the smell of incense and pot, and the ugliest statue I ever saw, of a group of straining, naked people holding an enormous boulder above their heads. It was a monument to the workers, apparently, but I always thought it was rather odd for a town whose most famous landmark was a gigantic crane. Anyway, Stefan knocked on a door. An illegal betting club, where they knew him well.

'"Who's your lucky charm this time, Stefan?" they said. I didn't understand. All I do know is that he turned my five thousand kronor into twenty thousand. How we got out of there without being attacked I don't recall. But as we stood beside a canal at dawn, what I do remember is that he took only a handful of the winnings.

'"We were going to split everything fifty-fifty," I reminded him.

'"What's the point?" he said. "Are you staying in Malmö?"

'"No."

'"So. It's no good to me on my own. I don't have your luck."

'He disappeared from my life as abruptly as he'd entered it, and for twenty years I enjoyed and increased my fortune. Then, five years ago exactly, Stefan Johansson reeled me in.

'I didn't even recognize the name at first, when he phoned me in Stockholm. I had stayed in Sweden, you see. I had made my fortune there, in the export of household design items, and just sent money back to Kent, where my family still has the orchards. He said on the phone, "I'm the man who made you" – which should have alerted me to his state of mind, I suppose. It was a remarkable choice of phrase, as I considered myself self-made. But, on the other hand, success has a thousand fathers, and many people have taken the credit for my achievements over the years. I had come to accept it as an aspect of human nature.

'He told me he had given up gambling years before, and was now a respectable scientist, working in genetic research. I attempted a few pleasantries, which failed. Small talk did not engage him. Urgently, he wanted to see me again, in Malmö. He had problems with his work and his wife was ill. Had I married? he asked. I said no, which seemed to annoy him. Any children by other means? Not that I knew of. Come anyway, he said. I was intrigued, I admit it. That long-ago night in Malmö was like a dream. So I invented some spurious business in the south-west, hired a plane, and flew down.

'We met again at the Bar Central, just for old times' sake. Neither of us recognized the other at first. He had aged badly since that summer night in 1971 – his back was curved, and his long hair was tied back in a grey pony-tail. My prosperity, meanwhile, had lifted me into a different world, where it is customary to look younger than your years. People now said I looked like Sting, which was pleasant. Stefan asked me to outline my career, which I did, although it was unnerving when he kept saying, "I knew it!" and thumping the table. What about his own life, his own work? It was hard to get him to talk about it. He said his wife Ingrid disapproved of his research methods, from which I assumed he worked with live animals. "Many women have soft hearts about laboratory experiments," I said. He agreed. "They like to think dumb suffering is unnecessary," he scoffed. "They take the view that no scientific progress in the world is worth an ounce of pain."

'Gradually, inevitably, our conversation turned to that interesting night when Stefan won the money and gave it to me. I assumed he wanted money, people generally did. So I said that if he had financial difficulties, I would gladly give him the money I owed him. If only it had been that simple.

'"Your money? You think I want your money? I could have had your whole life, don't you see that?" he said. He seemed very angry. "You're so stupid you don't see it. We were the same age, we looked alike, we had the same prospects. In those days, if we had looked in the mirror, we'd have seen each other! Now look at us. But I lacked something you had. Tell me what I have, George. What am I good at?"

'I said that, from what I knew, he was good at gambling, and had a superb analytical brain, also a photographic memory.

'"And what else does a gambler need? What else does everyone need in life? What divides the haves and the have-nots more than any other factor in the world?"

'"Money," I said.

'"No."

'"Charm. Good breeding. A secure childhood in the Garden of England. A resemblance to an international film star."

'He took me by the shoulders. "Luck."

'I shrugged. I couldn't believe he meant it. Luck happens, I said.

'"Yes," he said. "But only to those who are genetically predisposed to it." He punched the wall, rather alarmingly, grazing his knuckles. And then he added: "Like you."'

Stefan (or George) took a long swig of wine while Linda put another log on the fire. A high wind raged outside. Unspoken between them was the knowledge that Belinda, upstairs, had been avidly reading this sort of Gothic story for the past three years and making it her speciality. Were she ever to know the truth of Stefan's background, or that he had shared his narrative with the cleaning lady, she was likely to gnaw off her own leg with rage.

'So why was Stefan telling you all this?' asked Linda. She had curled herself small on the sofa, and was holding a cushion across her chest as a kind of shield. If something nasty was going to happen in this story, she wanted to hide behind the maximum amount of upholstery.

'Well, he was mad, you see,' said Belinda's husband, matter-of-factly. 'Quite insane. He started to outline his research, how for years he had been working to prove luck was genetically transmitted. In opposition to Darwinian orthodoxy, he argued that luck alone was the basis of evolutionary selection. So we talked on, and the bar grew hotter, and every so often he would pull at my hand or my arm, literally pinching bits of flesh. Once he picked a hair off my jacket and laughingly said, "Can I keep this? It might help me get safely across the road."

'I couldn't make him see things differently. Rational counter-argument simply incensed him. He said, quite simply, that I had the luck gene, and that it would be his life's achievement to locate it. Which was when I lost my temper, finally. I stood up and threw down some money for the bill. Luck gene? I said I'd had enough of this. "You're raving mad," I told him. And I marched outside into the cool night air, with Stefan scampering behind me.

'Walking into the main square, I calmed down. Children played in a fountain, women laughed. It was all so normal that I thought fondly of Stockholm, and how I would be home again next morning. This sad, grey man at my side would be soon forgotten. If not, his crazy ideas would provide amusing chat for a dinner party, nothing more. It occurred to me to feel sorry for him. Being the object of envy has its consolations. Though he might want my DNA, he simply couldn't have it, could he? I certainly couldn't give it to him. His envy was therefore a merely futile, self-sabotaging emotion. The more he hated me, the more he hurt himself.

'"Will you come to my house?" he said. "Ingrid would like to meet you. I told her you looked like a movie star."

'"Did you?"

104

'"Yes. She's looking forward to it."

'And so a susceptibility to flattery was my real undoing. I already had a soft spot for Ingrid, since she disapproved of her husband's work, and so did I. But I went to see her, if I'm honest, because I believed she would find me good-looking, and after the abysmal evening I'd had with Stefan, I needed a boost. Also, having lived in Sweden for twenty years, I recognized what a rare honour it was to be invited home.

'"Where do you live?" I asked, as we headed south again. Despite the influx of immigrants changing the shops, despite the substantial rebuilding of the city, familiar landmarks were passing. In the darkness ahead, I spotted those awful naked bums and the boulder, and I can't say the sight reassured me. We were in the Möllevången, once more.

'He produced a key, opened a door, and there was Ingrid, finally. We found her in the sitting room of their anonymous ground-floor apartment – a dull little woman, dark-haired, sour, and I knew at once the mistake I'd made. She was not a Terence Stamp fan. She just looked up at me without much interest, and said to her husband, "You were right. This one's better-looking." And when I turned to Stefan to ask him what she meant, he struck me on the head with a Carl Larsson reproduction he had snatched from the wall. I staggered, and he struck me again. I saw blood on my shoes before I passed out. I have never liked the saccharine work of Carl Larsson, incidentally. This scene, as you can imagine, did very little to boost him in my estimation.

'Concussed, I was bundled into a makeshift laboratory in the cellar, where – well, where I was subsequently kept imprisoned, the subject of innumerable experiments, for the next eighteen months. Yes, eighteen months in a room that stank of rat poison and surgical spirit! My life snapped shut on that night in Malmö. I guessed Stefan would kill me, sooner or later, because his experiments would fail. How

I survived those terrible times is a miracle to me, even now.'

Belinda's husband had been staring at the fire as he spoke. Now he turned to Linda, who shut her mouth when she realized it was hanging open.

'You don't believe me,' he said. 'You think I'm making it up.'

'Stefan,' she said gently, her face contorted with pity. Tears were in her eyes. 'Oh, how terrible. Condemned to death by your own luck!' She reflected on it and patted his hand. 'What an irony!'

'Mm,' he replied. He had stopped being struck by the irony of it quite some time ago. 'I never understood the science of his work, but suffice to say the luck gene stayed lucky. It evaded all Stefan's attempts to find it. I soon realized that Ingrid had been the cause of his obsession with genetic defect − hardly blessed by her own genetic inheritance, she had nevertheless refused to reproduce with a man who had no lucky aspect anywhere in his double helix. I think, to her, DNA was something like astrology. Since I was mostly shackled, I was obliged to converse with her for hours by the clock, and I can honestly say I never met anybody so unpleasant in my life. She was selfish and moody, and got her own way by crying. "Oh, Stefan," she would weep to her husband, "I'm so unhappy!" God, I hated her. She started to fall in love with me, of course. Wanting my babies was what this was all about from the start. "How lucky is this?" I wanted to point out to Stefan. "Your dwarfish wife now lusts for my helpless body! How bloody lucky is this?"

'I don't know what they did with the bits they cut off. To be fair, they were clever and discreet in removing only tiny little bits that wouldn't show − from the back of the ear, or the inner thigh, or the underside of a toe. All I know is that Stefan would go out to test his luck after injecting himself with something derived from me − and come back every time poorer, or beaten

106

up. Once he was so sure he had isolated my luck gene that he played chicken with the traffic and got run over. My luck was simply not transferable, it seemed. Meanwhile Stefan still went to great lengths to convince me of his theory, making me read his thesis on the biology of chance and testing me on it. Oddly, he seemed to place no value on his work if I didn't subscribe to it. Ingrid alternately provoked and pouted – taunting him in front of me, and then weeping when he hit her. And when we were alone together, she would paw my face and caress my body, saying she never stopped thinking about me, she loved me, she wanted me.

'I suppose I had been there a year by then. Kept mentally alive by *Monty Python* reruns that they let me watch on the telly. Entertained by watching the rats die, and by observing that Stefan's cuts and bruises were generally far worse than mine. They gave me reindeer sandwiches every day, which I can never forgive. Can you imagine what it's like, day after day for a whole year, trying to think of a joke that starts "I'll have a reindeer sandwich and make it – *what?*" You wouldn't think so, but it was this chronic inability to make a joke out of a reindeer sandwich that, throughout my captivity, brought me closest to despair.

'My own identity, meanwhile, had been easily disposed of by Stefan. I was dead, found in the canal two weeks after my visit. Somebody else's body, of course, I don't know whose. Anyway, when this corpse turned up, Stefan, being the police's favourite consultant pathologist, made extremely short work of the genetic fingerprinting. There was a small piece about my funeral in the papers, which Ingrid thoughtfully pasted beside my bed. My estate was claimed by Stefan – he made me sign a phoney will – my ageing parents grieved, which caused me terrible anguish. Meanwhile Stefan brought home to Malmö a Ferrari from the auction of my effects, and taunted me with the keys. He really was a sad case, Stefan. He deserved to have terrible luck, I mean it. Despite his undeniable genius, he deserved to be outwitted, as he subsequently was, by a man totally at his mercy.

'Because one day I put it to him, the answer to this conundrum of life. The time was right. Ingrid was getting unbearably frisky, and Stefan had just sawn off a quite visible piece of my elbow, and I suppose I thought enough's enough.

'"Look, Stefan," I said. "This *grand guignol* thing has been going on long enough. I've had a much better idea."

'Stefan laid the piece of elbow in a sterilized dish, and folded his arms. "What?" he asked.

'"It's obvious," I said. "The time has come for me to kill you and take your identity."

'"Why?" he said.

'"Because this outcome alone will confirm your theories of survival and be the crowning achievement of your work. Moreover, by transferring *all* my lucky genetic material into the identity of Stefan Johansson – instead of tiny, ludicrous slivers of it – we can ensure that the Johansson work will become famous and win prizes. Johansson will be a struggling, luckless nobody no more! He will be handsome and charming and his wife will adore him, and the world of science will fall at his feet."

'I held my breath, waiting for Stefan to burst into maniacal laughter and saw my leg off. But he didn't. He was genuinely struck by this idea. He could see the logic in it. His mind raced, as he considered the implications. I would have to work abroad, of course, where nobody knew Stefan's face. I must learn enough about Stefan's work to persuade people. I must learn to love Ingrid.

'Of course, I agreed to everything.

'"But let's not tell Ingrid yet," I urged him. He agreed. He said it would be a wonderful surprise for her, to find herself married to me. And, as he started fiddling with my sore elbow, I smiled and said I had a feeling he was right.

'"What are you doing?" I asked.

'"Shouldn't I sew this back on now?" He held up a sliver of flesh, the size and shape of an anchovy.

'"Keep it," I said. "I've got loads more where that came from."

'Stefan looked at me admiringly. "I wish I could be like you," he said.

'"You're soon going to be exactly like me," I said. And we hugged, man to man, in the one-way fashion available to people who are not equally free to move their arms.

'You can imagine my surprise that my ruse had been so successful. I even started believing in my luck gene. For a week or two, I was convinced he would wake one morning and realize he'd been tricked. But he didn't. Because he hadn't been tricked, not really. Genetically, my suggestion made excellent sense to Stefan. I was bound by my genes to do this thing. And if there was one thing Stefan never argued with, it was biological destiny.

'Actually, our conversations over the next six months about how I'd kill him and replace him were our very best times together. How we laughed! Stefan would banish Ingrid to the sitting room, and bring some beers, put Abba on his portable stereo. The words to "Waterloo" were particularly apt in the context, funnily enough; it's about fate, you know. He'd free one of my hands, which was nice. And then together we'd discuss the merits of various homicidal methods. I favoured shooting, for example, because it was quick and noisy, and because I might not have the stamina for strangling after such a long time horizontal. He fancied something more drawn out and Scandinavian.

'It was rather a bizarre situation, I suppose. I knew he was in earnest, though. He started to buy clothes for me. He bought a forged passport. He even registered my DNA as Stefan Johansson's, opened an account at Ikea and registered my signature on a new bank account with all our joint money in it. He was more animated than I had ever seen him. In planning all the details of how I would supplant him, he was illuminated by a kind of mad joy.

'And then one day Ingrid ruined it all. Just a week before the day marked on the laboratory calendar with a hangman's noose, the bitch came in and released me. It was a Saturday afternoon, Stefan had popped across to Copenhagen to buy me a last, parting gift – a rather nice briefcase I'd picked out from a catalogue – and she saw her opportunity. "Go away," I begged, when I realized what was happening. But by now she was mad for me, you see. Gagging. And what could I do? It was all frightfully embarrassing. She brought candles and arranged them around the room. She called me "big boy" if you can believe it. Drunk as a skunk, of course. She comes in, turns the light out, and climbs on top of me, and then starts moaning, "Hold me, hold me."

'"Ingrid," I say, fighting for breath and squirming, "I can't hold you. I'm tied up. Control yourself. You're sitting on my diaphragm."

'"I love you," she says. "And I'm so unhappy." At which point she starts unbuttoning my pyjamas and caressing my privates in what I can only describe as an electrifying manner.

'"You're always unhappy," I point out, through gritted teeth, as my neck flushes and my ears catch fire. "You can't blame me for that. You're Swedish."

'"Hold me, hold me. Don't you love your Ingrid?"

'"Get off me," I squeal. "Think of Stefan."

'"Stefan!"

'And then the unthinkable happens. With an ugly pout, which I assume she intends as coquettish, she unties my hands and puts them on her chest. I can't believe it. My hands free, after all this time. I waggle and flex them against her puddingy, jiggly breasts, as I try to absorb this enormous change in my circumstances. Suddenly, after all this time, there is only a drunk, lascivious small woman interposing her body between me and freedom. Moreover, all I have to do is push. I press tentatively, and she moans. I press harder, and she makes a bloodcurdling noise, like the miaow of a cat. I press again and she licks my face.

'"More," she whispers.

'So I gather all my feeble strength and push as hard as I can.

'"Take that, bitch!" I cry, as she slides drunkenly off my bed and on to the floor. She says, "What?" but that's all the resistance she offers. Once on the floor, she passes out.

'Blood thumps in my ears. I don't know what to do. I can hardly shackle myself to the bed again before Stefan gets back. Shall I run for it? I surely won't have the energy. Besides, when I stand up my pyjama bottoms fall down, revealing that I have been fully aroused by these exhilarating proceedings. At which point, as I dither half naked and priapic above his supine wife while candles twinkle romantically around the room, Stefan enters, waving the new briefcase, only to be frozen to the spot as he surveys the scene.

'"Ingrid, what has he done to you?" he cries, sinking to his knees. She lies before him, evidently lifeless. Oh, the times I have recollected this train of events! So many tragic turns!

'"Ah, Stefan, glad it's you," I bluff cheerfully, as I try to pull my trousers up. "Look, the first thing you need to know is that this needn't ruin our plans. This isn't at all the way it looks. I can still kill you exactly as we arranged with the rat poison. In fact, why don't I do it now?'

'"No!" he shouts. "Ingrid, are you all right?"

'"Of course she's all right," I snap.

'"I'm so unhappy, so unhappy," she whimpers from the floor.

'"There you are," I protest. "Perfectly normal."

'But he's not listening. He's distraught. And although he's unaware of it, his pony-tail has just caught light from one of

III

the candles. As he turns away from me, I see that the flame is travelling up his old brittle pigtail like a fuse on a stick of dynamite.

'"Stefan!" I yell, and hurl a glass of water at him.

'He turns to look at me, nonplussed by such a strange and puny act of violence. I will never forget that quizzical look on his face, not as long as I live. Especially when we both realized the water was in fact pure alcohol, used for disinfecting my wounds.

'"Bugger it, your hair's on fire, Stefan," I say, apologetically. And with a final cry of "Ingrid! You see? You see how unlucky I am?" Stefan Johansson goes up in flames.'

Belinda's husband paused for a breather. He had been talking solidly for an hour, and when he turned to look at Linda, he discovered she had all her fingers crammed in her mouth.

'I suppose you guessed all this?' he asked.

She shook her head. She'd had an inkling he wasn't Swedish. It wasn't the same. 'What happened?' she squeaked. 'Did he die?'

'Oh yes,' said Stefan. 'But it wasn't at all what we'd planned. Dying like that made it terribly difficult for me. Police came, and fire engines. I barely had time to flee the place before they arrived. Luckily Stefan had put all the relevant stuff in the briefcase already. Passport, bank account. The clothes were in a suitcase, and the keys to my Ferrari were in the hall. I staggered to the car and drove it a couple of miles before I dared to breathe. Then I got changed and drove like hell. I took a ferry to Denmark, drove to France. And here I am. Those albums were in the boot of the car. They're all I've got to remind me of Lucky George. It's awkward that I share an identity with a dead man whose demise was so spectacular, but since the alternative was to be scraped to the bone by mad people with no sense of humour, I can't say I mind too much.

'My only regret is mentioning Ingrid to Belinda. I can tell it hurts her. But somehow I could never contain my joy that

Ingrid was locked up in Malmö. They found bits of me all over the house, apparently. Bits of other people, as well. I wasn't the first, I knew that. Genetics in Sweden has never really recovered from the exposure. Ingrid was found to be wearing a locket containing a piece of my left buttock the size of a pound coin. Well, you can imagine the consternation.

'So that's my story,' he said finally, with a smile. 'I hope I haven't been boring you?'

Linda whimpered. 'No,' she said, in a very small voice.

'Promise you won't tell Belinda? She loves Stefan, you see. How can I tell her I'm somebody else? I love her so much.'

'You can't tell her.'

Stefan massaged his elbow through his sleeve, but mercifully did not offer to show Linda the place where the anchovy was cut off.

'And you don't mind pretending to be Swedish all the time?'

'No, it's easy. Tell people you're Swedish, and the amazing thing is, they never ask a follow-up question. Belinda has never asked me to tell her the Swedish word for anything, or wondered why I have no Swedish friends. No, it's fine, fine. The only trouble is, Linda,' – his voice lowered – 'there's been somebody watching me this week, and following me to work.'

'Who?'

'I don't know.'

'Why?'

'I don't know. He's young and smartly dressed. A boy with no hair. He's been following me quite openly. He hasn't learned very much, I know that. In fact, I think he knows only about my taste in Habitat comestibles. But if he comes near to uncovering anything about me – well, I don't know how to say this without sounding absurdly melodramatic!'

He laughed, and Linda waited. 'Go on,' she said.

'Well, Linda, I can't help it. I'll have to protect Belinda. If he uncovers the slightest thing about what happened to me in Malmö, I think I'll have to kill him.'

Part Two

One month later

Chapter Seven

Since they worked for the same newspaper, it was natural for Tanner and Leon not to recognize each other on the flight to the Malmö airport of Sturup. The newspaper world is like that. Leon had written about sport for the *Daily Effort* for fifteen years, and he had known altogether only eighteen colleagues by sight. Five had been sacked, and two had collapsed heroically at their desks during the World Cup in 1998 endeavouring to meet the first edition, so now he knew eleven. Leon loved the buzz and even the heartlessness of journalism. When his own time came to die, he cheerfully expected to be checked into heaven with Fleet Street's highest hallelujah, 'Copy fits, no queries.'

However, since he and Tanner sat beside each other on three separate occasions that Monday morning in March – first in the City Airport's café eating damp croissants, then in the departure lounge (both scanning the *Effort* with a professional eye and making 'Tsk' noises), and finally on the plane – it was odd that it took quite so long for them to speak.

Leon, for his part, was lost in thought. Four weeks had passed since Maggie sent him away, but he had dwelt on it ever since. He had become a changed man – as his eleven close colleagues would tell you. His reports from all round the globe were now peppered with strange words (removed by the subs)

117

like anal and penile. He washed his hair more often. He began one 600-word report from a UEFA Cup match with the words 'We forget sometimes that many quite intelligent people aren't remotely interested in football', and had found next day to his astonishment that his philosophical musings were reduced to a functional photo caption.

Oh, Maggie. He would lie awake at night in Budapest or Monaco, remembering the way she sighed and huffed whenever he spoke. She was so exotic, and spoke with such fabulous vowels. He was quite sure he'd once seen her in something, even though she'd told him it was impossible if he never went to the theatre. When he felt like cheering himself up, he would just remember that surprising moment when she kissed him rather violently in the car and whispered, 'Come and stay the night.' (Maggie had characteristically forgotten her own leading role in the seduction.)

Meanwhile Tanner's reasons for not speaking to Leon were even more prosaic. He was asleep. To return to the Stefan Johansson story was a bore, especially by comparison with the intervening month, which had been spent deputizing on Fashion. He'd had a wonderful time. When the fashion editor finally returned refreshed (and a bit green) from a French seaweed-therapy health farm, she discovered that in her absence the *Effort* had seriously commended men to wear pinstripe sarongs to the office, and that the editor had sent a memo to everybody in Features saying, 'More stuff like this, please.'

Jago had been impressed, not to say wildly jealous, and took the first opportunity to dispatch Tanner to Sweden, even though his passion for the clone theory had burned out long ago. No, sending Tanner to Malmö was now more a means of removing the young turk temporarily from the office. It is not unknown for people in Jago's position to arrive at work one day and find a Tanner in their chair. To find a Tanner in his chair *in a sarong*, however, would be more than Jago Ripley could stand.

So, whereas last week he'd been in Paris hobnobbing with tomorrow's designers (also known as today's bedwetters), now Tanner was heading for Malmö to meet a madwoman. No wonder, then, that bored by his demeaning mission and peeved that he'd been refused an upgrade by the airline, he no sooner settled into his seat than he produced a YSL-monogrammed satin blindfold, donned it, and started snoring.

Maggie, why? thought Leon, as the plane taxied to the runway. He tossed aside his Swedish basketball magazine, and squirmed between the punitive arm-rests, which dug into his hips. A man of his size was bound to dislike air travel. His enormous body was now squeezed awkwardly into the restricting window-seat, while the long, spindly Tanner alongside could loll with space to spare.

What did I do wrong? he continued. For the umpteenth time he rehearsed all the events of his wooing routine: it was driving him crazy. The fluffy racing car, the generous show of affection, the bottle of Cognac. Over in Oshbosh, he'd confided his interest in Maggie to a tabloid colleague called Jeff, who had advised him brilliantly, telling him to appear all the things he wasn't: i.e. thoughtful, sexually self-confident and enormously entertaining. 'You're not exactly a self-starter, are you?' Jeff had guessed, rather woundingly. 'More of a human waterbed. Well, women don't like that. Especially actresses. They like you to show fire and initiative and a decent profile.'

Since Jeff had been married three times, once to a lady wrestler, Leon assumed he knew what he was talking about. The trouble with Leon was that, being (indeed) no self-starter, he always took advice if he considered it well meant, regardless of whether it was any cop.

So he had burst into Maggie's flat as Mister Personality – and look what happened. Maggie had virtually thrown him out. But perhaps she hadn't liked him in the first place, either. Recollecting that night at Jago's, he was forced to remember he'd ignored the golden rule of social chitchat – that to be interested in motor-racing you must first own a pair of testicles. Also, he had told Maggie with some confidence that Rembrandt was not a household name, which now made him squirm to remember. It's always the same when you're categorical. Since making this silly statement, he had, of course, seen Rembrandt toothpaste in every corner of the globe.

'She's in love with that Swede, that's the real trouble,' he told himself. And no sooner had he formed this ridiculous, petulant theory than memories rushed to corroborate it. My God, here was the answer – at long last! In the car home after Jago's, what had Maggie talked about? Stefan. At dinner, with whom had she swapped private jokes? Stefan. And in her bedroom – how blind can a broadsheet sports correspondent be? – whose picture did she have in an elaborate frame surrounded by fairy-lights? Well, it wasn't Damon Hill. Maggie was in love with the Swede who talked funny. Who'd solemnly informed Maggie in front of everybody that she had been 'the absolute dog's bollocks' in a play he'd seen. Leon shivered at the thought of him, this man who had captivated Maggie with his silvery tongue. Who was, moreover, a slim, blond, exotic academic; the very antithesis of a bulky, swarthy hack who was also a human novelty mattress.

Tanner snored in his seat, annoyingly. Leon had taken care to reserve a position by the aisle, but had arrived to find Tanner already asleep in it, with all his paperwork piled beside him. Clambering over the gangly boy to the window, he'd had to move all the papers on to the floor. Now that the cabin staff were serving food and drink, should he attempt to wake this annoying man? Sleeping on such a short flight was preposterous. He'd taken off his shoes and everything.

'Rolls, mate,' he said companionably, in Tanner's ear. By dint of weary experience he was an expert on airline food. 'One roll with egg mayonnaise, and one roll with a slice of unidentifiable grey meat. And, seeing as it's northern Europe, a small square of chocolate.'

Tanner slept on.

'Coffee, mate. Lukewarm coffee in a cup with a silly handle you can't hold without sticking your elbow out so that it jabs into people.'

Nothing. The plane tilted violently to the left, as it always will when liquid refreshment is served.

'Coffee and rolls, mate. Whoopsadaisy. Nearly got some on your skirt.'

But Tanner slept on, so Leon ate two lots of rolls and drank two lots of coffee, and was just fiddling under the seat for his laptop when a file of Tanner's caught his eye. He blinked with astonishment. It had the name 'Stefan Johansson' on it – surely the name of Maggie's preferred lover!

He gasped. Could it be the same Stefan Johansson? No, no. There would be millions of them in Sweden. Millions. There were three, at least, in the national basketball team, a fact that had caused famous confusion on several occasions.

Yet he couldn't help it. He picked up the file, to examine it closer. And what he saw was:

Stefan Johansson, the Full Story
of a Cunning Clone
or The Wild Goose Chase of the Century
by Michael St John Tanner
chief investigative reporter of the *Daily Effort*

Leon frowned and gulped so hard that some of his egg mayonnaise came back. A cunning clone? What did that mean? A clone was a sheep, wasn't it? Blimey, if Stefan was a sheep, he was very cunning indeed.

Surreptitiously, still awkwardly bending to reach the floor, he opened the file and found that it was virtually empty. No dossier as such; certainly no manuscript. In fact, it had just three dog-eared items in it, which Leon – unable to control himself – memorized. The first was the address of a secure unit in Malmö's university hospital, with the note 'Ingrid J, Tues, 2.30'. The second was Laurie Spink's home phone number scribbled on the back of Jago's business card, with the note 'Ring any time, we're paying plenty.' And the third was a sheet torn from a notebook, with 'cookie' and 'nuts' written on it in appalling shorthand. Leon perused all three items and grimaced.

That he had never heard of Laurie Spink goes without saying. Leon was unashamedly ignorant of everything except sport. Once, at the time of a Northern Ireland summit, he had spotted the headline 'Adams in talks', and had been genuinely disappointed when the Adams in question turned out not to be Tony, the Arsenal and England defender, renegotiating his contract. So until genetic modification became an issue in Chinese swimming (a development not too far off, actually), he wouldn't know the first thing about the subject that had been filling features pages for the last five years.

As the plane banked and the seatbelt sign was illuminated, all Leon knew for certain was that he didn't trust the Swede. Was he a cookie? Was he nuts? It would explain a lot. Beside him, Tanner removed his eyemask, folded it neatly, and placed it in his inside pocket. 'Ah,' he said airily, when he realized Leon was looking at him. 'See you're admiring my sarong.'

He looked very young, Leon thought. Son of a successful father, no doubt. The sort of arrogant Oxbridge tyro who overtakes you professionally the same way Michael Schumacher overtakes people on the race-track – by ramming into them, sailing past, and getting away with it.

'Excruciatingly uncomfortable,' Tanner said, stretching his arms.

'Mm,' agreed Leon.

'Idiots wouldn't give me an upgrade.'

'Right. You going into town?' said Leon. 'We could share a cab and get two receipts.'

Tanner put his head on one side and thought about this proposal for about fifteen seconds — proof positive that he had been in journalism no more than a couple of months. 'All right.' He extended his hand, so that Leon could notice his bespoke cufflinks. 'Tanner of the *Effort*, pleased to meet you.'

Leon shook his hand enthusiastically. 'Are you Tanner? That's marvellous!' he cried.

'Why?'

'I'm with the *Effort* as well. Jago asked me to look out for you in Malmö. And here you are all along!'

The Armadale Road job was proving extremely easy for Linda. In short, she loved it here. Belinda's life had so many vacuums, all of which Linda was very, very glad to abhor. No wonder Belinda continued not to recognize her as a malevolent double like the ones in books, even when Linda posed for author photographs, liaised with a new agent, and signed a deal with a toy manufacturer. Except for those rather alarming wah-wah occasions when she threatened to walk out, Linda was a diligent, selfless, trouble-free sweetheart with a talent for home-making. Also she didn't charge much, which was astonishing when you consider the extra-mural commitments. Had Mrs Holdsworth ever been asked to effect an impersonation of Belinda on the *Late Review*, double-time would have been mentioned almost at once.

Only six weeks had passed since Linda's arrival. It seemed hardly possible, when so much had happened. Linda continued to rustle up smoked haddock in filo pastry, also to shop and to clean. But she had been stupendous on television, which no one could have predicted. Smart as a whip, with an infectious giggle, and no swank — she was spotted at once as a natural. The producer was impressed: he mentioned the possibility of a documentary about literary doubles, to help promote the book. To top it all, he even invited the Johanssons to dinner; and what a night that was for everybody. Stefan looked breathtakingly gorgeous in a blue suit Linda bought in Bond Street. Linda had her hair cut by Nicky Clarke. And while her dear, wonderful ambassadors were engaged in their selfless mission on her behalf, Belinda worked contentedly all evening, amazed by her own good fortune.

To be honest, Belinda did a rather wicked thing that night. When she heard her envoys return home by taxi at two a.m., laughing and drunk, she used her two-way listening device to eavesdrop. It was underhand, and reprehensible. But she was desperate to hear what (albeit vicariously) Belinda Johansson had been up to.

'When Alan Yentob turned up, I thought I'd die!' exploded Linda, filling a kettle.

'But you were brilliant,' said Stefan. 'He thought you were great. And the Marquess of Bath wanting you for a wifelet! Wait till Belinda hears.'

As Belinda now sat happily, day after day, at her lovely new desk, the only fly in her ointment was a niggling sensation of guilt connected with the quality of work she was producing. Because perhaps it was not enough, finally, to get your hands on Virginia Woolf's pure and rounded pearls. Perhaps you needed a smidgen of Virginia Woolf's talent as well. You had to be able to dash off *The Waves*, or *Mrs Dalloway*, or something. Sometimes she wished she could knock off another Verity book, to boost her confidence. She had ideas for Verity continually. But she took Linda's point that she must stop churning them out. Linda was organizing a new uniform edition of her back-list, and had everything in hand.

But this doubles book, how good was it really? What if it were second-rate tosh? What if duality were too complex a subject for her to reduce to seven types? Asking other people to sacrifice themselves in the cause of a bad book was an awful imposition. How would Linda feel when she found out she'd dedicated herself to such a hollow cause? How would Stefan feel, after suffering all those celebrity dinners with television controllers and the master of Longleat? It didn't bear thinking about.

Oh well. For now, it was terrific. Except for lavatory breaks, Belinda had scarcely left her first-floor office for the last six weeks. She had not left the house at all, or been downstairs, and had mostly kept the thick curtains drawn all day to exclude draughts. Mother was right that she was putting on weight: since Linda had started thoughtfully supplying crisps and Twixes, she had thickened at the middle, but it was a development that did not much alarm her. Bodily things were such an irrelevance. Besides, everyone says that when you write a book, you put on a stone or two, in the way women formerly lost a tooth for each baby they bore. Her burgeoning waistline was a badge of her intellectual fecundity, therefore. It meant she was 'with book', which was lovely.

Talking *ad nauseam* about the ex-cleaning lady was not what Dermot had envisaged when he first seduced Viv; and to be honest, it was a bit like being married to her, which wasn't the idea. But he certainly sat up and took notice on the afternoon when – as the adulterous pair sat in flowery dressing-gowns at the kitchen table one day in March – she finally explained to him why losing Linda had been such a phenomenal blow.

'The thing is, she was doing my job at the hospital,' Viv confessed, sobbing.

'What?' In his alarm, Dermot poured coffee down his front, leapt up and stubbed his toe. '*What?*'

'I don't know how it happened. It's just that I didn't really need a cleaning lady. I liked doing all the things in the house myself. I'm good at cooking and shopping and tidying. I gave her the credit and everyone believed me. I stencilled the bathroom and said it was her. I even made all the Roman blinds!' The thought of such abject domesticity reduced Viv to a further outburst of tears.

'Jago doesn't know,' she added. 'He must never know.'

Dermot reeled with shock. He gripped the edge of the table. His toe throbbed horribly. 'This is outrageous, Viv. For God's sake, is Linda medically qualified?'

Viv shook her head and blew her nose. She couldn't speak.

'Viv, she might have killed people.'

'I know.'

'Just so that you could sit at home joining bits of chintz!'

'There's a lot more to Roman blinds than that, Dermot!'

'Viv, listen to yourself!' He jumped up and started striding about.

'I know, I'm sorry. I know.'

'What you did was criminal.'

'I know. I'm sorry. I know.'

Viv made him another cup of coffee. She was glad her secret was finally out, but at the same time rather shocked to discover she'd forgotten quite the magnitude of it. Human beings can become habituated to the most horrible and unnatural things. Custom, as the Czech people so rightly aver, takes the taste from the most savoury dishes. So, by the same de-seasoning process, it had become normal in Viv's life to watch her cleaning lady take the car to the Royal Southwark four times a week, wave to her as she joined the traffic on the South Circular, and not think much about it beyond 'Time to get the sewing-machine out, hurrah.'

After all, Linda evidently did a marvellous job in Viv's place. She had been twice promoted. Surgeons regularly commended her, and told her she had far outstripped their expectations. The only difficult part of the arrangement was that when Viv gave dinner parties, Linda had to hang around until midnight pretending to work, and take credit for the puddings, when she had early appointments next day at the hospital.

However, if Viv was used to the idea, Dermot (as yet) was not. In fact, he was clearly horrified. 'But how could she do it? How did she know what to do?'

'Well, she took an interest, you see. She's like that – she listens and learns. And she admired my medical ability. It didn't just happen overnight. She asked me lots of questions, and really got very expert on the subject before—' Viv stopped.

'Before what?'

'Before sticking a needle in someone.'

Dermot clutched his head in anguish.

'Don't you have colleagues, Viv? Isn't medicine quite a small world? How could she pass herself off as you?'

'Well, it all worked out very neatly. The day I got the interview for the Royal Southwark, one of the boys needed a costume for school, and I didn't want Linda to make it, even though she was very happy to. It was a Viking, with a horned helmet, and I just wanted to do it myself, and not have Sam tell his friends that his mum was too busy. So Linda attended the interview instead, just as a lark. But then, when she got the job, we thought, why not go for it?'

'Why not go for it?' Dermot repeated, slowly. For an intelligent man, he was taking a long time to accept quite a simple proposition.

'We expected to be found out sooner or later, of course. I was ready for that. I knew I'd be struck off, possibly imprisoned. And Linda – well, the thing about Linda is that she is completely without ego. She genuinely lives to serve. So everyone was happy, you see. Linda and I could discuss cases. I could maintain an interest in the professional sphere without having to go to work every day and face all those decisions. It wasn't as bad as it sounds, honestly.'

This wasn't how Viv had anticipated this discussion. She

thought Dermot might feel sorry for her, or agree to help her persuade Linda to come back. Instead of which, he remained obstinately horrified.

'Don't look at me like that, Dermot. Women are in a very strange transitional state at the moment. We're feeling our way. "Having it all" sounds excellent in theory, but it turns out to be utterly ghastly. The choices are getting impossible to make. And some of us career women just can't stand to watch other people having all the fun with the rufflette and the spice rack.'

Dermot closed his eyes. 'I've got to be somewhere else,' he said, and left the room, Viv following him upstairs.

'Don't hate me,' begged Viv. 'Nobody got hurt. I'm only telling you so that you'll see it's happening again. She's taking over Belinda now. Mrs Holdsworth says Belinda is never seen any more. Linda is taking things further than ever. Dermot, she went for Belinda's smear test!'

Dermot, sitting on the bed and buttoning his shirt, said nothing. He was staring at the wall, thinking. 'How long did you say Linda was at the Royal Southwark?'

'Two years.'

'I knew it.'

'Knew what?'

Dermot had turned white. 'You know my appendectomy?'

'I do.'

'That bloody impostor gave me my pre-med. I knew I'd seen her before.'

How Stefan fitted into Belinda's life of monastic seclusion (or didn't) was awkward because she loved him more than she loved her book. That blue suit made him so handsome that when he popped in to say, 'How's this for a glamour-puss?' she nearly swooned with longing.

Loving Stefan was so easy. Belinda loved even all the little pits and scars he'd picked up (so he said) at his dangerously progressive kindergarten in Sweden. When first they were naked together, she had swarmed over his body finding the little dents, until she knew them so well she could draw a map. There was a place in Stefan's left buttock where you could insert your finger or your tongue – it was the most intimate thing she'd ever known.

'Did Ingrid do this?' she asked once, out of the blue. She meant, of course, 'Did Ingrid stroke you this way?' but it was a tricky moment before Stefan latched on.

'Forget Ingrid,' he said. But how could she do that, when he made mention of her so often in his sleep?

'Ingrid, no!' was the usual nocturnal shout. 'No, Ingrid!'

Since Belinda's idea of Ingrid was of a doe-eyed neurotic who cried a lot and finally sank into depression, she was stung by these cries. It was no use telling herself that being retrospectively jealous of such a poor, broken person was an unworthy emotion. 'Stefan is bound to love his first wife still, it's only natural,' Maggie advised, memorably. 'You're very selfish, Belinda. You want everything.'

But she was still upset, she couldn't help it. The first wife had been Swedish, for a start. Whatever happened in the rest of their lives, they would always have Hoola Bandoola.

So she assumed that in those bloodcurdling cries of 'Ingrid, no!' Stefan called to his poor lost wife as she slipped into madness, the way Orpheus called to Eurydice as Hades reclaimed her. She could have no idea that in fact the cry was accompanied by nightmare images of a dumpy psychopath advancing with a scalpel.

'You still love Ingrid, don't you?' she asked him, the morning after his confession to Linda. He'd made love to her in an unusually urgent way, and when she caressed his dimpled buttock with a fingernail, he screamed.

'Why on earth do you say that?'

'You ought to go and see her.'

'You really are going loco, Belinda. Ingrid is history. I have put up the shutters and, when the chips are down, drawn a line in the sand.'

'Malmö's not far.'

Stefan snorted. 'You have no idea where Malmö is, Belinda. It's one of the things I love about you.'

'She must miss you so much, Stefan.'

Stefan shrugged. 'I'm sure she does,' he said darkly. 'But look at it from her point of view. She'll always have a little piece of me.' With which enigmatic comment he left for college.

So now Belinda was alone with the second-rate book of tosh, uneasy about her work and uneasy about Stefan's cruel streak, when for all the world it was obvious that her cleaning lady was taking her life. Dostoevsky would have noticed it at once. But Belinda – well, Belinda was a woman with a shaky ego and took a different view. Having a double to do telly appearances on your behalf entailed no existential terror, it was absolutely marvellous. She looked at her Virginia Woolf postcard with quite different eyes since Linda came. She had pearls, pearls and more pearls, thanks to Linda.

And take the way Linda dealt with Mother. It was miraculous. Initially suspicious of Linda, Mother was now in love with her! She called her, rather pointedly, 'the daughter I never had'. Linda was pretty and well groomed. In Selfridges, she didn't sigh and drag her feet while Mother browsed: she grabbed the sleeves of smart suits and said things like 'What lovely buttons.' Linda modelled clothes beautifully, accepted gifts graciously, and best of all, never asked, 'Something up?'

Linda came to remove the filo haddock plate, which had been scraped clean, as usual, in the lavatory.

'No anchovy sauce these days?' said Belinda, brightly.

'No,' agreed Linda, unconsciously rubbing her elbow. 'No, I've gone off anchovies.'

'You never talk about yourself, Linda.'

'Have you ever asked?'

'I suppose not.'

Belinda wondered whether this was an invitation. But if it was, it was soon revoked.

'Do you need any Mars bars?'

'Well, I can't pretend another dozen wouldn't be nice.'

'I'll pop out later. Did I tell you I'm seeing Maggie? She rang up again. I said I'd meet her for coffee at the Adelphi. It's a friends thing,' she added, noticing Belinda's puzzled expression.

'You don't have to do that, Linda. After all, she's my friend.'

'Nonsense. I'd be glad to. You've got all those justified sinners to worry about. And I'm collecting the photos of your birthday tea.'

'Great. Oh, look, sorry I missed that tea, Linda. I got so absorbed—'

'No, it was fine. We had a lovely time. I shall be like Paddington Bear, having two birthdays.'

'Maggie doesn't mind about today, I suppose?' There was something odd about Linda supplanting her with her oldest friend, but she couldn't put her finger on it. Such issues were very confusing, these days.

'Would you prefer to go instead?' Linda offered.

'Right this minute?' Belinda was only half dressed, despite the late hour. She hadn't worn make-up in a month. There was chocolate on her jumper. 'No. Look. Give her my love, or something. It's just that you shouldn't do everything!' she urged, at last. As a protest, it was transparently feeble.

'But I want to,' said Linda. 'And you don't. That's why we're made for each other, isn't it?'

At the hospital in Malmö, Ingrid whimpered in her straitjacket. She had been trying to gather genetic material from the other patients again, though luckily only with the aid of plastic cutlery.

'I'm so unhappy,' she told the young nurse in Swedish.

'Yeah, yeah,' replied the nurse, bored.

'Stefan loved me,' she said. 'He was always unlucky!'

'You can say that again.'

Ingrid squirmed in the jacket and yelled, 'Stefan! Stefan! They tell me you are dead! What wickedness this is!'

'He *is* dead, Ingrid. You saw him die.'

'No, no! I'm so unhappy.'

'Yeah, yeah.'

'He's not dead.'

'Yes he is.'

It was dreary in Malmö when Leon and Tanner got their taxi into town. And the wind was piercing, like being lanced by icicles. As a seasoned sportswriter, Leon had judiciously worn a warm coat and thick boots; meanwhile the fine leather soles on Tanner's hand-made shoes sent him skidding into a bank of trolleys the moment they stepped on to the ice outside the arrivals hall.

'I'm getting my own column, you know,' said Tanner, in the gloom of the cab.

Leon could believe it.

Grey functional Malmö buildings flashed past. The radio played Euro music, and the driver tapped the wheel in rhythm.

'Whoever heard of Malmö?' said Tanner.

'Well, anyone who remembers the 1992 European Football Championships,' said Leon. 'England lost two-one. "Swedes two, Turnips one" – you must have heard that? It was Gary Lineker's last international appearance and Graham Taylor took him off. The fans trashed the town afterwards.'

Tanner looked at him with contempt. 'Do you really retain trivia, or do you look it up?'

'I was here. I remember it.'

'Good heavens.'

'So you're here to visit mad Mrs Johansson, is that right?' Leon asked, airily. 'Need me to come along? What's the story?'

He held his breath in the dark, wondering whether Tanner would trust his friendly tone. He did. 'Look, Ripley thinks Johansson is a clone.'

'A what?'

'A double. You know. The original Johansson died in a fire in Sweden yet here he is in London, pretending to have an academic post. So Ripley puts two and two together – or one and one together, if you see what I mean. This Johansson was an expert on cloning, you see, and a madman. Bits of pulsating human genetic material found all over his lab and house when he died. Signs of unethical practice. Bodies under the floor, I don't know. The wife went mad, and that's all there is to it, except – you'll like this bit – that the so-called clone is married to ... Well, guess. He's married to one of Ripley's *best friends*.'

From the way he spat out the last couple of words, Tanner evidently disapproved of nepotism in Fleet Street. Which was a little hypocritical of him, in the circumstances.

'Can you believe it?' said Tanner, nonchalantly tapping his passport on his leg. 'Nonsense. Utter bosh. This man is not a clone, there's just a mix-up. Do you know how many Stefan Johanssons there are in Sweden?'

'How many?'

'Well,' stalled Tanner, who hadn't checked, 'just say it's better to ask how many Swedes *aren't* called Stefan Johansson. Ripley's not too bright, that's all. It's my opinion that this Johansson declined the offer to write in his idiotic genetics supp, and the only explanation Jago finds plausible for such behaviour is that the man isn't human.'

Much as he instinctively disliked and distrusted the stuck-up boy, Leon was still impressed by such a fine grasp of Jago's personality.

'Do you like basketball?' he asked. It was a shot in the dark.

'Yes, actually,' said Tanner. 'Adore it. You don't play, surely?'

Leon ignored the way Tanner was looking him up and down. 'No, I don't play. But I'm here to cover it. Malmö Meerkats and Cincinnati Sidewinders. A slightly uneven contest. But Sweden's mad for basketball. It will be a good event.'

'The Cincinnati Sidewinders?' Tanner's eyes opened wide, and for the first time he dropped his world-weary act. In the cab, the music changed to Abba's 'Waterloo'. At the thought of the famous Sidewinders, Tanner suddenly looked twelve years old.

Leon hid his smile by looking out of the window. Sports journalism was such an odd job. Half the people in the world thought sport was an utter irrelevance, and the other half wanted to climb into your suitcase. Either they looked at you blankly and backed off a pace or two, or were so jealous they burst into tears. With Tanner, it could have gone either way.

'The Winders?' Tanner repeated. 'The Winders are in Malmö? With Jericho Jones?'

'I can get you to the press conference, if you like.'

'No!'

Leon pretended to check in his file for the time of the press conference, but he already knew it. 'It's tomorrow at two thirty. Are you free?'

'Yes!' Then Tanner's face crumpled. 'No! No, I'm not! Damn, damn, damn.'

'What's up?'

'That's precisely when I meet Stefan Johansson's mad old lady.'

'What a shame. Your one chance to meet Jericho Jones, I suppose.'

Tanner agonized. Leon watched him with considerable enjoyment. It was going to be simple to reach Mrs Mad Johansson before Tanner. When the time came, it would be a simple matter of swapping roles.

As the cab drew up at their cheap hotel and the driver charged them the three hundred kronor Leon had agreed at the airport, Leon felt optimistic for the first time in weeks. Maggie was pining not only for a married man but some sort of undead person! He could rescue her from this terrible delusion. And then the rest would be easy. How could he put it, in a poetic metaphor she would understand? He could slam-dunk her heart, he thought. He could slam-dunk her heart, while sky-walking.

Chapter Eight

When Jago saw Laurie Spink's fourth column, he was furious. This had gone on long enough. Not one reference to monstrous boobs had yet appeared in Spink's submissions; not even a mention of monstrous dicks, which he'd assured Spink would be a satisfactory second-choice subject, if sensitively handled. Although he worked for a mid-market newspaper, Jago had been promoted especially on his talents as a tabloid thinker, as a man with a direct psychic link to the least-educated person on the Clapham omnibus. He had kept the Viagra story going for twenty-eight months. The picture desk adored him.

'Damn it, Spink,' he bellowed now down the phone. 'If I'd wanted a piece about free will and predestination in the scientific age, I'd have asked the Archbishop of Canterbury. In fact, hang on a minute.' He tapped his keyboard and studied his screen. 'I *did* ask the Archbishop of Canterbury.' He tapped some more. 'Jesus,' he exclaimed. 'Have you any idea the money that man gets? I could get God for less. Listen, Spink. I want this again in thirty-five minutes or I rewrite it myself.'

'I've got a tutorial,' Spink objected.

'You've always got a tutorial.'

Jago slammed down the phone, and dialled Dermot, the Archbishop's literary representative. He loved playing tough-talking newspaperman like this. Sometimes he opened his desk drawer to gaze for a few seconds at a little picture of Edward G. Robinson, to fire him up sufficiently.

'Dermot, it's Jago. What the fuck do you think you're doing?'

A lengthy pause at the other end, while Dermot fought panic. It had to happen one day that Jago would discover the affair. Sweat formed on his brow.

'Dermot?'

'Yes.'

'I'm talking to you. This so-called Primate of All England of yours. Who exactly does this guy think he is?'

Stefan ate his third nut cookie of the morning and put down his *Teach Yourself English Slang*. He had felt better about himself since his late-night confession to Linda. He wished sometimes he could drop the Swedish act, but he was right about Belinda's attraction to him as a Swede. Belinda could never love a man called George; she'd admitted as much. When they saw a production of *The Importance of Being Earnest* in the early days of their relationship, he tested her afterwards.

'You don't mean to say that you couldn't love me if my name wasn't Stefan?'

'But your name is Stefan.'

'Personally, darling, to speak quite candidly' — he did his Wildean dialogue pretty well — 'I don't much care about the name of Stefan. I think there are lots of other much nicer names. George is a charming name.'

But true to Oscar Wilde, Belinda said that George had no music and didn't thrill, and that she pitied anybody married to a person called George, and that she could never love a George, and so on. They were laughing, of course. It wasn't serious. But Stefan already loved Belinda so much that he couldn't take the risk. What always amazed him was that she didn't penetrate his phoney Swede act anyway. True, he'd lived in Stockholm for twenty years, but when his wife asked him (for example) who was the Swedish Alfred Hitchcock, or the Swedish Jack the Ripper, or the Swedish Kenneth Williams, it was surely obvious he was making up the answers.

'Bo Söderberg,' he told her recently, with great authority, when she asked who the Swedish Enid Blyton was.

'Didn't you say Bo Söderberg was the Swedish John Travolta? I'm sure you did.'

'No, that was his brother Nils,' Stefan had replied, thinking quickly. 'Nils Söderberg. Brother of Bo. Marvellous clan, the Söderbergs. All blond and extremely clever. Kerstin Söderberg is the Swedish Barbara Woodhouse, while Jonas Söderberg won the Eurovision Song Contest in 1958.'

Luckily, his wife trusted him. She did not ask for an invitation to Stockholm, to meet the Magnificent Söderbergs. And luckily he also loved researching idiom. Throwing back his head now in the Habitat café, all the better to concentrate and memorize, he resolved to work into casual conversation today *codswallop, cold feet* and *colour of your money. A load of cock*, he discovered, was 'less polite than *cobblers*'. How interesting to consider either of these terms by their degree of politeness. And which of these two excellent turns of phrase would Stefan authentically choose? Or would he (as it were) cock a snook at both?

'No bald-headed boy, these days,' he remarked to the girl selling coffee. It was true. A month had passed since Tanner had appeared. Stefan felt free to breathe again.

She smiled, uncertainly. 'The one who kept watching you and making notes?'

'That's the one.'

'Gone to Sweden,' she said.

Stefan blenched. 'What?'

'He rang just now from a place called Marmite, and asked me to let him know if you'd done anything remotely interesting in the last four weeks. Those were his exact words. I wrote it down, look. I said no, by the way. What a nerve.'

'Marmite?'

'Sorry.' She consulted her notes. 'Malmö. He mentioned two dots.' She looked at him. 'Are you all right?'

'No.' Stefan had swung his scarf around his neck. 'Did he tell you his name?'

'Tanner.'

'Right. Tanner.'

'Of the *Effort*.'

Stefan stopped in his tracks. 'The newspaper?'

'I suppose so.'

The boy was from Jago's paper!

'Oh God in heaven,' he said.

Dermot put down the phone from Jago and took a deep, steadying breath. Life was certainly teaching him a lesson – not to have sex with your clients' wives. Not because it was morally scummy, or anything, but when the husband rang you in a flying rage about something else entirely you needed to lie on the floor to recover.

Dermot felt very uneasy about Jago. He could handle feelings of disloyalty, of course; and he was actually deeply fond of lying. What he hated most about the present situation was having to keep from his best newspaper contact Viv's phenomenal secret. A potentially lethal criminal fraud had been perpetrated by Jago's wife, and he couldn't tell anybody. Viv had exonerated her conspiracy with Linda, if memory served, by invoking the beauty of the resulting soft furnishings. He wondered whether even the Calvinists in their heyday had ever considered such a belief system. Justification by Tie-back, they would have had to call it. Expiation by Kapok.

Right now, he was supposed to be calling the Archbishop with the *Effort*'s demands, so he got up off the floor, put his feet up and started to count to 500 instead. This was his usual practice. He would just wait a few minutes and then phone Jago back, saying the Archbishop was a tough nut with titanic financial commitments who refused to bend over for the *Effort*, not now, not ever. He knew Jago would capitulate when met by superior rhetorical force: Jago liked to impersonate Edward G. Robinson, but it was all an act. Come back at him as Arnold Schwarzenegger, and he rolled over like a puppy.

'Archbish says no dice,' he snarled realistically, after making and drinking a nice cup of peppermint tea. 'You made one primate very, very angry, my friend. He said he'd personally excommunicate you.'

'Shit,' said Jago. 'Really?'

'Just back off. OK?'

'OK.'

Dermot took a deep breath. He had to say *something* about what he'd learnt of Linda.

'Listen, I hear your friend Belinda's on *Late Review*, these days. She's a big hit.'

'So?'

'So I hear she's looking like Kylie Minogue. You should snap her up for the *Effort*.'

'Kylie Minogue? Belinda?'

'That's right.'

'Belinda looks like George Orwell.'

This was unkind, but not entirely untrue.

'Well, I'm just tipping you a wink.'

'You're doing what?'

'Tipping a wink.'

'Oh.' Jago wrinkled his nose. He had no idea what to make of this. He couldn't relate to anything cryptic. That Linda was impersonating Belinda he already knew, because at home Viv spoke of nothing else.

'OK. See you. Oh, name some flowers, I'm in a spot.'

'Aster, rose, daisy, clematis, camellia.'

Jago made tapping noises at the other end, and put the phone down.

Dermot looked at the dead receiver and shrugged. By his own meagre ethical standards, he had certainly done his best.

Four bad weeks had passed for Maggie since she threw Leon out of her house. Her therapy had intensified to such a degree that now it had more of a life than she did herself. She was therapy's tool, nothing more. As she sat at home with the cats in the evenings, she was a mere husk, stroking the fluffy racing car, watching mindless television and snivelling.

The trouble was, the well-intentioned Julia had a no-nonsense hard-hat approach to therapy. Demolish the person, inspect the foundations, and then rebuild to a new and better spec, using a selection of the original materials. No matter that a shower unit and a bit of cosmetic crack-papering might actually suffice. Instead, methodical and painstaking, she dismantled Maggie's personality brick by brick, examining the mortar, preserving bits of cornice, and making careful notes of the archaeological layers in the wallpaper. The only problem was that, while the process was ongoing, Maggie felt exactly like an abandoned human building site, with wind rustling her tarpaulins. No roof; no walls; no floors; fireplace and toilet exposed for all to see. It was no wonder, really, in these conditions, that a squatter quickly got in.

Because although Noel had been banned from Julia's programme of therapy – lookalike role-playing was absolutely ruled out after the first experiment – Maggie slept with him anyway. She didn't mean to. It just happened. He kept phoning to tell her he cared about her, and that she was lovely and talented, and that she didn't deserve to be exploited by married men who stayed only an hour. And then, one day, he brought a thoughtful cat-toy for Miranda, which broke down Maggie's weakened defences. Noel now came to see her twice a week, each time for fifty-five minutes. And it was awful. Not knowing how much it upset her, he brought her extremely cheap presents, such as a copy of the *Big Issue*, or a paper bag with two oranges in it. Presumably he hoped to repeat the effect of the cat-toy, but instead she felt demeaned. 'He thinks I'll do it for a bag of Bombay mix,' she said miserably to herself, as she put her hand down his trousers. 'And if I'm doing this, I suppose he's right.' These days, when Maggie looked in a mirror she was reminded of a line in a Restoration comedy she did at college: 'I'm like an old peeled wall.'

As she prepared to meet Linda for coffee at the Adelphi, she wondered how much of this to tell her. None of it was very flattering, after all.

'Obviously, if I'm sleeping with you, I must leave Julia,' she said to Noel, after his second visit. He was putting his coat on and consulting his watch. Having washed his hands twice, he was still sniffing his fingers with a quizzical expression, as if he couldn't identify the smell.

'You can't do that,' he exclaimed, with panic behind his eyes. He took her by the shoulders, his hands heavy against her neck. 'I mean, she'll want to know why, and you can't tell her. I hope you're not that selfish, Maggie? To hurt Julia? After all she's done for you?'

'No, no. But—'

'Besides, you must never curtail therapy unnaturally. It's incredibly dangerous, psychologically.'

'I know.'

The problems of leaving therapists had plagued Maggie for the past ten years; she was an expert on its double-binds. 'This isn't working,' you say. To which they reply, 'We must discuss this urgently. Is Tuesday afternoon still good?' 'You're not very bright,' you object. And they look at you pityingly and say, 'But it's exactly this kind of judgementalism that is blighting your life, don't you see that?'

'Sometimes I think Julia will never let me go.'

Noel laughed. 'Join the club.'

'But I'm not married to her!'

He assumed his solemn expression again, and she knew she was in for a lecture. As a member of the therapists' union, Noel had sworn on a stack of Freuds never to let such heresy pass unchecked. 'What you could have with Julia is better than marriage, Margaret. If you would only accept it, only open yourself up! You refuse to experience transference! But if you did, you'd see that Julia is completely on your side.'

'Is she?' Maggie sniffed.

'Of course. Shame you're shagging her husband, really.'

As she remembered this scene, Maggie felt tears of shame roll down her face. And what had she said to him next?

'What I need, Noel, is to have a *man* completely on my side.'

'Pay me thirty quid an hour and you might get one.'

'I wish we could talk.'

Noel kissed her forehead lightly. 'Talk to Julia,' he said. 'Gotta go.'

There was a time when Belinda had never really heard of Malmö. A Söderberg might be a crispbread. But now her beloved Stefan was going back on a sudden visit, and she had to bite her lip and be brave while he packed for his journey.

'Is it Ingrid?' she whispered. 'Is she — worse?'

144

Stefan took her hands and held them warmly in his own. 'Not possible,' he said, gravely.

'Oh, Stefan. I can't help feeling guilty about her. We're so happy and she's so—'

'I know. Don't say it.'

He threw some warm clothes in a suitcase, and checked his watch. He was catching a flight to Copenhagen in two hours from Heathrow.

'Oh, Miss Patch, I love you. You do know that? I must come clean. You give me collywobbles.'

She grinned bravely. Of course she knew that. She really appreciated it, too, when he remembered to call her Miss Patch. Even if Audrey Hepburn never weighed thirteen stone, smelt a bit, and got dizzy standing up.

'I wish I could come,' she lied.

'No, no. Listen, Belinda. You have fears that you will cease to be before your pen has gleaned your teeming brain. This is what you tell me. I respect this. It is not codswallop, I think?'

'I hope not.'

'So don't get cold feet. I know what you think, Belinda. But your book will not be common or garden. Or cobblers.'

'OK.'

He stood in the doorway, gazing at her. He really didn't want to leave. Not only did he have genuine affection for his strangely ballooning wife, but he had found no way of incorporating 'a load of cock' into the conversation.

Jago couldn't believe it. He was having a very bad phone day. Tanner had been in Malmö just two hours, and already Stefan had discovered what was going on.

'Who is Tanner of the *Effort*, please, Yago?' Stefan demanded, without preamble. In the background to the phone call were giveaway airport noises. 'And why is he in Malmö?'

'Oooh,' stalled Jago, whose mediocre skill at lying was rightly famous. 'Tanner? Tanner. No, I can't think. How's that lovely wife of yours, incidentally? I hear she's quite foxy these days.'

'He has a bald head, like a footballer.'

'Bald head, bald head, bald head. Oh, I know! Fashion! That's right. Couldn't think who you meant. Yes, Tanner's our great young style guru. Must be in Malmö for – er, Scandinavian Fashion Week. Snoods are back, apparently. Is there a problem?'

'Well, yes, Yago. This bald-headed Tanner fellow has been following me. And I don't think it's because he studies my outfits.'

'He follows you? What for?'

'He spooks me, Yago. In fact, between you, me and the doorpost, I think this Scandinavian Fashion Week story may be a load of old cock.'

'No!'

'Can you call him off, please?'

'I'll try. But why?'

'I must go, Yago. But please, help me! I helped you many times. Please. I don't know if I am coming or going!'

'Which way *are* you going, by the way?' Jago tried to make it sound like a pleasantry.

'What?'

'Are you coming or going, Stefan? Are you in Malmö?'

The line went dead, and Jago buzzed his secretary. 'Get me a flight to Malmö, quick! And name me some flowers while you're about it!'

'You've got to get out of this Noel-Julia situation, Maggie,' said Linda, firmly. She poured milk into her coffee, and took another cake from the plate. What a shame Belinda never came out these days. She'd have liked the Adelphi. Linda sometimes felt she knew Belinda's preferences better than Belinda knew them herself.

'It's the first rule of survival,' she added, brushing icing sugar from her fingers. 'Never have anything to do with people who drain the life out of you.'

'But they each have my best interests at heart.'

'Is that what they told you?'

'Of course.'

'So you feel really great, do you?'

'No, I feel terrible.'

Maggie felt rather awkward talking to a stranger in this way. But it was odd. This woman was far more supportive than Belinda was. She had the knack of applying herself to somebody else's situation. She seemed to think loyalty the principal virtue of mankind. She said Maggie had enormous potential as an actress. Already, in fact, Maggie was ready to call her the best friend she'd ever had.

'Can I ask your advice, too, perhaps?' asked Linda. 'I would love to know what you think about something.'

'Who, me?'

Maggie brightened for the first time that day. Her advice was never sought by Belinda. Even when freely offered, Maggie's bitter, sour-grapes opinions were consistently ignored by all her friends.

'It's just that you've known Belinda for years. Do you think she secretly wants children?'

Maggie barked with laughter at the thought of it. 'No.'

'Why's that?'

'Because she's incredibly selfish.'

'But Stefan would make such a lovely father. Strange that a geneticist would waste such genes.'

'Oh Lord, you're right there. When I was Olivia in *Twelfth Night*, do you know the part I couldn't cope with? It was when Viola said to me, "Oh, lady, you are the cruellest she alive, if you will lead these graces to the grave, and leave the world no copy."' Maggie swallowed. 'It used to make me cry.'

'That must have been very effective on stage.'

'Oh, yes. Except that it's more of a comical moment, really.'

'Oh.'

Maggie pulled herself together. 'But that's what you mean about Stefan? He's bound by sheer good taste to reproduce?'

'Yes.'

'I think you're absolutely right.'

Jago phoned Tanner on his mobile, and heard strange sports-hall echoes in the background, like a ball bouncing and the squeak of rubber-soled shoes, an organ playing, and lots of cheers.

'Tanner? Whatever time your appointment is with the madwoman,' he barked, 'you've got to bring it forward!'

'Sorry?' yelled Leon. The noise of the basketball warm-up event behind him made chatting difficult. Tanner had gone to buy a coffee and left his mobile on the desk. Leon had helpfully answered it. 'This isn't Tanner—' he began.

'What's that noise? Tanner, where are you?'

'What?'

'This is Jago Ripley, for fuck's sake! You've got to go and see the loony as soon as possible!'

'What?'

Leon had heard this clearly enough, however. 'What?' he yelled. He was quite enjoying this. He had never liked Jago much.

Jericho Jones performed a graceful sky-walk slam-dunk, and the place went wild.

'Stefan's on his way!' screamed Jago, amid the approving roar of the Swedes.

'Sorry, you're breaking up,' Leon said, then switched off the mobile and dropped it back on Tanner's desk.

'Who was that?' asked Tanner, returning with hot drinks on a paper tray.

'No idea,' shrugged Leon, and looked at his watch. Things were going rather well with his Maggie mission. He just had to get to the hospital before Stefan Johansson.

Meanwhile, back in London, Jago chewed the edge of his desk with excitement. It would be accurate to say that his interest in this story had been revived. Stefan had a secret, all right! He was acting like a guilty clone! And, with any luck, the whole story would unfold within the extremely short range of Jago Ripley's twenty-four-hour attention span.

When Mother popped in to see Belinda, she found her methodically cleaning her keyboard with finger and spittle.

'Damn. I mean, hello,' said Belinda, guiltily. Lucky her mother had not entered earlier and found her counting her Mars bar wrappers. Writing had not been very good today. In fact, according to her word-count software, she'd added fourteen words in total to her manuscript, and two of those were 'Chapter Three'. But on the bright side, she had enough Mars bar wrappers for a free scratch card, and the function keys and space bar had never looked so shiny.

'Busy, dear?'

'Yes, yes,' said Belinda defensively. 'Very busy. Quite a lot of my time is spent just thinking, you know. It's not all tap-tap-tap. That's typing, not writing.'

'Yes, of course. That's why all your work takes so long, I expect.'

'Mm.'

Mother cleared a number of books from Belinda's couch and sat down. She chose this spot because it was the furthest from the radiator. Gently, she stroked her own cheeks upwards towards her ears, like a cat washing itself.

'Something up?' asked Belinda, automatically.

Mother ignored her. 'Belinda, it isn't easy to say this, but I feel I must.'

'What?'

'I feel you have let yourself go. There. I've said it.'

'Let myself go?' Belinda laughed.

'Yes.'

'Nobody says that any more, Mother. It comes from the days when people wore corsets and plucked their eyebrows, and lived in L-shaped rooms.'

Mother harumphed. 'You're not even offended! Oh, Belinda, you're beyond hope.'

'What do you expect? I haven't "let myself go". Actually, it's an interesting phrase, when you think about it. It can be a very good thing to let yourself go. Go on, Mother. Let yourself go!'

'But it's what you've done,' she protested. 'You've let yourself go. You used to be quite slim and sexy, and now Stefan can hardly bear to look at you. And I don't blame him. It pains me to say it when you're my own daughter, but in that cardigan you look absolutely disgusting. I can't think where you get it from. Have you *ever* seen me wear a cardigan? Even Auntie Vanessa never wears cardigans and she's got the worst dress sense of anyone in this family.'

Belinda swallowed hard. The metallic taste of the keyboard dirt made the action all the more unpleasant.

'Look at your nails! When was the last time you went to the hairdresser? I can't stand by and watch it any more. This room smells. When I think of how beautifully Linda dresses.'

'What's Linda got to do with it?'

'My own daughter, a human barrage balloon. In a V-neck cardie with pockets. I bought you that beautiful nylon Prada coat last autumn and I found it under the stairs today. It had spiders in it. It was streaked with what I can only describe as snot. I'm having it cleaned, and then I'm giving it to Linda.'

'Stefan says I'm lovely.'

'Can't you see he's just saying that?'

'No, he isn't.'

'Well. You don't see the way he looks at Linda when you're not there. But I can tell you, he can't take his eyes off her.'

Belinda gasped. This was too much. 'Well, now I know you're just being spiteful,' she cried, and – hardly knowing why she did it – she secretly switched on the two-way baby-listener, so that Linda would hear downstairs in the kitchen, where she was known to be rustling up a delightful dish of squid stewed in tomatoes and lemon before popping off to Broadcasting House to review a new film of *Dr Jekyll and Mr Hyde* for Radio 4.

'Repeat what you just said to me!' she told her mother, in a loud voice. 'What are you implying about Stefan and Linda?'

'I'm merely saying that if you continue to bloat in the dark in extra large T-shirts with Wallace and Gromit on the front, your husband won't be able to help himself. Linda is a very attractive young woman, who also happens to be a lot nicer than you are, as well as more talented, and with excellent connections in the worlds of both the media and fishmongery. And, being only human, she fancies Stefan as much as we all do.'

Mother stood up and left the room, leaving Belinda to stare down at her extra large T-shirt in a state of confusion. Her mother had all the wrong values, surely? Stefan had told her just an hour ago how much he loved her. He was extremely supportive about the book, too. Besides, who would be interested sexually in a deputy when he could have the real thing? No, Mother was a silly, interfering woman with artificially arched eyebrows who would find any excuse to disparage her own daughter because she was jealous of her intellect. In fact, Belinda was just about to whisper into the intercom, 'Linda, did you hear all that? What a ridiculous person my mother is!' when she overheard Mother entering the kitchen.

'Linda! Darling!' she said, as if she'd just come home from a terrible day. 'Can I help with anything?'

Belinda knew she ought to switch off the device, but somehow she couldn't. Instead, she placed the speaker on her desk, to hear it better. It was crackly, a bit muffled. But good enough to picture the scene. A scrape of a chair told her that her mother was sitting down. A kettle was filled and switched on. Chopping commenced on a wooden board.

'You're looking lovely, Linda,' Mother said. 'I was just telling Belinda how lucky she is to have you doing everything for her.'

'That's nice,' said Linda, clattering some pans. She sounded strangely brisk. What was up? Surely she'd been flattered by everything Mother had said. It was true that not many people bridge so gracefully those two distinct worlds of the television studio and the fish shop. Belinda notably had contacts in neither.

'May I say something?' Linda said, at last. Sizzling and stirring could be heard.

'Of course.'

'I think you're a wicked person,' said Linda, in a level tone. 'I couldn't see it before, I thought we were all on the same side. But I heard what you said to Belinda just now, and I have to tell you I think you're a cow.'

Belinda was glad she couldn't see Mother's inadequate expression of mild surprise, but was torn nevertheless. Should she rush downstairs to make the peace? Or make sure she didn't miss anything by staying put? She found she had very mixed feelings at hearing Linda call Mother a cow. She wanted to boo and cheer at the same time.

'I think you should leave the house and go back to your flat,' Linda continued. 'You've been very good to me, which makes this hard to say. But I see now you are hurting Belinda, and if you hurt Belinda, you hurt her work. We all know it's very important for Belinda's work that she's not upset.'

'But Belinda's work isn't worth twopence!' exclaimed Mother, brightly. 'Face it Linda, you're twice the person she is.

You're the person everybody likes. Stefan thinks you're gorgeous.'

'Take that back,' warned Linda. She sounded angry.

'Don't be absurd,' said Mother.

'Take that back.'

'No.'

Belinda couldn't believe it. Were they both mad?

'Put down that frozen salmon, Linda!' said Mother, her voice rising.

'Make me,' said Linda.

At which point, unbelievably, there were sounds of a scuffle.

'Oh God,' whispered Belinda. 'They're fighting!'

She stood stock-still, staring at the speaker on her desk. She heard a chair knocked over. Bits of crockery fell off the table and smashed. And throughout there were gasps and squeals. There was violence in the kitchen!

'Linda!' she yelled into the intercom. 'Mother! Stop it!'

But the scuffle continued, with the sound effects of oven doors and broken plates until a loud 'Aieee!' from Mother announced that something very serious had happened.

'My face!' Mother yelled. 'Linda, you bitch! My face!'

Belinda realized it was time to leave the sidelines. Sometimes it's all right for an author to abandon her desk — for example, when her loyal cleaning lady is downstairs mutilating her mother. So she loped to the landing, puffed and clung to the banister when she saw stars, then struggled downstairs, reaching the kitchen just in time to see Linda wield a side of frozen salmon round her head, like a claymore.

'Linda?' Belinda said. 'Put down the fish.'

Linda's arms went limp. It had gone very quiet suddenly. Between them on the kitchen floor Mother already lay unmoving, her face upturned and strangely beautiful. She was dead.

Why did she look so strangely beautiful? As Belinda later

153

learnt, a sudden exposure to the heat of the boiled kettle during the scuffle had made Mother's features drop perfectly into place for the first time since the lift-job. In death, therefore, she looked natural and not a bit surprised, and the irony was profound. Nobody would ever say, 'Something up?' to Mother again. In the turmoil she had slipped on a piece of raw squid, banged her head on the corner of the kitchen table and died instantly. By the time Belinda arrived at the kitchen door, the celestial Fenwick's had already claimed her mother, its cash tills ringing in praise.

Linda's eyes were round holes in her face. Belinda thought afterwards it was the first and last time she ever saw Linda frightened.

'Put the fish down, Linda.'

Linda looked at the salmon as if she had no idea where it came from. 'I didn't—'

'I know.'

'It was her that was angry. It wasn't me. I told her to go, that's all.'

'I heard.'

'She wasn't good enough to be your mother, Belinda. She said I was twice the woman you are! What sort of mother says that?' Linda's dismay choked her. Tears rolled down her face. 'Look,' she still managed to say, 'I did this for you, Belinda, and if you're not happy about it, I'll go.'

Belinda felt her head swim. She had to be happy about *this*? It was a bit of a stretch from being happy about a daily diet of eels and haddock to being happy about seeing your mother lifeless on the kitchen floor. Linda really didn't know where to draw the line, did she? The problem with this situation was that neither of them had the faintest idea where to draw the line.

'Belinda? Don't say you're not happy about this. Please. I don't want to go. How could I live with myself?'

'Oh God,' said Belinda. 'Come here.'

And as she hugged her insanely loyal cleaning lady, who sobbed in her arms, she noticed with a kind of glum horror that Linda was still cradling a slab of frozen fish.

Chapter Nine

Leon's fifteen years as a sports writer sometimes meant that people made the wrong assumption about him. They considered him a *career* sports writer, whose life was a perpetual memorizing of results and whose death would be a final whistle of three long blasts. This wasn't how he saw his own life, however — not at all. True, he liked his job and was good at it. True, he could remember without effort the salient events of Malmö in 1992 or Headingley in 1981. But as far as Leon was concerned, such things did not define him. They weren't *him*. The last thing he wanted was to end up like his journalist father (quite a famous chap in certain circles), who became so preoccupied by his own status within the world of sport that by the end of his sad, peculiar life he was arguably deranged.

'Who was that on the phone? Was it Bobby Moore?' Dad would call from the shed, while Mother burst into tears, and the boys pretended not to hear. 'Did I tell you Seve Ballesteros gave me this sombrero? I taught Jack Charlton how to fish.'

The effect on his sons had been interesting, however. While his softer, younger son Leon had decided to try sports writing himself, if only to prove that madness need not be the profession's inevitable conclusion, the older son Noel became a psychotherapist, to prove that delusional madness is everywhere, not just in people who swan about at the World Cup without paying. Dad had died without being impressed by the achievements of either child, of course. His last words, dutifully relayed by the mystified night cleaner in the terminal ward, left no message to his family. They were instead 'Tell Pele I'll get back to him', from which the family were obliged to derive comfort of a kind. At least they could tell themselves that Dad had been Dad, right to the end.

As a result of their divergent paths in life, Leon rarely saw his brother these days — they had so little in common. But each brother was perfectly aware of the other's existence. When Maggie first told Noel he looked exactly like a man called Leon, he could (and should) have cleared up the mystery at once. But he didn't. He chose instead to be mystified and sceptical, because he enjoyed exploiting Maggie's confusion, and delighted in insisting that Leon did not exist. This was why the sight of her stroking that bloody fluffy racing car made him irrationally angry. It would be true to say that he didn't like Maggie at all, in fact. She just represented something about his annoying younger brother, whom he had discovered (as all older siblings discover sooner or later) he could not literally murder without the risk of incurring awkward questions.

So trashing Leon's girlfriend was a more subtle means of exercising his jealousy, and had the benefit of not being criminal. One should try to feel sorry for Noel, really. It can't be easy when your younger brother is always in Nevada watching sell-out fights with apocalyptic overtones ('Judgement Night III' 'Resurrection Night IX' 'Seven Bowls of Wrath Night') while you spend most afternoons passing tissues to snivelling inadequates in a basement off Tooting Broadway.

'I've got to go out somewhere,' yelled Leon above the basketball din, putting his coat on.

'You can't,' yelled Tanner. 'You've got to cover the match.'

Half-way through the evening was indeed a bad time for

Leon to desert his post, but there was no alternative. 'File it for me,' he told Tanner.

Tanner pulled a bad-smell expression. 'Sorry, don't write about *sport*,' he said.

'It's easy,' Leon assured him, ignoring the put-down. 'They only want four hundred words, and I've done most of it already. Call it LEON when you file and they'll never guess. Mention lots of statistics and get the names right. How many words can you do in an hour?'

Tanner made a wild guess. 'Two or three thousand?'

'Really?' Leon raised an eyebrow. He was impressed.

'I mean, two or three hundred.'

'Oh. Right.'

'I mean, twenty or thirty.'

'Well, whatever,' said Leon. 'Have you used one of these?' He indicated his laptop.

'Of course,' scoffed Tanner. 'My dad's company pioneered the software.'

'Then have fun. I'll see you back at the hotel.'

Outside the sports hall, Leon consulted his Malmö map, straining to hold it against the icy wind. By his reckoning, the University Hospital was an easy walk from the Baltiska Hallen. He gathered his coat against the biting gale and stomped north, wishing he knew more about genetics or, indeed, more about insanity. Blagging his way into unlikely places he was good at. You just carried a coffee in a foam cup, consulted your watch in an exaggerated manner, and shouldered through swing doors as if you knew exactly what to expect on the other side. But what do you do when confronting an insane Swedish woman who holds the key to a genetics mystery? Unless she had the particular delusion that she was the first person Gordon Banks phoned up after the 1966 World Cup final, Leon's first-hand experience would be sorely inadequate.

'Bugger,' he said, leaning into the wind and adjusting his

earflaps. Was this really such a good idea? His toes were numb already. Was it possible for eyeballs to freeze this far south of the Arctic Circle? Inside the hall it was cosy and warm and bright. Out here it was like being X-rayed by weather.

But he thought of Maggie and a surge of romantic sappiness warmed his toes and carried him onward. How helpless the poor girl was! In love with a man who had taken cynical advantage of a terrible tragedy in this poor Ingrid's life. Stefan must be exposed; there was no doubt about it. As he plunged into the neighbouring area known (unpronounceably) as the Möllevången, he tried finally to gather his thoughts. 'Nice statue,' he commented absently, as the appalling boulder-and-bums confection in the Möllevångstorget came into view. And with that excellent critical judgement behind him, Leon forged on against the wind.

'I must see Ingrid Johansson,' demanded Stefan, in rather good Swedish, at the hospital reception desk on the ground floor. 'I have come all the way from England, and I won't take no for an answer.'

The dumpy duty nurse looked at him as if he were speaking Urdu. The order of some of the consonants made sense, but the vowels had been picked at random by a chimpanzee. It was a bit like reading someone else's shorthand. 'I mist sew Oongrud Johinssin,' was what it sounded like. 'Oy hyve cim oll the whoa fram Inglound.'

'Do you speak English?' asked the nurse, at last.

'Of course,' said Stefan.

'Thank God,' she said. 'What is your name, please?'

'Stefan Johansson.'

'Stefan Johansson?' She wrote the name down and underlined it.

Stefan had second thoughts.

'I mean George Colwan. C-O-L-W-A-N.'

She narrowed her eyes.

'George Colwan?'

'Yes.' Her pen was poised for crossing out. 'Not Stefan Johansson?'

'That's right. That's somebody else. He's dead.'

'He's dead?'

This nurse's English was irritatingly good, Stefan decided. She could do all sorts of intonations just by repeating everything he said.

'Will you wait, please?' she said, and dialled an internal number. '*Hej!*' she said into the phone, in the brisk salute he remembered from his twenty years in Sweden, and then began to speak too quickly for him to understand.

He had never quite got used to '*Hej!*', he recalled. When he did business in Sweden, he preferred to say, 'Hello, how are you, sit down.' But the Swedes said, '*Hej!*' and that was it. It was funny how it all came back. Arriving by boat from Copenhagen this evening, he'd gone straight to a shop to buy a map and had found himself in an automatic '*Hej! Hej!*' exchange with the youthful shopkeeper. It was only when the man carried on in Swedish, commenting lengthily on his choice of map, that Stefan admitted his Swedish wasn't so good any more. 'No problem,' confessed the youth in English. 'It was yust bullshit.'

'Do you know Ingrid? Is she – all right?' Stefan asked the nurse, when she had finished with the phone. It was weird that, here in Sweden, he didn't need to pretend to be Swedish any more.

'Yes, Ingrid is well. She is not my patient, of course, because she is my friend. I have known Ingrid thirty years. She worked here, you know, during the years of her marriage.'

'I didn't know that.'

'When she was suspended on suspicion of stealing cotton swabs and Petri dishes and scalpels and bandages, I spoke up for her. We were like sisters. Ingrid and Birgit! I knew her husband Stefan very, very well.'

Stefan tried not to look too closely, but there was something rather odd about this Birgit. For one thing, she was cubic in shape, and seemed to shrink in height the more he looked at her. For another, her top lip kept twitching. 'Really?'

'Ingrid is as sane as you or I. Yust upset by Stefan's murder, as who would not?'

'I see. Murder? I see.'

'All those stories about Stefan's experiments were made up.'

'Good. Yes.'

'So,' she said, with an emphatic exhalation. 'Will you wait in here, please?'

Stefan was puzzled, but followed the nurse along a corridor. She opened the door to a small room, ushered him inside, then locked it.

'Do you know how unhappy Ingrid is?' she said, through a glass panel in the door. 'She is *so* unhappy. And you know who she blames? You! Lucky George! You set fire to her husband! You threw her on floor! You get blood on her Carl Larsson reproduction! Your luck yust ran out, Lucky George!'

'Hey!' he yelled, through the glass panel in the door. But the only person who heard him just said, '*Hej!*' back again.

At which point, Stefan saw the inexplicable sight of Leon – from Jago's dinner party – barge past Birgit and through a swing-door, carrying a cup of coffee.

Back at the sports hall, Tanner was having a few difficulties writing his 400 words. Because, just when he'd settled on a rather good line about Sidewinders being sidelined, just when his account of the match had reached the important 350-word mark, with ten minutes to deadline, Jericho Jones stopped the match and announced his retirement from world sport. His son had been expelled from school in Cincinnati on suspicion of dope dealing, and it was time to stop bouncing a ball. He apologized to the miffed Meerkats. He apologized to his millions of fans. He recalled the words of his first coach, 'Strut' Schwarz, to the effect that 'No man is in Ireland.' And then he led his astounded team back to the dressing room.

As all around him reporters grabbed phones and started shouting, Tanner wondered what his precise responsibility was here. 'They won't need me to write about this, will they?' he asked a chap from the *Guardian*, who had been helpful up till now.

'Get me the news desk,' snapped the chap.

Tanner looked at the 350 words he had already accumulated, and felt a bit sick. Rewriting the whole thing in ten minutes was out of the question. Whereas if he continued at the current rate, and changed nothing, he could just make it. Much as he enjoyed sport, much as he admired Jericho Jones for his splendid eloquence, he was horrified by the reaction of his colleagues. Was this really so important? Surely only time would tell? 'News will pick it up,' he told himself. 'If it's important, News will do it.'

He was right, of course; but also wrong. Unfortunately, if there was one thing that defined Tanner, it was his refusal to be part of any mass brute reflex. So, disdainful of his colleagues who yelled urgent things like 'What's the son's name?' to each other, and 'Who fought the battle of Jericho? Was it Cain or Abel?' while tapping their keyboards at indecent speed, Tanner took it easy. Insouciance above all; that was the aim. A sense of perspective. Thus it was that his last fifty words mentioned that Jericho Jones had sadly marred this excellent game with a sensational and inappropriate retirement speech which, on mature reflection, did not deserve the oxygen of publicity.

Tanner signed the story in Leon's name and filed it. He shut Leon's computer, packed his bag and left the building, fighting his way between newsmen waving bits of paper, and dodging the lighting cameramen who waited outside shouting, 'He's got to come out this way!' and 'Someone said he had a car at the back!' and 'This is the biggest thing that's ever happened in Malmö!'

Tanner shook his head at such depressing evidence of pack mentality, hitched his skirt a bit, and set off to walk northwards, through the Möllevångstorget, back to the hotel.

Jago's taxi driver was in heaven. Already the fare was two thousand kronor. Apart from disliking the peremptory way the driver had greeted him with '*Hej!*', Jago was pretty comfortable, too. Because this was the way to do journalism, in his opinion. Get the taxi driver from the airport to tell you everything you need to know, including facts and figures. This driver was either the best bluffer in the world, or really knew the exact number of bars in Sweden (*cf.* Finland and Denmark), the exact distance to Copenhagen, and the dates of the city's buildings and statues. By contrast, back in England, Jago recalled that his airport driver had told him with similar confidence that English was spoken by everyone in the world until the eighteenth century, when the French came along.

'So this is the place, huh?' said Jago, peering from the cab at a dilapidated front door with '8B' above it. The windows were dirty. Old snow adhered to the doorstep. 'The real Stefan guy died here?'

'No one lives since,' said the driver. 'Even the rats left, they say. It was terrible story, yuh? Mad scientist chopping people to bits? Mister Yekkle, yuh? Dr Hyde.'

'Any idea he might have produced clones? That was his work, wasn't it? You know the word clone?'

'Clones, yuh. Dolly Sheep. We Swedes read more newspapers than any peoples in Europe.'

'Yeah?'

'Oh yeah. We top list also with coffee consuming, eating frozen food. We are yust third in reading books and owning telephones.'

'And killing yourselves.'

'No, this is not true,' said the driver, solemnly. 'We are eleventh only in world at killing ourselves. We are statistically very happy peoples.'

'How much do I owe you now?'

'Three thousand.'

'I understand why you're happy.'

The driver didn't laugh, but put the car in gear.

'You're wrong, though,' said Jago.

'No, no. I check all this. Eleventh only.'

'No, I mean you're wrong that there's nobody living here.' Jago gestured to 8B. 'There's a light on.'

The driver pursed his lips. 'No, no. Not possible. We go now?'

'Yes, there is. Look. Sort of a glow.'

The driver looked. Jago stepped out of the cab and peered in at the window. Not only was there a faint light inside, but there was movement, too. The front door flapped open.

'So,' called the driver, whose manner had changed. 'That's enough fun, yuh? Now I think we get out of here.'

'Not yet,' said Jago.

'Get in, please. In.'

'Look, pal—' he began.

At which point the driver slammed the Volvo in gear and drove off, leaving Jago outside 8B without his luggage, listening to the howling of the wind.

Leon had done extremely well in infiltrating the hospital. In fact, he had done too well. The cup of coffee trick had worked wonderfully, and he had ignored all calls of '*Hej!*'. Eight sets of swing doors had succumbed to his mighty shoulders, including the last one, which was clearly marked in Swedish, 'EMERGENCY EXIT TO CAR PARK'. He barged through this final set into the cold night air, hearing the doors swing back into place with a nasty click before he realized what had happened. Damn. He had gone through that hospital like a dose of salts, and right out the other side.

His phone rang. It was the office.

'Hi!' he said, quite pleased. He stomped his feet and sipped the coffee. 'Good job I brought this,' he said aloud.

'Leon?'

'Hey!' said Leon, glad to hear the familiar voice of his boss in London. He didn't usually get calls about minor events in Europe that were only worth 400 words. But, on the other hand, he was good on basketball. His favourite sportsman was Jericho Jones, and he'd written some decent stuff about him today — about how he was still at the top of his form, and would be splendid presidential material. 'So how's the piece? Should I have rung yet for queries?'

'Queries?' yelled his boss. 'Queries about this *shit*?'

'What?' Leon was confused. He had left Tanner with about 300 words already written. How could the boy have messed up so badly?

'What are you playing at, Leon?'

'Oh, no, don't tell me I said anal again.'

'Very funny. You're fired.'

'What?'

'I haven't got time for this, Leon. I've covered up for you long enough. You've been losing your grip for weeks.'

'What?'

'Stop saying "What".'

'What?'

And then the phone went dead.

Leon sat down on an old box and sipped his coffee. Meeting Maggie had not been too good for him, he had to admit. A lot of things seemed to have backfired since then. Take today, for instance. One minute he was a well-liked *Effort* man on a mission. The next he was jobless in a foreign delivery bay where he might conceivably freeze to death. Funny how life takes turns of that sort. Getting back into the hospital and locating Ingrid Johansson seemed a pretty remote possibility right now.

'They never called my stuff shit before,' he reflected aloud. But he had little time to dwell further on the mystery before alarm bells and sirens began to ring and wah-wah within the building, and lights to flash on the wall. A shower of dust and grit landed on his hat. Looking up, he dimly saw a dark figure with a rope, abseiling down the sheer wall towards him at considerable speed. It was Ingrid Johansson. She had escaped.

'Tanner!'

It was the editor of the *Effort*, phoning from London.

'Uncle Jack!' said Tanner. 'How are you?'

Back in London, the editor shut his office door. 'Where are you, Tanner? Someone said you were in Malmö. Is that possible, in our hour of need?'

'I am. Although I can't think why. It's freezing, and I've just been looking at the most hideous statue I think I've ever seen.'

'Look, this is a long shot. Just say no, if you like. Do you know anything about basketball? The thing is, there's a huge story about Jericho somebody. Our man completely let us down — Sport are fuming, they've sacked him. I said I'd help. What can you do?'

Tanner bit his lip. It was terrible when ambition wrestled with honesty like this. 'You mean I can save the day, Uncle?'

'Exactly.'

'Gosh.'

As the man who had imperilled the day in the first place, Tanner was playing things exceptionally cool.

'How long can I have?'

'Three hours maximum. Good boy. Is Jago Ripley there?'

Confused, Tanner looked around. What a strange question. 'No. As I said, I'm in Malmö.'

'When you see him, tell him I'd like a word. Between you and me, Tanner, he's upset the Church of England.'

Replacing his phone in his skirt pocket, Tanner felt so good suddenly that he felt like dancing. It was a shame about Leon, but on the other hand, for someone who clearly had no connections at board level, Leon had done pretty well for himself over the years. It amazed Tanner that ill-connected people bothered to try in most professions when it was so obvious they wouldn't succeed.

'Tanner!' he heard, through the noise of the wind. He stopped and looked around. Sounded like Ripley. But where?

'Over here!'

Tanner scanned the empty street of three-storey red-brick tenements, and saw nobody. And then he jumped in the air. Because Jago was inside an apartment, peering out of the dirty window, a faint glimmer in the room behind, as if from a candle. In the light from the street lamp, his face looked pale, almost green. Perhaps he had found a seaweed-therapy place.

'Why aren't you at the hospital?' Jago yelled, his words muffled by the glass.

'Going tomorrow.'

'I told you to go today.'

'You didn't!'

Not surprisingly, Jago was finding it hard to impress his authority on Tanner. 'This is the house where it all happened!' he yelled. 'You'd better come in. We may find something. Jesus, I'm freezing my balls off. I've got to get something on Stefan.'

Outside, Tanner was clearly dithering.

'I said, come in! It's not housebreaking. The door was open.'

Tanner thought about his big chance, writing a lead story for the editor, and weighed it briefly against helping Jago with his stupid clone theory. 'Actually, rather not, if it's all the same.'

And then, from Jago's perspective, something very unpleasant happened to Tanner's face. His look of boyish superiority dissolved, to be replaced by a look of terror. 'Aaaagh!' he yelled, pointing directly at the executive features editor of the *Effort*.

'What?' said Jago.

'Aaaagh!' screamed Tanner, somewhat louder. And before Jago could turn round to see what Tanner was screaming at, he'd been lightly bludgeoned from behind by an old, charred Carl Larsson reproduction.

An alarm at the hospital. People in white coats running around. Through his window, Stefan couldn't hear much but he could see Birgit, in tears, confessing something to a man in uniform. She raised an arm and pointed towards him, and a porter ran to unlock the door. 'Ingrid Johansson has escaped,' he said.

'Oh, fuck,' said Stefan, with feeling.

'That's the man,' said Birgit. 'He killed Ingrid's husband. I told her he was here, and she went – she went—'

'Loco?' suggested Stefan.

'No,' said Birgit, with dignity. 'She went out of the window.'

'Men did this to her!' she wailed. 'Men are to blame!'

Everyone looked at her. No one could dispute the passion of her opinion, but the logic was lost on those who knew Ingrid.

'Where's she gone, Birgit? Where do you think?'

'To the apartment. In the Möllevången. I am sure.'

Stefan staggered. 'The apartment is still there?'

'Why not?'

'Oh God,' he said, and put his head in his hands.

*　　*　　*

'Aaargh,' said Leon, as Ingrid landed on top of him. Her rope had been a bit short, and she had fallen with some force, knocking him flat. However, with typical selflessness, he quickly righted himself and staggered to her aid. She was curled up, moaning. The alarm bells were still ringing, and the lights flashing, and both had instinctively scuttled into the shadows.

'Are you all right?' he shouted.

'My ankle, my ankle.'

It was odd being dropped on in this way, and Leon didn't really know the etiquette. 'I'm sorry,' he yelled. Like most English people, he was only comfortable when things were his fault, somehow. He had broken her fall and saved her life. Naturally, he should feel responsible. He helped her to her feet. 'Can you walk on it?'

'No!' She squealed with pain. 'Oh, I am so cold! So cold! And so unhappy! This noise!'

Leon looked at her for a second or two – a shivering small Swedish woman with frizzy hair and pyjamas – and found he was taking his coat off for her.

'Here,' he said.

'Your yacket?' she said, her eyes wide.

'You said you were cold,' he shrugged. 'I'll be OK.' He patted her hair a bit and tried to think straight. Who was she? Even to someone as trusting as Leon, it was clear from her flimsy ward clothes and novel method of evacuating the building that she was not Director of Operations.

'Are you a mad person?' he yelled, as she buttoned his enormous coat. 'Are you Ingrid?'

'Yes.'

They heard footsteps inside the building, heading towards Leon's swing door. In a minute, if they did nothing, they would be caught.

Leon bit his lip. 'I could carry you,' he offered.

*　　*　　*

That the real Stefan Johansson was not dead was something nobody had considered except Ingrid. And Ingrid, of course, was dangerously insane. But now Jago was downstairs in a basement-cum-dungeon, face to face with the real, breathing (wheezing) remains of Stefan Johansson, and for the first time in his illustrious career, the words 'Listen, did you sell your story?' somehow refused to form on his lips. Jago was out of his depth. Like everyone, he'd seen *Silence of the Lambs*, but much as he now racked his brain, he couldn't remember any practical lessons from it. He recollected something about blood dripping in an elevator, but that was it.

'Who are you?' asked Stefan, from the shadows. 'Why are you here in my house?' His voice was a low croak. His disfigured, blackened face looming behind Jago was what had frightened Tanner and made him run off – to come back soon, presumably, with the police. Stalling Stefan until help arrived wasn't going to be easy, however.

'Hey,' Jago replied to Stefan's questions. He held up the palms of his hands, and tried to remember how he'd been taught in New York to defuse scary situations. 'You're OK. I'm OK. I'm Jago, you're Stefan, OK. OK?'

'Neither of us is OK, I think,' said Stefan, solemnly. 'I should be dead in my grave, and you, Yago, should definitely be elsewhere. You trespass, you snoop, you tell the boy outside you will "get something on Stefan". Not OK.' He swayed from side to side. 'Not OK.'

Jago's right knee was shaking uncontrollably. In the dark, he saw a flash of a scalpel in Stefan's hand.

'I was always so unlucky,' said Stefan. 'I wanted to die, and look at me. I wanted my wife to be happy. Hah. Are you lucky?'

'Me?' Jago thought quickly. 'No. Never.'

'I'm sorry.'

171

'No, I'm like you, Stefan. Abject son-of-a-bitch. Nothing goes right.'

Stefan set down the scalpel and picked up a large knife, something like a saw. From his faraway expression, as he ran his thumb lightly along its blade, he seemed to be remembering happier times.

'I yust wanted some of his luck!'

'Tch!' agreed Jago, his eyes swivelling. 'Not much to ask.'

'And this is what happens! Ingri-i-i-id! Ingri-i-i-id!'

His call was like a reindeer, or possibly a meerkat, howling across icy wastes.

'Look, can I ask you something, Stefan?'

'What?' He seemed suspicious.

'I'm on your side, Stefan,' Jago assured him. 'God, yes. Believe me. I just think you should know there's someone impersonating you in England. Calls himself Stefan Johansson, married my friend Belinda, talks like a Swede – you know, kind of better than everybody else. Sort of guy that has all the luck. Tall, blond. You know?'

'Really?' Stefan's eyes lit up. 'I made it!' he whispered.

'So. All I want to know is, he's a clone, right?'

Stefan's eyes widened. 'A clone?'

'See, I have to tell you this, I'd like to write your story, Stefan, I really would. Let me tell you, your fame is going to be phenomenal! What do you say?'

'A clone of who?' Stefan asked.

'Of you.'

'Does he look like me?'

'Well, no. But, without being offensive, I mean, nobody looks like you, do they? Except maybe the toast-guy in *The English Patient*.'

Stefan started to chuckle. 'A clone?'

Jago was getting fed up with this. 'It's not funny,' he said.

'But you are funny, Yago,' Stefan said. 'A clone of me!' And he burst out laughing again. 'You think I am yeenius, yes? I make little Stefans in test tube! All to be unlucky like me! Very, very funny, Yago!'

Jago pursed his lips. Being ridiculed for his ignorance was never his favourite pastime. He wasn't too keen on being called Yago so much, either. He had enough of that at home. 'So he's not a clone? He's an impostor?' Stefan's laughter only increased. He was beside himself, and Jago couldn't stop him. 'Look, OK, I made a mistake. I'm only human.'

'Only juman! Ha ha ha.' Tears rolled down Stefan's cracked cheeks. 'Ha ha ha,' he continued, mercilessly, while Jago pouted, waiting for his recovery.

Only a noise from upstairs made Stefan stop. A creaking on the floorboards.

'Stefan?' whispered Belinda's husband. As Jago and Stefan listened, the voice was familiar to both of them. 'Stefan, it's me.'

There was a pause, and Jago closed his eyes.

'I mean, it's you,' he said, as his legs came into view on the stairs. And finally, as Belinda's husband reached the basement, 'I mean, Stefan, it's us.'

Chapter Ten

Surprisingly enough, Belinda's husband had quite positive feelings at finding Stefan Johansson alive in the Möllevången. In fact, since he had come hotfoot from the hospital expecting only to confront the escaped Ingrid, he was quite delirious with relief and joy to discover his old friend. This profound attachment between a victim and a tormentor has few parallels in common experience, so may perhaps seem odd. But somehow, when you not only adopt someone's identity but also feel responsible for hurling flammable liquid on them when their hair was on fire, it turns out that the feeling you have for them is – love. Especially if you used to listen to Abba with them as well.

True, Stefan had sawn pieces off his body and held him captive for eighteen months of his life, probing his DNA and feeding him those damn joke-resistant reindeer sandwiches, yet this couldn't stop Belinda's husband from believing that, together, the Stefans were a team. The Stefans. The Incredible Stefans. The Incredible Genetically Modified Stefans. Thus it was that, aware Stefan was holding a serrated knife, Belinda's husband still hugged him. Aware that Stefan's facial skin was dangerously unstable, he still kissed him. And sadly unaware there was anyone else in the room, he rolled up his sleeve and said, 'Look at my buggered elbow, you old bastard, did you think it would grow back?' and burst out laughing. It was strange but true. Only in the company of Stefan Johansson of Malmö, Sweden, did he really feel free to be himself.

'You are Stefan, too, now? It worked?' said Stefan, in the darkened basement, the light just perceptible in his eyes. 'You are Stefan Johansson, in London? Rich, lucky, handsome, famous, *Swedish*?'

'*Hej*!' said Belinda's husband, raising his hand.

'*Hej*!' said Stefan, striking it.

'Oh my God,' said Jago, unseen, under his breath. He backed into the deepest shadows.

'So. Big-shot Stefan. You make how many Stefan babies?'

'Ah. None yet.'

Stefan was disappointed. 'You must. It was our agreement. Your luck gene!'

'I know. I will. But my wife is not entirely herself at the moment. It's complicated.'

'Oh. Not entirely herself. Like Ingrid. *Ja*.' Stefan seemed to understand.

'Well, not exactly like Ingrid.'

Belinda's husband smiled and tried to broach the subject of Ingrid's escape. He couldn't. 'I'm so relieved and happy to see you, Stefan. This is the first time I've relaxed in years.'

'I am pleased to see you also. I can hardly believe it. This knife in my hand. You there. Me here. Yust like old times. Remember how we talk for two months about the rat poison? And then we do not do it! I'm so unlucky, I tell you. Always.'

Belinda's husband looked around. 'Any of me still here anywhere?' From the faint light reaching the room down the stairwell, he could make out a surface, the sink, his old bed, the shackles in the wall.

'They took it all,' said Stefan. 'Blackened my name. Burned my notes. I was denounced as a mad scientist, George! Me, mad! It was a bad time. Typical bad luck that I should live through it regardless. But you know what kept me going? Knowing I was you. Knowing Stefan Johansson was free. How you get free that day, by the way?'

'Ingrid untied me.'

'Ah.'

'She fancied me, Stefan. I'm sorry.'

'Ah. I knew it.' Stefan was being brave. 'Did you like the briefcase?'

'I'm still using it.'

'Good, good.'

Belinda's husband coughed and fidgeted. Upstairs, the last candle flickered and died, leaving them completely in the dark. Somehow the blackness gave him courage. 'Look. You do understood why I had to leave in a hurry that night when your head caught fire?'

'Sure,' shrugged Stefan. 'No skin off my nose, *ja*?' And both the Stefans laughed like drains, while Jago, incredulous in the blackness, moaned, 'Oh God,' and vowed never to leave the office for a story again.

'Can I ask you something, Ingrid?' Leon puffed. He was now carrying her piggy-back fashion, which was awkward because she kept rocking back and forth and moaning, while clasping her gloved hands in front of his eyes.

'You are big man,' she remarked.

'Thanks,' he puffed. 'Where are we? I mean, where do we go next?'

She looked around vaguely, and told him to head right. Were they travelling in circles? Big though he was, Leon was no human carthorse, and carrying Ingrid was hard work. He was sure they had passed this statue several times already. Added to which, his phone kept ringing and cutting off before he could put Ingrid down and answer it.

'You have a question, big boy?' she reminded him.

'Oh yes. You see, there's a man called Stefan Johansson who's living in London. I know there must be thousands of Swedish men with that name—' He stopped, panted, and set off again at a slow walk. It was odd talking to somebody who was on top of you like this: you couldn't see if they were listening. It was like looking in a mirror and seeing the back of your own head.

'Anyway,' he continued. 'Anyway, the point is, it's not *your* Stefan, obviously, because your Stefan is dead. That's right, isn't it?'

There was no response from above. Leon decided to carry on.

'So *this* Stefan is married to a woman called Belinda. And he's very, very happy and has a nice car and a good job and lots of money. But the thing is, he's got other women in love with him as well.'

Leon stopped again, for a breather. 'I'm sorry. Is this boring?'

'Not at all.'

'Anyway, that's why I'm here, you see. I came to see you. I don't think he should do that. It's not fair. There's a woman called Maggie who loves Stefan, too. Are you listening?'

Above his head, Ingrid was looking very strange. Her English wasn't quite up to this level. However, she had just heard the shattering news that her husband was not only alive but involved with foreign women – moreover, English women, who were notoriously loose. Just as she had always suspected, Stefan had survived that terrible night, after all. And then he had made a new life abroad, leaving her to rot in Malmö.

'Ingrid?' He wriggled his shoulders, to make contact. She clamped her knees to his ears. It hurt.

'What car does he have?' she asked.

'Can't hear!' he yelped.

She loosened her knees.

'You said a car. What car?'

'Are you interested in cars?' Leon was pleased.

'No.'

'Oh. Well, it's a Ferrari. An old one. He loves it.'

She let out an involuntary cry, and tried to turn it into a cough. '*Ja,*' she said. 'So what is question?'

'Well. Did Stefan do any work with cloning? You know, making clones? Because all we know is, he dies in the middle of a lot of genetic experiments, and then turns up in London. The man in London could be a clone.'

'Clones? What is clones?'

'Like Dolly the sheep,' Leon explained.

'Stefan made sheep? No.'

'No, not sheep. I mean, did he make any little Stefans? Baby Stefans?'

'I don't understand,' she said. But he could feel something different about her. She was like a dead weight now, as if slumped. He hoped it wasn't his fault. He always hated to make women unhappy, because he didn't want to be like his dad.

But Leon had made Ingrid very unhappy, despite his best intentions. In fact, Ingrid was so wounded by the news that she could hardly breathe. Stefan! Having never known of the novel agreement between Stefan and Lucky George to transfer all George's genetic material by the simplest of methods, it would never cross her mind that the Englishman had taken Stefan's identity. All she could think of were the little Stefans that had been made without her, and the little Stefans she never made. Like Banquo in the Scottish play, she saw them stretched out in a line – a dozen little unborn Stefans, all with curved backs and long grey pony-tails with penknives in their hands, all so sweet. Rearranging herself on Leon's shoulders, she managed to kick him in the face.

He recoiled. 'Sorry.'

'OK,' she replied, in a dream.

They trotted along in silence for a bit, while Leon tried to

179

think of something cheerful to say. 'The hospital people never caught us anyway,' he said. 'You could have jumped out of that window any time, Ingrid.'

'I wish I yump out the window the day I arrive,' she said. 'Over there!' And she pointed to the door across the deserted street with '8B' written above it.

Stefan had not come unaccompanied to the Möllevången, of course. He had entered the apartment alone, that's all. Security men, Birgit, and a variety of people in white coats had charged into a nearby sauna to await his signal. 'Wait for my signal!' he told them – though unfortunately without mentioning what the signal might be. And so they huddled inside, sweating, while Birgit stood at the door. A sauna was hardly the ideal place to wait on a night so cold: clad in sensible coats, they were now succumbing to the heat. In fact, while Birgit stood sentry and attracted a fair amount of passing trade with her nurse's uniform, she twice heard behind her the wheeze and thud of hospital security men sliding down the walls and fainting.

'Here is Ingrid now,' she reported in a whisper (in Swedish). 'She is riding a man like a gorilla.'

'I saw that man in the hospital,' replied one of the doctors (also in Swedish). 'I assumed he had legitimate business, but I realize now I was fooled by the confident manner with which he carried his hot beverage.'

'Mm,' agreed Birgit.

Outside, down the street, Ingrid was dismounting from Leon. He helped her to the door. 'That's far enough,' she told him. 'I want to go in alone. I have things to say to Lucky George. I have things to say to Stefan, too. I will come to London.' As she passed his coat to him, she took a note from the pocket and studied it. Then she put it in her pyjama pocket.

'Stefan's dead,' said Leon, gently. 'You know that. The man in London isn't your Stefan.'

'Thank you for ride,' she said, and stamped on his foot.

'Ow!' he said. 'Sorry.'

She hobbled to the door, and turned. 'You can go now,' she said.

'I'll wait,' he said. 'I'll wait.'

'Ingrid! My chicken! Can it be you?'

As Ingrid hobbled and groped her way in the dark down the stairs to the old lab, she let out an involuntary sob of unhappiness, which her husband recognized straight away.

'Ingrid!'

'Stefan!'

A *clonk, clonk* on the stairs.

'Ingrid! I thought I'd never see you again!'

'Stefan! They told me' – *clonk, clonk* – 'you were dead!'

As Stefan signalled to him to hide, Belinda's husband automatically backed into the shadows and crouched beside his old bed. He was happy to oblige. Having come between these people once before, he didn't fancy doing it again. He felt guilty at spying on their reunion, but on the other hand, he could scarcely make an excuse and leave. The only trouble was, as he leant back into a more comfortable position, breathing softly in the consuming blackness, he realised, with a plummeting heart, that he was leaning against something that was not only warm and soft, but alive – which enveloped and clutched him. The surprise produced an interesting sensation. All the hair on his body stood up and subsided again, like a follicular version of a Mexican wave.

'Hi!' whispered the body, in a kind of squeak. It had covered itself in a camouflaging blanket. 'We'll all laugh about this one day, right?'

'Jago?'

'Hi, Stefan,' said Jago, muffled. 'I can explain.'

'Jago, you shouldn't be here! It's very dangerous.'

'Jesus, you're telling me.'

Belinda's husband peered across the room, and saw Ingrid groping her way to the bottom of the stairs. Evidently, she was unable to see anything yet. She stumbled, and her husband caught her, but then instantly let her go again. Stefan was in agony. He loved his wife, and had missed her painfully. But he couldn't bear for her to see his disfigured face, or touch his scaly body.

'Ingrid! I thought I'd never see you again,' Stefan repeated.

'Stefan, let me hold you! I thought Lucky George would be here, not you! Birgit saw Lucky George! I will kill him if I see him, for what he did to you!'

Stefan gulped audibly.

'Are you all right?' said Ingrid. 'Can't we put a light on?'

She reached for the switch, while across the room, Jago and Belinda's husband both spasmed with alarm, clutching each other.

'No current,' Stefan said. 'Not for years.'

The pair in the corner slumped with relief.

'We must get out of here. We will be found,' said Ingrid.

'I'm tired, Ingrid. I have been living like a dead person. Since they took you, my life has been so terrible, so empty!'

'Really? No little Stefans, then? No Belinda?'

'What?'

Ingrid's tone had changed. They all noticed it.

'It's just that I heard some things. I heard you made little Stefans without me.'

'What are you talking about?'

Belinda's husband watched with horror as Ingrid started to survey the room. Her eyes must be getting accustomed to the dark. She wasn't picking out details, but she was seeing shapes. On all fours, she had edged her way to a table with old, rusty instruments on it.

'I'm not mad,' she told Stefan. She was nearer now.

'Of course you're not.'

'I mean, I'm not stupid.' She picked up a scalpel and twiddled it, so that the blade found the only glimmer of light in the room. 'How was London? How was Belinda?'

'I haven't been in London. I've been here. In Malmö. Going out after dark, stealing food and candles. An odd dabble in vivisection my only entertainment. Waiting, waiting for you. Dead and alive. And I have to tell you, Ingrid. Now we're back together again, I'd like to move to somewhere a bit more interesting to be dead in. Like Belgium.'

'Ha.'

Hauling herself vertical, Ingrid sat on the mouldy bed and started to cry.

'I trusted you, Stefan. I believed you loved me. You remember how happy I always was?'

There was an awkward pause.

'Well, I seem to remember—'

'I was *happy*, Stefan!'

'Of course, my dear. I remember.'

'And now you are happy with somebody else, and you make little Stefans.'

'No!'

'Yes! I know all about Stefan Johansson's high life in London with the Ferrari!'

'I deny it. I can explain!'

The tension in the room was as thick as the darkness. Belinda's husband had started to tremble, and Jago was hyperventilating. So it was a spectacularly bad moment for Jago's phone to ring. Especially as he had programmed it to play *The Ride of the Valkyries*.

'What's that?' screamed Ingrid, as the electronic Wagner trilled with unseemly volume.

'Oh God,' said Stefan.

Jago stood up in the dark and, with a mumbled 'Sorry, sorry – God, isn't this always happening?' wrestled frantically with the inside pockets of his coat, while the Swedes both watched him open-mouthed.

'Ripley, you're OK!' shouted the voice from the earpiece. 'I knew you would be.'

It was Tanner. Two hours after he'd seen Jago struck by a picture-frame in the Möllevången, he had allowed conscience to prick him at last – as his star blazed in the Fleet Street firmament at home, and Jericho Jones boarded a private jet at Sturup. For in the interim, Tanner had saved the day for the *Effort*, and was extremely pleased with himself. Sitting on the steps of the ghastly statue's plain granite plinth, he was attempting to get his bearings.

'Tanner. I'm going to kill you,' said Jago, and hung up.

'Ripley!' said Tanner, but the phone had gone dead. He tapped it against his leg.

Jago realized both the Swedes were still peering in his direction. He swallowed, and resolved to tough it out. 'I'll call him back,' he confided in a whisper, dropping his blanket neatly over Belinda's husband. He started to walk nonchalantly towards the stairs, on legs that wobbled. 'Mobile phones,' he said, with a shrug. 'Big industry here in Sweden, yes? Taxi guy told me. Nice to meet you, Ingrid.'

Ingrid pounced, but her ankle betrayed her. Jago had never moved so quickly in his life. He reached the stairs and was gone.

'Stefan, who was that, please?'

'Just some guy,' Stefan explained, lamely. 'Guy with a phone. I found him here. He's gone now.'

'Anyone else back there?' asked Ingrid. 'The Malmö Meerkats? Lucky George?'

'No, no.'

But Ingrid did not believe him. She started to grope around.

184

She fingered the blanket that covered Belinda's husband, so close that he could smell her.

'Why are there no candles down here, Stefan?' she asked. 'Is it because – all those years ago, me and Lucky George?'

'Yes.'

'It was all his idea, you know. To make babies. I never wanted anyone but you.'

'Mm.'

There was a long pause, while Belinda's husband sat rigidly still and prayed to the god of luck genes. He tried to imagine himself one of those human statues in shopping centres, painted all over in blue or gold. He imagined the Woolworth's and the children in football shirts trying to annoy him, and the smell of frying onions wafting from a van.

It can't have worked, however.

'Stefan,' said Ingrid at last, twitching the blanket, 'I can hear breathing. I know there is somebody here.'

Turning up outside the apartment and meeting Leon and Jago, Tanner was disappointed by his reception.

'You stupid little transvestite bastard!' yelled Jago, who had just emerged from the building. 'I could have been killed down there! I could have been fucking killed! Where the fuck have you been?'

Tanner sighed. The excitability of journalists was beginning to annoy him. 'Actually, you'll be very impressed when you know. I was persuading Jericho Jones to return to sport. Got an exclusive for the *Effort*. Took longer than I expected, that's all. The editor said you should call, by the way,' Tanner added, smoothing his jacket, which Jago had grabbed by the lapels. 'Something about Lambeth Palace going bananas.'

'What? I don't believe this. There's a mad bitch with a knife down there, and you're talking about the Archbishop of Canterbury?'

Leon intervened. 'Ingrid? Is Ingrid all right?'

'You know Ingrid?' Jago swung round to look at him. He hadn't registered Leon's presence before. He was confused. 'What the fuck are you doing here?'

'Well, I carried her here from the hospital. She was hurt.'

Jago gave him a long, incredulous look. 'Listen. Leon. That your name?'

'Yes.'

'Well, Leon, fuck off. One minute you're the most boring dinner guest I ever met, and the next you're helping a psycho on the worst night of my life. You're fired!'

'I'm fired already.'

'Well, you're fired again! But you're going to help me first, OK? And as for that smug son-of-a-bitch — Where did he go?'

Leon looked around. They both did. Tanner had disappeared. At the doorway of the sauna opposite, there appeared to be a commotion — people in uniforms spilling out into the night air, as if gasping for breath. For a few seconds, Leon and Jago ran in all directions, looking for Tanner, until it occurred to them that, for some unaccountable reason, he had chosen to go inside.

'Help!' Jago yelled. 'For fuck's sake, somebody help!' And the people from the sauna came running.

What Belinda's husband always said afterwards was that he heard the merest scuffle and that was it. Before Leon, Jago, Birgit and a herd of rather light-headed security men could hammer down those stairs with their torches and loudhailers, Ingrid had lunged fatally for Stefan with her knife. That's what he told everybody, anyway. But there was more to it than that. Much more.

'I can hear breathing, Stefan,' Ingrid had repeated, tugging at the blanket. Belinda's husband closed his eyes. It was all over. He would never see Belinda again, or work 'under the cosh' into a

186

conversation. It struck him as terribly sad, suddenly, that Belinda would never know he wasn't Swedish. She would never sing 'Angeleyes' to him again, or be disabused about the Söderbergs.

But as Ingrid pulled the blanket ('I think I just see if Lucky George—') a curious thing happened.

'It's all true!' yelled Stefan.

'What?' said Ingrid. She dropped the blanket.

'It's all true! I'm so sorry, Ingrid. I went to London. Yes, I did. I always hated Malmö, it's so cold and boring! And I always hated *you*!'

'Stefan, how could you?'

Belinda's husband felt his bowels turn to water. What was Stefan doing? What was he saying? He had been devoted to Ingrid all his life. He loved Malmö. This was suicide!

'And I've been married for three years to a beautiful woman called Belinda,' Stefan continued. 'And we've got two little Stefans, and lots of money and—' Stefan's ingenuity was beginning to flag '—and we didn't even go to the Carl Larsson retrospective when it came through, and the car is still running very well indeed and – *aargh!*'

'Stop!' Belinda's husband yelled. He threw his blanket over Ingrid's head and circled her with his arms. But he was too late. As he held the hooded, wriggling Ingrid, he was obliged to watch once again as his namesake Stefan Johansson expired in this bloody nasty basement in Malmö.

'No!' he cried. With a pang of grief and shame, Belinda's husband noticed that Stefan had laid down his kitchen knife in the dark. As Ingrid ran to attack him, he had made no effort to defend himself.

Tanner was watching in disbelief from the stairs.

'You!' said Belinda's husband. 'Go away. This is all your fault.' But Tanner didn't move, because he couldn't. Upstairs cacophonous people were approaching, swapping instructions in Swedish, and trying to switch the lights on.

Ingrid wriggled, but he held her tight under the blanket. Stefan hadn't wanted her to see the state he was in, and now she never would.

In his final moments, Stefan reached out a scaly hand towards Belinda's husband. As he remembered it afterwards, it was like a blessing, an apostolic succession of Stefanhood.

'You are Stefan now,' he whispered. 'Make more Stefans, for my sake!' And then, just as Birgit and the others came running with their lights and noise, he gagged, and his eyes rolled, and he died.

They arrested Leon for aiding Ingrid's escape, but then let him go. Tanner's story made the last edition, while Jago made his peace with the Archbishop of Canterbury by offering him a weekly ontological spot on the puzzles page. Leon asked Tanner politely about his encounter with Jericho Jones, but found it hard to bear. All his life, Leon's father had fantasized about sharing a flat with Roger Bannister or telling Gary Player he should try wearing black. Leon had always hoped to make that dream come true. And now Tanner had simply bumped into Jericho Jones on a windy night in Malmö, and was deciding when to take up the offer of the trip to meet the folks in Cincinnati.

'I was running off to call the police, of course,' said Tanner. 'But there he was, looking up at that awful statue. What could I do? The editor had asked me to save the day. Jerry made them stop the car when he saw it.'

'Jerry?'

'Mm. He said the figures straining to hold up the boulder reminded him of life at the top in basketball. He cried, actually. I mentioned it in the piece.'

'I should think so.'

'Yes. Cried on my shoulder. But I simply told him he should pull himself together, and in the end he saw my point. He's a great fan of the sarong, incidentally. Offered to model one for the *Effort*. It could have been anyone who gave him the courage to carry on, obviously. But funny how it was me.'

Meanwhile, in the basement, Belinda's husband sat for hours on his old bed, feeling bereft, lonely and shaky. He had been an inch from death when Stefan had intervened and drawn Ingrid's wrath away from him. What should he make of Stefan's bizarre sacrifice? Should he admire it or deplore it? Did it set him free, or obligate him for the rest of his life? And how could he ever share it with the woman he loved?

Jago put his arm around him, but found that even in this extreme situation, his unreconstructed maleness prevented him from going for the full hug. So he converted the gesture at the last minute into a matey shove at the back of the neck. 'Stefan? You OK?'

Belinda's husband smiled grimly at the appellation, but didn't contradict it.

'I've got to tell you,' said Jago. 'I got this all wrong. I had no idea. I thought you were a clone.'

'What? That's a bit far-fetched, Jago.'

'I know. I'm sorry. I got carried away. I had no idea it would be something straightforward like you taking the identity of a Swedish guy who cut chunks off you.'

'He loved me, you know.'

'Yeah? It really looked like it. I hope no one ever loves me that much.'

'We were very close.'

'There's such a thing as too close.'

Jago helped him to stand up.

'Promise me you'll never tell anybody about this.'

Jago pulled a face. This was too tough a promise to make. 'I'm only human, Stefan! Jesus!'

'Please, Jago. I left all this behind. Belinda thinks this kind of thing only happens in books. She thinks doubles are some sort of literary convention! And it was your fault it all happened.

That boy you sent to spy on me? Why did you do that? When I think of the things I've done for you. The times I supplied you with names of Swedes!'

Jago felt like a heel. 'OK,' he agreed, softly.

'What?'

'I said OK. I won't tell anybody. I'll go nuts, but I won't tell anybody.'

They sat together on the bed, Stefan still hugging the blanket. He sniffed it. It smelt of surgical spirit, reindeer sandwich, rat poison and ancient mould. In short, in a funny old way, it smelt of home.

Part Three

Three months later

Chapter Eleven

From her sparkling attic window, one morning in the last week of June, Belinda observed the arrival of the cleaning lady. Mrs Holdsworth came three times a week, these days. She entered without noise or bother, and was no longer permitted to smoke except in the garden. Swearing had been prohibited. In the intervening months, Linda had trained her to Hoover and dust, tidy and polish, and do simple shopping for haddock and eels. According to reports, the rest of the house was like a palace. Linda had also instituted a Time Wasting Box, into which Mrs H must insert 50p if she tried to start a conversation up the loft ladder. Belinda felt a twinge of sadness at this. A nice old philosophical chat with Mrs Holdsworth about why God made lungs so complicated would have been pretty welcome, the way she was feeling right now.

Far away downstairs, a phone rang. Belinda strained to hear it. When Stefan and Linda were both out, sometimes she would drag herself to the top of the loft-ladder to hear more clearly, but usually she just stopped tapping the keys for a minute. Today, as she paused midway through 'The quick brown fox jumps over the lazy dog', the muffled voice leaving a message was her new agent praising her 'Up the Duff' column in the *Effort*. Belinda liked the sound of this new agent: he had parties for clients and, on occasion, even came to the house with good news and a bunch of roses. The phone rang again almost immediately, with a different voice but the same congratulation. This time it was Julian Barnes.

Wow, thought Belinda. She had no idea she knew Julian Barnes.

Three months on, Belinda still could not believe her luck. Linda had continued to remove from her every worry and obstacle of life – including some she hadn't even admitted to herself. Look at the way Linda disposed of Mother, for example, then forbade Belinda to feel bad about it. 'If you grieve, then I'll feel guilty,' Linda explained. 'And if I feel guilty, I'll have to leave. Which I assume you wouldn't want. Besides which, grief always saps creativity, and we can't have that. So buck up, Belinda. Look, as far as the world's concerned, you're dealing with the bereavement brilliantly. Honestly, I'm congratulated on my surprisingly high spirits everywhere I go!'

That Mother had died through the dreadful accident of slipping on a piece of squid had been accepted by the police and was, in any case, the truth. But the incident had linked Linda to Belinda in a complicity that made both of them uncomfortable. Belinda's move to the attic took place within a day, and was mainly Linda's idea, but it made sense to them both to separate Belinda totally from the life downstairs. Especially if she kept crying, and getting on everyone's nerves.

'I did it for you!' Linda would remind her. 'Her love wasn't unconditional. Conditional, judgemental love – well, it isn't worth having.' And although Belinda secretly disagreed (she rather liked the idea that love should be deserved), she had to admit that a great weight had been lifted from her psyche with the death of Mother. Yes, she blamed herself for not intervening more quickly when she heard the fight downstairs on that fateful night. She wished she had been a better daughter. But she did feel better in some ways. No longer was there somebody in the world who automatically thought badly of her. As an incidental symptom of this reaction, her attitude softened towards squid. She still couldn't eat it, of course, but nowadays it was certainly welcome in the house.

Meanwhile, look at this block about babies, too. Again Linda had blazed the trail. Why had Belinda been waiting to have children, putting things off? Because she felt inadequate? Because she felt unqualified, not good enough for motherhood? Fortunate, then, that Linda entertained no such weaselly doubts on the subject.

'But you will make a marvellous mother, Belinda,' she'd said, on that momentous day conception was confirmed. 'And Stefan will be over the moon about it. You know what he was like when he got back from Sweden.'

'Am I the first to know? Oh, Linda!'

'Of course. Do you want to see the test-kit thing? I can get it from the bathroom.'

'Oh yes, please.'

'How do you feel?' Linda gave her a conspiratorial wink.

'Fine. No different. I can't really believe it.'

'Belinda, I'm so happy for you. I have to say it. I think you're doing absolutely the right thing. Especially when there's been a death. New life! Congratulations.'

'Thanks.'

'And I'll do everything, as usual. Eat coal, whatever. I'm fit and strong.'

'You're marvellous. When you first came, I would never have thought one day you'd have a baby for me. Tell Stefan I'm blooming.'

And now Linda was making Belinda famous with this column about the pregnancy, and earning more in a month than Belinda expected to receive when the doubles book was finished! It was amazing how life turned out, really.

The only fly in the ointment — it was now more like a gluey knot of drowned bluebottles — remained the book. Because after spending several months devoting herself entirely to it, Belinda found to her astonishment she didn't give a damn. No one could have predicted this development, but the more she studied the literature of doubles, the less she saw anything remarkable in it. It was Dr Jekyll and Mister Bleeding Obvious, as far as she was now concerned. Even her formerly favourite story, the Hans Christian Andersen one about the shadow, seemed curiously pointless. Given the choice, she read 'The Ugly Duckling' and 'The Princess and the Pea' instead. Her notes had started taking a sardonic turn, and she had written 'so what?' in big letters across the front of her Dostoevsky. 'Existential angst, my arse,' she surprised Linda by saying once, when she popped up to borrow some Sartre.

Sensing the problem, Linda had offered to help out, and had started reading *The Confessions of a Justified Sinner* in her weekly BBC car before the *Late Review*. But, secretly, Belinda was thinking of dropping it altogether. They didn't need the money, after all. And she had to admit that in the context of the high profile Linda had acquired for Belinda Johansson in the media, the doubles book was going to look rather dull and earnest when it appeared under her name – rather like the bathetic little tomes on Euclid that Lewis Carroll turned out, when everyone was expecting more *Alice*. Lumbered with *The Dualists*, Linda would have to do such a lot of explaining next time she was invited to Number 10. If the book simply evaporated, it might be better for everybody.

So, up in her converted loft (thankfully with *en suite* facilities) she just typed a lot about quick brown foxes jumping over lazy dogs, and tried not to ask herself three hundred times a day whether the quick brown fox was the *alter ego* of the lazy dog, or a totally separate entity with its own agenda. Bloody doubles. Why was everyone so obsessed with them? Even Jago Ripley, the man who admitted to the attention span of a zucchini, had got interested recently, apparently.

'Hello?'

Belinda jumped with fright. An intruder on the landing!

'It's me. Viv.'

'Oh fuck,' cursed Belinda. She looked in panic around her attic room. Apart from jumping out of the window, there was no way out.

'Belinda, can I come up?'

'No, you can't.'

Belinda regarded the trap-door with horror. From the telltale clanking sound, Viv was already ascending the ladder.

'I've got to see you,' came Viv's voice. 'I need to talk.'

'Bugger off. Who let you in?' Belinda's heart was racing.

'Please, Belinda. I'm coming up. This ladder's terrifying. There'll be an accident on this one day.'

Belinda realized there was nothing for it. As Viv's head appeared through the trap door, Belinda picked up a carton of Mars bars and emptied it over her, simultaneously yelling, 'Help!'

'Belinda, you bitch, ouch!' cried Viv, retreating.

She crawled to the window, flung it open and yelled 'Help!' again. Thank goodness, Linda was emerging from a taxi in the road below, with a half-dozen Harvey Nichols carrier-bags. She looked up and saw Belinda at the window. 'What's wrong?'

'Help!' she yelled. 'Linda, help! Come quickly! Viv got in!'

Linda shoved money at the driver and raced indoors, but was too late. Viv had taken fright at the bombardment of confectionery, run downstairs and escaped through the back door — presumably with the help of Mrs Holdsworth.

'Are you all right?' Linda called, as she tackled the loft-ladder. It clanged and swayed as she mounted it at top speed. 'Belinda, I'm so sorry this happened. Viv must have gone mad.'

Belinda caught her breath. 'I'm OK,' she said. 'I'm OK now you're here.'

Linda took her podgy hand and patted it. 'Of course you're OK. You're lovely. Everyone loves you.'

Belinda reached for a tissue in her velour tracksuit bottoms. 'It was a shock, that's all.'

'Of course. How did you get on today with the book?'

'All right, I suppose. It's taken an interesting animal turn. Foxes and dogs.'

'That's interesting.'

'Mm. Julian Barnes phoned, I think. To say he liked the column.'

'Well, there you are. *He* likes you.'

Belinda rolled over on her stomach. It was her most comfortable position, these days. 'I'd love to read my "Up the Duff" column sometime,' she said, gently. She knew it was an awkward subject.

'I'd be so embarrassed, though. You're the real writer, Belinda. I'm only pretending.'

'Mm.' Belinda picked at a lump of congealed tomato sauce on her T-shirt. 'It was really scary just then, Linda. I suddenly saw what this looks like to Viv. Me upstairs on my own, you downstairs with Stefan, me getting so fat and slobby, and you having the baby. You telling me all the time that I'm lovely. If she didn't understand this was all for my sake, she could so easily get the wrong idea. She'd think you were stealing my life, or something far-fetched like that!'

Linda smiled. 'You're not getting fat.'

'I am, a bit. I had to have my wedding ring sawn off, didn't I?'

'You're lovely. You were too thin before, that's the truth of it.'

Belinda glanced around for a mirror but then remembered Linda had kept them all downstairs, for fear of accidents. 'Mother never thought I was lovely. She said I'd let myself go.'

'That's a silly expression.'

'She wasn't right, was she?' Belinda sniffed.

'Never. Maggie sends her regards, by the way.'

'Does she ask after me?'

Linda hesitated. 'Well, not always. But I tell her anyway. She's on the mend, I think.'

'Oh, good.'

'I think she's going to be happy, at last.'

'That's nice.'

After Mother died, something happened to Linda. She stopped being an enigma. On that ghastly March night, after the police had been and gone, keeping them up for hours with questions, she let down her guard. At precisely the same time as Stefan told Jago all about his dual identity in Malmö, Linda finally sat down and talked about herself, prompted by Belinda.

'All those things you told the police,' Belinda said. 'I didn't know any of it. I felt so stupid that I knew so little about you. You never said your real name was Janice. Or that you grew up in Crawley. That sort of thing changes everything.'

'Does it? I don't see that. I'm Janice from Crawley, not the last of the Romanovs.'

'No, but tell me. Please. When did you change your name?'

'When I came back from France, when I was thirteen.'

Linda got up and opened the oven. She was baking the salmon, compelled by sheer force of habit.

'Go on,' said Belinda.

'I never talk about this.'

'Just this once.'

'You promise not to laugh?'

'Of course.'

'You see – look, it's not a big deal. Don't expect much.'

'OK.'

'Well, when I was thirteen, I went on an exchange visit for a month to Grenoble.'

'Yes?'

'I know, lots of people do it. This was a direct swap, though, which we later discovered is quite unusual. I had a great time in Grenoble, although I was homesick. A month is a long time to a thirteen-year-old. The trouble was that, when I got back, something quite upsetting happened. I turned up at the house in Crawley and – well, my parents barred the front door and told me they preferred to keep the French girl.'

'What?'

'I know. I was devastated. I just stood there with my suitcase. I'd brought them souvenirs! Mont Blanc in a snowstorm, that kind of thing. Individual chocolates with alpine flowers on. I was looking forward to showing off my French. But they said they'd thought about it quite hard and decided the French girl was more interesting than me, and that she fitted in better. They had all had a lovely time without me.

'I didn't realize they were joking, you see. Especially since they'd piled my stuff in the front garden. Guitar, recorder, teddy bears, jewellery box. Mum said afterwards that my face was a real picture! All the neighbours had come out to watch. The French girl said, "*Au revoir*, Janice," and they shut the door.'

'Linda, that's dreadful. How could they be so cruel?'

'The French girl had talked them into it – apparently she'd persuaded other families before, and told them it was always hilarious when the kid got home. But it wasn't hilarious this time, because I burst into tears and ran off. I took it so seriously. Well, after she'd gone, and my stuff was back in the house, my parents told me they were really disappointed in me for not seeing the funny side, for not trusting them. "We are shocked and hurt, Janice," Daddy said. He had gone all white around the mouth. He was furious. "You let us down very, very badly."

'So that's the story. Obviously, in the end, I felt so guilty about hurting them that I ran away.'

Belinda was appalled. Her own mother had undermined her gently, over decades, like a lone termite gnawing her foundations. Linda's parents, by contrast, had gaily picked her up by the heels and dropped her down a lift shaft. 'But you didn't hurt them,' she said. 'Think about it, Linda. They hurt you. They should have apologized to you, not blamed you.'

'You don't have to take my side, Belinda. I've thought about it a lot, and I take theirs. I know what I did was wicked. I doubted their love. I thought love could be switched off, you see.'

'Can't it?'

'No.' Linda sounded quite fierce. 'Anyway, you asked me why I changed my name and left Crawley, and that's it. That's all. Now you know.'

The evening of Viv's unexpected visit, Stefan came home as usual at six thirty. Three months had passed since Malmö, and a lot of things had changed. As he came through the door this evening, for example, he did not carry a book of English idioms, determined to incorporate 'How green was my valley' or 'Go and chew bricks' into the conversation. He carried the poems of Tomas Tranströmer, Sweden's 'buzzard poet', a book with a discouraging monochrome snowscape on the front. For reasons connected with the demise of the real Stefan, he had gone terribly Swedish all of a sudden.

At weekends, for example, he haunted Ikea in Croydon, correcting people's pronunciation, explaining the effect of the little bubble on top of the vowel. Twice security men had asked him to leave the building, because they thought he was warning people not to buy the kitchen cupboards. He watched Bergman films on video with masking-tape covering the subtitles, and read biographies of Strindberg, for fun. He hummed Abba's 'Chiquitita' as he walked down the road to the bus and wore his moose-hat at unlikely hours of the day and night.

'But you're not Swedish,' Linda hissed to him tonight, as he selected for the umpteenth time the CD of Swedish football songs, *Mama, Take Me Home to Malmö*.

'I need to do this,' he said. 'You understand. You do love me, Linda?'

'I do love you, George. Yes.'

It was inevitable that Linda and Stefan should make a bond, when Linda knew his secret. True, Jago now knew some of his story, but only to Linda could he confess his feelings. Jago's idea of sympathy was to push the back of your neck so hard that you almost dislocated your head. Belinda's now total absence upstairs threw him increasingly into the company of Linda, too – especially at the literary festivals and the New Labour media parties. And it didn't help his relationship with his wife that, shortly after Stefan's return from Malmö, Belinda had overheard them talking about Ingrid, and jumped to the unflattering conclusion that the subject of their discussion was her.

'It's her selfishness that was always so hideous,' he said.

('Hideous!' gasped Belinda.)

'Yes,' agreed Linda. 'It's hard for anyone to be happy around selfish people.'

'She always refused to make little Stefans – that's the point.'

('He wanted little Stefans,' she yelped.)

Belinda had wept bitterly when she heard this, but nowadays comforted herself by eating a Mars bar in a suggestive manner. Looking around at the life Linda had given her, the life she'd desired so badly, she felt a familiar pang of loss and confusion. Because although she might have said she wanted lots of peace and quiet, and may even (oh God) have wanted her mother to disappear, when exactly had she told anybody that she didn't want sex any more?

She stroked her own enlarged breasts, absently, and tweaked

her nipples. More than ever she desired Stefan; her body ached for sex, grieved for it. But by becoming physically gross and affecting tracksuits, and by moving upstairs after the death of Mother, and moreover by being hideously selfish and refusing to have little Stefans, she'd somehow removed herself from the carnal world. It would be obscene to caress Stefan now; to lick him all over, as she formerly did. Such a gorgeous man would need to be tranquillized first. However much it hurt her, it made sense for Stefan to partner Linda. He wanted babies, suddenly. In fact, he was broody. Linda was young, fit, sexually desirable, talented, and keen. Belinda had to face it: she herself was none of these things.

Meanwhile Stefan felt wounded and rejected by Belinda, who had moved upstairs just when he needed her most urgently. Returning from Sweden on the plane after the basement ordeal, all he could think of was how furiously he would fuck Belinda, the first chance he got. He pictured himself, naked in the moose-hat, driving himself into her on the hall floor, again and again, sucking her breasts and clutching her wrists until both of them exploded. But instead he'd got home and found a big empty bed, and a wife in the attic who said, 'No, don't, I'm too yicky,' whenever he tried to touch her.

'You are not yicky, Belinda,' he assured her. 'I don't marry yicky women.'

'I am. I'm so selfish and yicky.'

'All right. Let's say you are. But I don't mind if you are yicky.'

'You should.'

'I love you.'

'I love you, too.'

'Then why can't I have you?'

'Because I love you too much to let you have sex with someone who's so yicky.'

'You feel guilty and confused because your mother died,' Stefan said.

'Yes,' said Belinda. 'Yes, I mean no. I mean yes.'

For a few weeks, the frustration experienced by both of them was intense. Belinda felt horny all day, every day, but tried to ignore it. This must be what it's like to be Michael Douglas, she thought. She wrote erotic poetry to Stefan; she crept downstairs when he was at college, and sniffed his clothes in the laundry bag. But in the end there was nothing for it but to speak to Linda, and beg her to help.

'But I can't make Stefan love me,' said Linda, embarrassed. 'It doesn't work like that. It's not like taking your place on the *Today* programme. He knows I'm not you.'

'He likes you, though, doesn't he? Tell me what you talk about downstairs all the time. You're always laughing.'

'Oh,' Linda blushed. 'He tells me about Sweden. This and that.'

'Haven't you ever wanted to touch him?'

'Belinda!'

'He's so lovely. And he's a flirt. He must have flirted with you.'

Linda closed her eyes and thought about the times they had danced together. 'A bit.'

'You see? If you didn't fancy him, I wouldn't ask you. But you do. He's so lovely. Tell me what you really feel about Stefan, Linda.'

'Honestly?'

'Honestly.'

'I love him.'

'Oh.' Belinda bit a lip and said, 'I knew it. I knew it, I knew it, I knew it.'

The two women looked at each other like Thelma and Louise before going over the rim of the Grand Canyon.

Belinda knew what she was doing. She was letting herself

go, totally. Linda would love Stefan, and make him happy. It was better to see him with Linda than lose him. The thought of Stefan making love to anyone else was torture. But the absence of Stefan would kill her.

'Stefan is a wonderful lover,' she told Linda, now. 'And you know he fancies you.'

'He doesn't.'

'Did he give you a nickname?'

'I can't believe we're talking like this. I don't like it. He's your husband. I would never hurt you. Nor would he. We're on your side.'

'Did he give you a nickname, though?'

'Yes.' Linda grimaced. 'I can't tell you what it is.'

'I know.'

That evening, Belinda heard such unmistakable moans and cries from the kitchen that she gave up trying to read Nabokov's *Despair*, and just listened. The woman who abhorred a vacuum had finally identified the last gap in Belinda's life and filled it. Whether it was remotely similar to doing the *Today* programme, Belinda never inquired. As for Stefan, as he swarmed over Linda, he felt an intense mixture of guilt and relief, revulsion and desire – in fact, he felt more authentically Scandinavian than ever before. It was both agony and ecstasy to make love to the desirable, sympathetic cleaning lady. When she told him she loved him, he wept like beans.

Afterwards, as they ate their steamed sea bass with ginger mayonnaise and kept kissing and touching each other without speaking, it occurred to Stefan that Linda was better than Belinda at everything; absolutely everything. He only hoped, for pity's sake, Belinda never knew how much.

Naturally, Stefan couldn't face Belinda after sleeping with the cleaning lady. He was grateful for her removal to the attic. Linda had moved into the bedroom; they made love discreetly, but all the time, and he thought about her constantly. The relief of being with someone who knew him as himself – and loved him for himself – was overwhelming. He suddenly wished he had friends and family for Linda to meet. He wished he could take her to Sweden. He phoned her six times a day, on her mobile, and made her laugh. He ambushed her in the shower, and wore her underpants on his head. Everywhere they went, people noticed their physical addiction to each other; jointly, Linda and Stefan gave off so much heat that the background wobbled. It was a thrill to touch her hand. Stefan was happier than he had ever been.

No wonder that he tried to banish Belinda from his mind. The only way to cope was to tell himself she had died. At Mother's funeral (which Belinda and Linda attended under obscuring veils, like something from a Victorian novel) Stefan buried a number of people, including his wife. He buried Stefan and Ingrid as well as Mother, and he shovelled like mad to put six feet of earth over Belinda.

'What was it Belinda used to say?' he asked Linda one night, as they cuddled on the sofa in front of *Fanny and Alexander*, while Belinda made faint tap-tap-tapping noises upstairs. 'The line from Keats. "When I have fears that I may cease to be before my pen has glean'd my teeming brain." I think that's exactly what's happened. It's an exact, gruesome description of what's happened to her. Her brain is still teeming, but she has completely ceased to be.'

So the last time Belinda saw Stefan was at the funeral. It was the last time she had seen anybody except Linda, now she came to think of it. Maggie had been there, with the lumbering sports writer from Viv's dinner party. Viv had attended, too, and even said a few words in the chapel, which was fitting, since Viv and Mother had always hit it off. She said Mother was a fighter, a trooper, who defied the tides of time. It made her sound like Horatius holding the bridge, not an ungenerous old woman who refused to have crow's feet. Everyone was terrifically impressed.

As a parting gift to her vain parent, Belinda chose to have an open casket for Mother, to show off the features that had cost so much, and that had finally settled so nicely into a beautiful face. All Mother's old friends were invited, so they could admire the handiwork for one last time and gnaw the pews with envy. The biggest shock had been seeing Auntie Vanessa, whose naturally ageing features had operated as a kind of Dorian Gray picture for Mother – showing precisely her alternative fate. One need hardly point out, of course, that with all her lines and saggy bits, Auntie Vanessa looked fine.

Meanwhile 'Age Shall Not Wither Her' was the chosen epitaph for the headstone, which had the benefit on this occasion of being literally true, and a kind of coded warning to future grave-diggers. Her undertakers agreed. Like the tanner discussed in *Hamlet*, Mother's facial construction would last in the ground nine years.

Over tea, Belinda had kept her veils on and watched how Jago made such a strange fuss of Stefan. Linda explained to her that the 'boys' had met by chance in Malmö and become firm friends. Aside from that, the funeral was socially a disappointment. Maggie and Viv both kept their distance; Stefan did not comfort her. She rather wished she hadn't come. But then Stefan chose his moment beautifully and read aloud a haunting poem by his favourite chap Tranströmer.

As always at funerals when people read poems, there was a lot of shrugging and coughing. But Belinda loved it. Her squeeze of congratulation when he resumed his seat was the last time she'd touched him. She'd have squeezed him longer, if she'd known.

And now it was June, Linda was pregnant, and Belinda weighed

207

fourteen stone. She hated all the academic books around her, and longed to write a Verity story, for a bit of excitement. But Linda had started writing them, to general acclaim, so what was the point? The publisher loved all the new developments in Linda's first draft. As Belinda quickly acknowledged, Linda had combined the original simple tone with a more sophisticated psychological insight – for example, explaining with bold strokes the pain of childhood rejection that drove Verity's rival Camilla to be so selfish. Linda had also (another bold stroke) killed off Goldenboy, Verity's number-one pony.

'You can't!' gasped Belinda, as she read it, weeping for the loyal pony, who rolled his eyes just one last time as he lay on his straw and offered a hoof of farewell. The fictional death of Goldenboy was as devastating to Belinda as the real death of her own mother. Tears rained down her cheeks. As always, however, she had to admit that Linda was right. Sentiment and complacency were all that had detained Goldenboy from this, his best ever fictional moment. Why had she never seen it? This horse was born to die! The postbag would be enormous.

Belinda wished she had some magazines to read. All these hours to kill, day after day, while Linda and Stefan assumed she was writing the *magnum opus*. Perhaps she could take up nail-painting. She wondered what they would think if they knew her favourite pastime was seeing how many pencils she could retain comfortably in the folds of her body and still move from one side of the attic to the other. Her personal best was twenty-two.

Unconditional love was what she had, though. She derived much comfort from that. This might look like a crummy life to anyone who didn't understand. But it came from, and amounted to, unconditional love. A dozen times a day she reread the poem Stefan had read at the funeral, pondering it. The whole of life and death was in it, in a gloomy Swedish kind of way. And she didn't mind thinking about death, particularly. Because here was another obstacle (the ultimate one) that Linda had thoughtfully cleared from her path. In the corner was a little box of medical, anaesthetizing stuff — bottles, needles, masks. It was left over from Linda's days at the hospital, when she was Viv. Belinda gazed at it for hours at a time, thinking about the oblivion it offered.

'If you ever want to go,' Linda said solemnly, one night, 'I'll help you. There's no greater love than that, Belinda. No greater love.'

Sometimes she dreamt of Stefan rescuing her from her attic, as if it were a fairy tale. He would climb up the outside wall, and burst in. He would kiss her and wake her from a sleep of years; shake her till the piece of poisoned apple dislodged; shatter the mirror from side to side.

But it wasn't like that. She wasn't a princess held in a tower by some magic spell. She was a fat woman in Battersea with no friends who was perfectly at liberty to come downstairs.

Chapter Twelve

Maggie rolled her eyes to heaven and said, in her deepest voice, 'Moscow!' It felt good. She said it again. 'Moscow! Moscow! Moscow!'

Leon applauded. 'That's very good,' he said.

Maggie sat down, still studying her text. 'You don't think the middle one should be like a question?' she asked, nibbling her pencil. 'As if she's saying "Yes! Moscow!" then has a doubt, "But do I really know what Moscow means? What if I don't like Moscow when I get there?" and then, "No, Moscow's fine, I'll settle for Moscow"?'

'I think the three howls were better. You can be too complicated, you know.'

'OK.'

Maggie made a note in the margin of her *Three Sisters*. The first day of rehearsals was tomorrow. In her experience, it was quite important to decide at this stage whether Irina really, really wanted to go to Moscow, or had already got bored with the idea, and was just saying it.

'Talking of Moscow, did I tell you I covered the world skateboarding championships in Red Square last summer?'

'You might have done. I don't remember.'

Leon shrugged. It was clear that Maggie had not yet

learnt to be fascinated by the astonishing global impact of American sports.

'Well,' she said, rather unkindly, 'you won't be doing that any more.'

'No.'

'This is such a sad play,' she declared, at last.

'Don't tell me,' said Leon. 'They never make it to Moscow.'

'That's right.' Maggie was impressed.

'Is it far?'

'Oh. I don't know.'

'Is there a train?'

'I think so.'

'Why don't they go, then?'

'Oh, you know how it is. I remember hearing an interview on Radio 4 with some people in a ticket queue in Leicester Square, once. A man and his wife, hoping to see *Cats*. The interviewer asked him if he often came to London, and he said proudly, "Twice a year, yes. We take in a show, and have a meal. Quite a ritual." "Where do you live?" asked the interviewer. And you know what he said? "Wimbledon."'

You had to hand it to Maggie. Once Leon had turned up on her doorstep from Malmö and uttered those epiphanous (if baffled) words, 'Hang on, what's my brother doing here?', it had taken Maggie just a few minutes to cast Noel from her life. What a heel that man was. He was Leon's *brother*? All along he'd known she wasn't deluded? Maggie opened the front door to find the two men colliding on the step: Leon in a rather fetching fur hat with ear-flaps, holding a presentation pack of gravad lax and an enormous Toblerone; Noel looking shifty in his old leather jacket, with a small ball of string. Sadly, her Shakespearean double-take training let her down once more, but at least she didn't faint. Instead of crying, 'Most wonderful!' at the sight of the Confusingly Similar Brothers, she just summoned up all her non-Shakespearean instincts and spat in Noel's eye.

'That's very good string,' he told her, as she snatched it and shut the door on him. 'I can explain all this,' he continued, through the letterbox. 'It's only because you are so fatally insecure that you can't cope with this without resorting to aggression, Margaret!'

The string found a use quite quickly, as it happened. With Leon's help, Maggie parcelled up all the insulting presents Noel had given her, and dispatched them to Julia without explanation. She reasoned that a trained psychoanalyst was surely capable of working out the connection between a pound of spuds, a dartboard with no numbers on it (evidently found in a skip), and three sample-size bottles of perfume (evidently Julia's own free gift with lipsticks, purloined from the bathroom cabinet.)

She hadn't wanted to hurt Julia. But on the other hand, short of hiring an assassin, this was the best way of breaking out of therapy that the human mind had yet devised. As a clinger, Julia could give lessons to barnacles. But now, with a single bound, Maggie was free. Free to stop maundering on; free to spend her therapy money on jackets and magazines and catfood; and, most importantly, free to survey the ravaged building site of her psyche and rebuild at her own speed.

And she made very short work of it, in fact. Didn't even bother with scaffolding. By the time she decided to become an item with the faithful Leon, just three days later, her psyche was virtually ready for carpeting. Fully roofed, it smelt of fresh magnolia emulsion, and was only waiting for the pointing in the chimney-stack to dry. True, Maggie's psyche was slightly wobbly, and some of the windows didn't open, but at least it was habitable once more.

'How can you do this to Julia?' Noel objected, on the phone.

'Bugger off,' said Maggie.

'Think of yourself, Maggie. You're not a viable personality! You need us! You need me!'

'Give your Bombay mix to some other poor sap,' she pronounced, with dignity, and slammed down the phone. Jettisoning Noel, she felt not only jubilant but intensely theatrical. Were she ever to get the role of Nora in *A Doll's House*, she would draw on the emotion she felt right now. How marvellous. Were Ibsen alive today, she felt 'Give your Bombay mix to some other poor sap' was exactly the sort of line he would be writing.

'Linda and Stefan have invited us to dinner tomorrow,' she told Leon now. It was a rainy Monday, and they had been together nearly three months, living at her flat.

Leon stroked Ariel, while trying to read a sports section. 'OK.' He winced, involuntarily, and fingered his hair. 'Can I watch Wimbledon, if the rain stops?'

'You don't like them much, do you? Linda and Stefan?'

'Well, you can't help noticing a pattern. Stefan's first wife is locked up in an institution. His second wife is locked up in the attic. And nobody cares about either of them.'

'She's not locked up in the attic. She wants to be up there. Did you know Viv tried to see her the other day, and Belinda told her to fuck off? You surely don't think any of this was Linda's idea?'

Leon harumphed. It all seemed pretty obvious to him. As they said in one of his favourite movies, 'Follow the money.' Belinda had a wretched, lonely, anonymous existence; Linda posed on magazine covers with her arm round Antonia Fraser. But then he was a very straightforward kind of chap. Malmö had been a perplexing time for him, what with getting the sack for something he hadn't written. He never understood what had happened there. All he knew was that it was his own fault for deserting his post, that Tanner came out of it with a promotion, and that he still felt sorry for Ingrid.

'Well, I've been thinking about it,' said Maggie, 'and it seems clear to me that Belinda is the Superego in that house.'

'The Superego? Maggie, *don't*.' Leon hugged the fluffy racing car and picked at it. 'You promised. It makes you sound like Noel.'

'I know. I'm sorry.'

'Dad really did know Bobby Moore, you know. He wasn't making it up. I met someone once who saw them together in the car park at Anfield.'

'But I'm not a bit like Noel. He accuses everybody of being mad. I don't do that.'

'No.'

'I observe things, that's all. And I can't help seeing that Linda is the Ego, and Ingrid is the Id.'

'Please don't!' Leon put his hands over his ears.

'Sorry.' She came and kissed his head, then settled down to read her text again.

'Do you think it's supposed to be funny that Irina can't remember the Italian for "window"?'

'What does she say exactly?'

Maggie found the place.

'"And now I can't even remember the Italian for 'window'!" The direction says "With tears in her eyes".'

'That's definitely funny.'

'Good.'

Whether or not Belinda was happy did not much worry Viv any more. She had known for ages what was going on in Armadale Road, and had long since ceased to care. Mrs Holdsworth brought her regular juicy news – about the burgeoning affair between Linda and Stefan, about a holiday in New Zealand the happy couple were planning, about the baby (of course) and the celebrity phone calls. Viv hated to admit it, but she rather approved of the Johanssons' arrangement. People should do the things they are good at. And, in her opinion, Belinda was good at being selfish and lazy, and letting other people take the strain of the practical stuff.

No, what had sent Viv scurrying up Belinda's loft-ladder was not sympathy or friendship, but alarm. Because she had just heard from Dermot. Her ghastly lover said he could no longer endure to be silent about the hospital scam. Every morning he woke from dreams of Linda in a surgical mask, advancing with a foot-long syringe, something like an antique enema pipe – and he just couldn't take it any more. He wanted justice, he said. He would shortly be 'doing something about it'.

What could Dermot do? He could tell the police, inform the hospital. Either way, Belinda ought to know that Linda was about to be exposed, and very probably arrested. But, of course, Viv's visit was thwarted by a torrent of Mars bars, and the message did not get through. In fact, the only consequence of her action was that her spy was sacked – Linda guessing, rightly, that Mrs Holdsworth had admitted Viv to the house.

'I'm going to have to let you go,' Linda told an affronted Mrs H, on the phone. 'I can't possibly put up with disloyalty. Please come to the house tomorrow, and drop off your keys while I'm out.'

Which was how it came about that, on the same rainy Monday, Mrs Holdsworth did a fine and glorious thing. As a parting gesture, she collected up all Linda's 'Up the Duff' columns and delivered them to the attic.

Belinda was lying on her stomach, with her arms at her side, practising her noiseless weeping technique, when Mrs Holdsworth's head poked through the trap-door. Work-wise, all Belinda had achieved that day was 'Now is the time for all good men to come to the aid of the party', repeated twenty-eight times. So she had got down on the floor, as usual – to think, and to feel sorry for herself, and to weep secretly for her deceased mum, and to gaze at the box in the corner with all the syringes and things. Objectively speaking, it was indeed the right time for all good men to come to the aid of this party. All Belinda got, however, was Mrs Holdsworth.

'Mrs Holdsworth?' said Belinda, rolling over to sit up, and wiping her eyes. 'Are you OK on that ladder? You don't fancy a chat, do you? Come on up!'

Mrs Holdsworth pursed her lips and looked around at the piles of dusty books, her employer impersonating a baby seal on an ice floe. 'Are you fucking having a laugh?'

Belinda thought quickly. 'It's just that I've been lying here wondering — er, why men have nipples. Any ideas?'

But Mrs Holdsworth merely set down the columns, dismounted the ladder, and left the house for ever. Belinda heard her cough and slam the front door, and the sound of departure made her sad. There was a time when the departure of Mrs Holdsworth would have been like having a nail removed from her head. How strangely life turned out. Recently, Belinda had been remembering the nice man from British Telecom — was his name Graham? Fancy ringing afterwards to check that she was all right. What a nice man. She was wondering if he would fancy a chat about Friends and Family. Ah, yes, friends and family. He might even be able to advise her on how to get some.

'Give me some days!' she had said to him. It was hard to believe she had ever felt like that, now that she had day after day after day. At her funeral, to which she had recently devoted much thought, she'd decided to have the congregation sing along to the old Kinks record, where Ray Davies says 'Thank you for the days'. Linda would understand. Linda was so wise.

Humming and snivelling some more, Belinda gave a cursory glance to the columns, with her own name blazoned across the top and a smiling picture of Linda. Should she read them? Did she have the intellectual energy? Lying there on her chest, she hadn't really been dwelling on the enigma of the male nipple. Really she had been exploring a dream, a dream she'd first had on meeting Linda; a dream in which she'd been gently placed

217

inside a washing-machine, there to float happily in the soapy, sloppy water, occasionally tapping on the glass as the drum rolled her right and left, left and right. 'Hello?' she'd called to Stefan, but he'd been absorbed in his breakfast. 'Hello?'

She remembered what her husband had said to her at the time. What would happen when the spin cycle started?

'They've invited us to dinner,' Viv told Jago.

'Linda and Stefan?'

'Tomorrow night.'

'OK.'

Viv returned to her treadle machine and her cloth of gold. She had volunteered to make all the costumes for an end-of-term Shakespeare. To add a bit of interest to the project, moreover, she had urged the drama teacher to set it not in some fustian bardic wasteland (sacking robes, and so on) but at the court of Louis XVI, with the hall of mirrors.

'You always have to overdo it, don't you?' said Jago. The living room was a sea of scarlet satin and costume pearls. The Ripleys were not speaking much, these days, except to snipe at each other.

'Leave me alone,' said Viv, completing a seam.

Agitated, Jago drank his coffee and poured some more. He hated his days off, especially if they were not at weekends. Viv was so madly domestic at present, as if to prove she could outdo the old cleaning lady. And as for him, he couldn't settle at home. He was frantic to know what Tanner was up to at the office. Every time he closed his eyes, he pictured Tanner trying his chair for size.

'So are you all right about Linda and Stefan?'

'What? Of course.'

'I take it you've stopped thinking Stefan's a clone?'

Jago put down his mug with a clunk. 'I never thought Stefan was a clone.'

218

'Oh, really? I thought you did.'

Belinda put down the cuttings and stared at the wall. Then she stared at the ceiling. Then she stared out of the window. She couldn't believe it. She felt sick. This reflects on me, she kept thinking, idiotically. I wouldn't mind, but this reflects on me.

To find oneself described in public print as the Bat in the Belfry was a shock, of course. No doubt Mrs Holdsworth thought it was this libel she needed to know about. But matters were far worse than that. Because, truth to tell, 'Up the Duff' was rubbish. Linda was writing liquefying compost, and under Belinda's name! The realization had so many implications! Belinda considered several of them rapidly. 'Good God,' she breathed. 'How will I ever explain it to Julian Barnes?'

There was nothing wrong with the genre of 'Up the Duff', as such. Even from the seclusion of her ivory tower, Belinda was aware that people wrote these domestic dramas in newspapers all the time, and sometimes executed them with effortless brilliance. Linda's tone, however, was as clunky as a piano dropped down a staircase. The eponymous Up-the-Duff (Linda herself) had comical misunderstandings with Nordic Dreamboat (Stefan), while Conversationalist with the Feather Duster (Mrs H) took meals to Bat in the Belfry (Belinda). Meanwhile Unborn Sprog caused mayhem of a predictable nature. There was no getting away from it. 'Up the Duff' was dire.

'Sprog?' Belinda shuddered. '*Sprog?*'

Dermot sat at his desk, twiddling a pencil and thinking hard. He, too, had noticed that 'Up the Duff' was dreadful, but this was not his only reason for wishing to spike Linda's activities once and for all. True, he had recently contracted an ambitious young woman writer who would be glad to fill many of Linda's commissions, were Linda abruptly to relinquish them. But by and large, he just didn't

approve of Linda posing as an anaesthetist without quali-
fications.

Yet it was by no means obvious what he should do. The
police must not be involved; Viv must not be dragged down.
As he now understood, the poor confused woman had only
responded to a biological urge to make cushion covers, after
all. So, weighing up all considerations, he just needed a story
about Belinda Johansson to scupper Linda's career. 'A story
about Belinda Johansson,' he muttered to himself. 'A story
about Belinda Johansson to scupper Linda's career.'

But what rumour could he circulate, to make all Linda's
editors and friends drop her? That she was an impostor? No,
that would merely intrigue them: they would ask her to write
about it. That she was a criminal? Ditto. An adulteress? A
transsexual? A matricide? Ditto, with knobs on. That she was
terminally ill? Dermot laughed nastily. Any hint of terminal
illness (even curable illness) would have them gagging for Linda,
and upping her fees.

It was frustrating for a man like Dermot to find he could
do nothing. Possibly the best-connected chap in London, he
need only break the story and it would be everywhere. Wild
fire looked sluggish in his vicinity. Yet he felt powerless. He
frowned and fiddled with his silver bracelet, ran a hand across
his smooth pate. Whatever a famous person admits to nowadays,
it merely makes him more famous, more *hot*. Unless . . . ?

Dermot felt the answer was coming to him. He pressed his
knuckles against his eyes. Unless . . . ?

Gingerly, he picked up the phone and dialled the *Effort*. The
editor was, naturally, one of his clients.

'Jack,' he said. 'Terrible news, I'm afraid. About Belinda J.'

'What's happened to her? Don't tell me those bastards at
the *Telegraph*—?'

'No, it's not as bad as going to the *Telegraph*, Jack.'

'Good. What is it, then?'

Dermot took a deep breath.

'The thing is, Jack, Belinda's dead.'

Linda got the news on her mobile. Dermot felt it was only sporting to let her know at the same time as her editor. She was at the fishmonger's, and in her dismay involuntarily sat down on a display of dressed crabs. 'You've said Belinda's *what?*'

'I've said she's dead, Linda. This couldn't go on. Fight it, and I'll tell everyone about your syringe secrets. You could be in prison for years. Tell Belinda I had no choice. People will be expecting a funeral, but that's your problem.'

And he hung up.

Linda felt her throat constrict. Everything she'd built up for Belinda was to be destroyed! A life so rich and fruitful! A life so happy! Running home, she phoned Stefan, in tears, and he promised to meet her there as soon as he could.

'Belinda!' she yelled, as she let herself in to the house.

'Belinda! Belinda!'

Belinda peered through the loft trap-door. 'I've got a bone to pick with you,' she said, waving the columns.

'You've heard?' squealed Linda.

'I've read it myself, thank you very much. How could you do this, Linda? I trusted you.'

'I'm so sorry. I'm so terribly sorry.'

As Belinda watched her cleaning lady climb the damn ladder for the umpteenth time, she was deeply puzzled. Confronting Linda about 'Up the Duff' was turning out to be a lot easier than she thought. She had feared one of Linda's weeping tantrums. Instead of which, she seemed the soul of contrition.

'This wasn't how I intended things to end,' Linda said. 'You've got to believe me.'

'End?' said Belinda. 'There's no need for them to end.'

But Linda wasn't listening. She was agitated. She kept picking up tissues and tearing them into shreds. 'Things are worse than ever!'

'Linda, are you all right?'

'How can you be so calm, Belinda?'

'Look, it's only a column.'

At which point Linda realized, with a sinking heart, that they'd been talking at cross-purposes. 'You said you knew,' she said, flatly.

'Knew what? About this damn "Up the Duff"? Yes, I do.'

'Everyone thinks you're dead, Belinda.'

Belinda laughed. 'But I'm not.'

Linda shrugged. 'Well, there's the rub. If I am, you are.'

'But you're not dead, Linda. You told me you've got a box at the Proms. Have you gone raving mad?'

'Trust me, Belinda. It's over. We're dead. No Proms, no nothing.'

'Why?'

'It's over. There's absolutely nothing I can do.'

In the Gemini café near Maggie's flat, Noel perused the ballet listings in *Time Out*. Visiting the ballet was not in fact his favourite pastime, but since Julia was a fan of dance, and since his marriage needed considerable attention since his wife found out about Maggie (if only he had not wooed Julia likewise with a pound of spuds!), he was quietly reading the listings, and circling events with a pen, when a strange woman caught his eye and smiled, as if he ought to know her.

She was sitting at a neighbouring table, nervously playing with a knife and flicking through a Swedish–English phrase book, but when she recognized Noel, she moved with awesome speed. Before he knew what was happening, she crossed over to him, grabbed his head and pressed it hard against her chest.

'*Hur länge har du varit här?*' she cried, impenetrably, and kissed the top of his head.

His face smothered by this strange woman's bosom, he tried saying, 'Do I know you?' but not much came out. The sense of fear and confusion was matched in intensity only by the taste of rough wool and the *déjà vu*. Another of his brother's conquests? Well, if it was, Leon's taste in women was coming seriously into question.

'Hello,' he said, uncertainly, as she released him from her excessive greeting.

She pulled his ears intimately, and danced a jig on the spot. Whoever this unattractive little Swedish woman was, she was evidently very pleased to see Leon.

'Birgit!' she called to another small woman, solid, who was bringing coffee.

'What?' said Birgit (in Swedish), sitting down.

'It worked! This is the man who carried me through Malmö, on the night of Stefan's death! The man who gave me his coat with the note in the pocket!' she said (also in Swedish).

Birgit slapped him on the back and saluted him in true Swedish fashion. '*Hej!*' she ejaculated.

'Er, hi,' Noel replied, and turned to Ingrid. 'Er, good to see you again. Last time I saw you, you were — um?'

'I had my knees around your head, *ja*?'

Noel laughed, and tried fervently not to picture the scene. 'That was some night,' he ventured.

'But I escape,' Ingrid explained, suddenly solemn. 'I escape to London. All Sweden looking for me! Mad woman on loose! Birgit help me.'

'Oh good.'

Noel's brain was whirring.

'I found this note in your pocket, describing this Gemini café!' She produced the note Maggie had scribbled to Leon all those months ago — the day she'd run into Noel in the Gemini. That poor sap Leon had evidently treasured it. 'So I come here to see you, beg you to help. I am so unhappy,' she added, unexpectedly.

'That's a shame,' said Noel. 'But only natural.' He assumed his sympathetic expression and, through force of training, handed Ingrid a paper serviette.

She took it, wiped her eyes, and lowered her voice to explain. 'Stefan is dead. I come for Belinda. Birgit help me. You understand? Then my work is done.'

Noel patted her hand, which still held the knife. He knew Maggie had been in love once with someone called Stefan. Belinda was her oldest friend. A plan was hatching, vaguely but very quickly. The fact that it plainly involved a dangerously mad woman gave him no particular cause for alarm. As Maggie so rightly pointed out, Noel assumed that everyone was mad. For the first time in her life, Ingrid's overtly dangerous insanity provided her with protective colouring.

'Where are you staying?' he asked.

'Nowhere,' Ingrid sobbed. 'We yust arrive.'

'There's someone I want you to meet,' Noel said, gently taking the knife away from her. 'I'll find you a place to stay.'

'How can you be dead?' Stefan paced the living room. 'How can you be dead?' he repeated. 'You just cooked salmon and samphire pancakes. We've booked for the Cleveland Orchestra. Dead people don't do that.'

Linda hung her head. 'Look at the flowers, George.' The room was full of sympathetic bouquets; the answering-machine flashed with thirty messages. 'Belinda doesn't seem to mind, that's the funny thing.'

'She doesn't mind that she's *dead*?'

'She's coming down later, for a chat.'

'A *chat*?'

'Don't keep repeating things, George. I'm worn out. I've had a pretty bad day, when you think about it.'

She certainly had. News of Belinda's demise had spread

quickly. Her new agent — a friend of Dermot — informed all her employers within the hour. In fact, when the first of the flowers arrived at the house, she was still in the attic delivering the thunderbolt to Belinda. 'You'll have to go down,' she told Belinda. The bell was ringing insistently downstairs. 'Quick!'

'I can't. I haven't been down for three months. I won't know how to find the front door.'

'Go on!'

'But who shall I say I am?'

'Who cares? Just act sad and shocked. Go *on!*'

'We ought to nip this in the bud. Tell everyone you're OK.'

'Please, Belinda. Nobody knows you.'

So Belinda hauled herself down the ladder, and crossed the landing, and made her way through the house. And the funny thing was: it was exactly as if someone had really died, or at least, abruptly disappeared. As she made her way to the front door, she tried to move noiselessly, yet was spooked by the silence. Unfamiliar pictures hung on familiar walls; she saw new objects on old shelves; she spotted the shopping left in bags on the kitchen table. A shiver rushed up her spine. 'This was how she left it,' was the emotional message of everything in the house. 'In the midst of life we are in death. Ingredients for salmon and samphire pancakes were found in the shopping. A macintosh still wet from rain dripped beside the front door.'

The doorbell rang, and as she reached for the door-knob, Belinda felt dizzy.

'I've got some flowers for Mr Johnson,' snapped the young man on the doorstep. He was in a hurry, and his pocky skin was wet. His double-parked van was blocking the road; a taxi braked behind it in the rain, and tooted. To Belinda, the combination of sensations was so intense that she staggered. It was like going from the reading room at the British Museum into the trenches of the First World War. The colour, the noise, the people!

'For Mr Johnson,' the man repeated.

'Mr Johansson,' she corrected him, automatically.

'Well, can you take them, love? My van's in the way. Are you all right? You look terrible.'

'There's been a death,' she explained, lamely.

'I'm sorry,' he said. 'It happens.' And handed her the flowers. She wrestled with the card, to see who they were from. It was Dermot, of course. 'Are you related to the deceased, yourself?'

Belinda thought about it. 'Not really.'

'Well, I'm sorry anyway. 'Bye.'

And now, while Stefan consoled Linda downstairs, Belinda considered how all this affected her. It wasn't too bad, actually. In fact, strange as it may seem, she felt rather chirpy. For one thing, dying made her feel a lot better about Mother. The phenomenon known as 'survivor guilt' no longer applied. Plus, being dead had stopped her from killing herself. Which had to be a good thing, really.

As she cast a quizzical glance at Linda's medical box, she could only think how strange it was to have fancied ceasing onthemidnightwithnopain,courtesyofLinda'sneedles.'   f3794"I have been half in love with easeful Death,"' she told herself, in astonishment. '"Now more than ever seemed it rich to die", *tsk, tsk*.' Add these morbid sentiments to all the frantic pre-death gleaning she'd been up to, and Keats had rather a lot to answer for, she reckoned.

Dying was definitely the best thing that could have happened. Dying made her tidy her attic, and sort her clothes. Books were neatly piled; manuscripts efficiently stuffed into black plastic bags. Belinda embraced nonentity with an energy that was quite inspiring. On her way back to the attic after the Interflora man had gone, she had gathered a few items together, including a mirror from the downstairs loo, and now she looked at herself

226

in it. She fingered its surface, pawed at her reflection, like an orang-utan in a perception experiment.

'Belinda, you're dead,' she said to herself in the mirror. 'You're dead, you are.'

She rubbed her teeth, and put some lipstick on. 'This is fucking fabulous,' she said.

Selecting an old cassette of Kinks records, she slipped it into an old machine, and wound it at top speed until she reached 'Days'.

'Bloody hell,' remarked Belinda, and played the track again. She'd often noticed in life how old pop songs came to mind just when their lyrics finally meant something to you. But wasn't 'Days' supposed to be about an affair? How could it at the same time describe so accurately an experiment in full transference with a cleaning lady that had ended in this unique paradox in a Battersea attic? The true potency of cheap music must have been sorely underestimated. As she listened to the lyrics for a second time, she felt an old familiar twinge in her abdomen. It was Neville. Oh God, the lovely rat was back. *Ta-da!* This was almost more solitary happiness than she could bear.

At midnight, Linda called to her. 'Belinda, are you mad?'

'Not at all,' Belinda called back.

'This is supposed to be a house of grief,' Linda barked. 'Some of us are quite upset, even if you aren't. Stefan just had a call from a very tearful Terry O'Neill in Mauritius. I was phenomenally well liked, you know. People are being so nice. Come down. Have some supper with us. We're worried about you.'

But Belinda couldn't help it. She didn't want to go down to the funeral parlour of the living room. Instead she played the song again, and turned the volume even louder. 'Thank you for the days,' she yelled. And, stooping slightly under the eaves, she danced and twirled and laughed.

Chapter Thirteen

Whether to persist with the dinner party was the Johansson household's chief concern. Arguably, the Johanssons had broken their fair share of new ground, etiquette-wise, yet here was a further ticklish point to ponder. If your best friends know you're not really dead, is it OK to ask them to dinner? Finally, they decided it was. So while Stefan spent hours on the phone, accepting sympathy in a courteous Swedish manner from a surprisingly large proportion of the Groucho Club membership, his late wife flicked listlessly through her recipe books, with unseeing eyes. 'I can't enjoy cooking now we're not alive any more,' she objected to Belinda. 'When I was doing it for you, it had a point. It was for you. But I've failed us, Belinda. I've let us down by kicking the bucket like this.'

'Buck up, Linda. I can't believe this attitude. It's not your fault. You were always a marvellous cleaning lady. Dermot's got it in for you, that's all.'

'I feel terrible.'

'Hardly surprising, in the circumstances. What did we die of, by the way? Was it an accident? It was very sudden.'

'How can you be so matter-of-fact about this, Belinda?'

'I don't know. You're right, though. I've never felt so matter-of-fact about anything. I'll pop to the shops later, if you like, seeing as you can't go out any more. Anything you want me to do on your behalf, just say. I owe you heaps. Fancy a Mars bar?'

Energized by the events of the last twenty-four hours, Belinda was pushing into new frontiers of tactlessness, but couldn't help herself. 'This often happens to people in grief trauma,' she puffed, having just run up and downstairs six times, for the exercise. (Linda was sitting with her head in her hands.) 'I heard about it on Radio 4. The bereaved generate masses of energy. Divorce does it sometimes too. Divorcees — particularly the victims — become human dynamos.'

Stefan watched her in amazement. 'You are in the pink, for sure, Belinda, even when we are taken to the cleaners,' he remarked. (Although it pained Stefan to readopt his Swedish guise for Belinda's sake, he did so with aplomb.) 'We will have to get you the enormous hamster wheel, or I'm a Dutchman.'

'I've thought of something you can cremate, anyway,' Belinda continued, red-faced, standing on her neck on the hearth rug and cycling her legs in the air. 'For the funeral. You can cremate my book. If you pile in the research notes and the Dostoevskys, it ought to weigh quite enough to fool everybody.'

'Your book?' wailed Linda.

'Well, let's face it. Thanks to your careless demise, I shan't be needing it. I always think it's spooky when books are published posthumously, don't you?' And with that she commenced a programme of rigorous Canadian Air Force exercises, with weights strapped fast to her wrists and ankles.

It was while Belinda was Hoovering the hall with a feather duster between her teeth in the early afternoon that the doorbell rang. Stefan was in the attic, reorganizing it for Linda. The Johansson *ménage* had come to the consensus that the attic would be an ideal place for Linda to hide from her admirers during the funeral and after. Meanwhile, in advance of the dinner, she was clattering pans in the

230

kitchen, and poking bits of dead fish in a desultory fashion.

'Hello?' Belinda opened the door to see Noel and two women who looked foreign and odd, like missionaries. 'Are you collecting?'

'Mrs Johansson?' said the smaller of the two women, with an accent.

'Johnson,' Belinda corrected. Then she thought about it, and laughed. 'No, you're right. Johansson. Sorry, I've not been myself lately. We've – er, we've had a death in the family.'

At this, the women exchanged glances.

'Do you remember me, Belinda?' asked Noel, warmly extending a hand to shake.

'Is it Leon?'

'You *do* remember!' he said, avoiding the outright lie.

'But you're coming tonight with Maggie, aren't you?'

Noel smiled. 'Mmm,' he agreed.

'Well, thank goodness you didn't bring flowers,' she said, ushering them into the living room. 'The place is stiff with them. If you'll pardon the expression.'

She looked at the two women expectantly, as they sat down on the sofa. She smiled in what she hoped was a reassuring fashion. What on earth were they all doing here? Birgit nudged Ingrid and indicated the moose-hat. Ingrid picked up the CD about going home to Malmö, and nodded meaningfully. They whispered briefly in Swedish.

'Aren't you going to introduce your friends?'

'Ah, yes. Of course.'

Noel took a deep breath. The outright lie could no longer be avoided. 'Agnetha,' he said, indicating Ingrid. 'And Anni-Frid.'

The two women both looked up and said, '*Hej!*'

'Like the women in Abba?' Belinda asked, amused.

'That's right.'

'How amazing. "Does your mother know?" Ha ha. Cup of tea?'

It was so long since Belinda had seen strangers that she was almost giddy with the novelty of it. Had strange dumpy Swedish women visited the house like this in the old days in the company of boring sports writers? She couldn't remember. It all seemed so long ago.

'You'll have to forgive me, but I feel a bit funny about Abba.' She smiled. 'My husband Mr Johansson used to be such a fan, you see. It means that Abba have rather painful associations for me now. I never stopped singing "Angeleyes" at one time. Is your friend all right?'

Ingrid was noticeably squirming in her seat. Evidently her identification with Agnetha in Abba did not extend far. She hadn't even bothered to wear electric blue satin or a crocheted hat. In fact, it was clear her potent Ingridness could not be suppressed for long.

'I'm so unhappy,' she blurted, as Noel shot her a warning glance. She was holding Stefan's moose-hat and caressing it.

'Me too,' said Belinda, brightly. 'Cup of tea, then?'

'My Stefan was here! My Stefan! With this fat Belinda! I'm so unhappy! I want to kill her!'

'Ingrid!' hissed Birgit.

Belinda froze, with the smile still fixed to her face. Alarm bells were finally tinkling; Neville had finally grasped his trapeze and started to swing. 'Could you wait a minute? I'll just put the kettle on.'

But as she raced upstairs to find Stefan, she was aware of rapid, scuttling movement behind her; and by the time she reached the loft-ladder, the front door had opened and closed. Thus, before Stefan could be alerted to the presence of all three of his wives in the house at the same time, the maddest one had thankfully departed.

*   *   *

It was a big day for Stefan, the day of the wake. Up in the attic, alone with Belinda for the first time in months, terrified by the knowledge that Ingrid had come to his home, he broke down and told his one true wife all about his three ghastly visits to Malmö. Without breaks or sustenance, this enterprise took him well over an hour and a half.

'Stefan, I'm so sorry!' she cried, when it was over. 'I mean, George, I'm so sorry!'

'Don't call me that,' he said, turning from her. 'You said you could never love anyone called George.'

'Did I?'

'After *The Importance of Being Earnest*. You must remember. You said the name George had no music. And then you went upstairs.'

'I never stopped loving you, Stefan. I can't bear to think what you've been through. On the other hand, I can't bear to think what I've been through either. And, Jesus, look what Mother's been through! Linda sorted her out rather too well, didn't she?'

'Linda is not to blame. She's a good, good person.'

'I know.'

'She just loves unconditionally. She never draws a line. She has no judgementalism.'

'I know. It stems from adolescent trauma. Do you want to hear something amazing? She offered to help me kill myself. I nearly took her up on it.'

'What a woman.'

They clung to each other, both their minds racing. Linda had caused so much appalling havoc in their lives, by being such a jolly nice person who never drew the line.

'And now Ingrid is here,' Belinda reminded him.

Stefan groaned. 'Was Ingrid's companion stocky and miserable, a bit like a Smurf?'

Belinda nodded.

'Birgit,' he concluded. 'She persists in thinking Ingrid is normal.'

Suddenly, a lucid memory of the Möllevången basement overwhelmed him. In his mind's eye, Ingrid twitched his blanket once more, while Stefan drew her attention fatally away, yelling, 'It's all true! I made little Stefans in London!' This was what finally drove Ingrid to kill her husband, he remembered. It was the notion of the 'little Stefans' that Stefan taunted her with, that drove her to murderous frenzy.

'We must tell Linda none of this,' he said. 'We'll deal with Ingrid together, you and me.'

Belinda was so struck by the phrase 'you and me' that she grasped her husband's hand and led him to the mirror.

'Oh Belinda, don't,' he said, and tried to pull away. He couldn't bear to look at himself. He'd been so selfish, so cruel.

'No, please,' she said. 'Please look.'

And so they stood before it, their eyes glancing right and left compulsively, as if in the dreaming state of sleep — looking first at each other, then at the couple they made, sometimes at themselves. It was something they hadn't done since they were first in love, gazing at each other with such seriousness in a mirror's reflection without catching the other's eye, without smiling.

'You and me,' pronounced Belinda at last, with a sigh.

'You and me,' Stefan repeated.

'What a bloody shame,' said Belinda, 'that I'm not writing a book about all this any more.'

Tanner knew he ought to be excited by the new job Uncle Jack had given him, but as he sat at his new desk, he still wondered whether he should be wasting his time in this ridiculous profession. From the absurd fuss Jago Ripley had made on his dismissal, anyone would think making newspapers was a remotely important occupation.

'You? In my job? You're the worst journalist in the world!'

Jago had yelled, while Tanner examined his nails in silence, waiting for Jago to collect his things and vacate the room.

'Jericho Jones has promised us a lifestyle column,' he'd told Jago. 'You've got to admit it's an improvement. We're replacing your terrible dead pregnant woman with an exotic superstar facing a new lease of life in sport. "Still Dunking", I call it. The editor loves the idea. Are you going to the *Telegraph*?'

Jago snarled, picked up his boxes and left the office.

'We'll always have Sweden, Mr Ripley,' Tanner called after him. 'I owe you for that, don't forget!' At which he settled himself in his new chair and prepared for his first editorial conference as one of the most important people on the *Effort*.

In the three months since Malmö, Tanner had mostly put the hazy events of that ghastly night behind him. So when Stefan Johansson called on his direct line, after Jago's departure, he was quite annoyed.

'Jago? Is that you?' hissed Stefan. 'Ingrid's turned up in London! I have to speak to Leon! He's harbouring her!'

'Mr Johansson? Tanner here.'

Stefan gasped and said nothing.

'Met in Malmö,' Tanner continued. 'Saw you throw a blanket over that murderess. You may remember my sarong.'

Stefan remained silent.

'Hello?' said Tanner. 'Mr Johansson?'

But just the muffled word 'Shit' could be heard, before Stefan hung up.

Tanner peered at the receiver, and reluctantly made some notes. Tiresome though this whole Malmö story was, he could see it had potential. 'Ingrid here,' he wrote, and circled it. 'Leon harbouring,' he wrote alongside. He underlined '*Shit*' three times, then set off for conference.

'This is going to be like a *wake*,' said Jago, as he rang the Johansson doorbell at eight twenty-five that evening.

Viv rolled her eyes. 'I think technically it *is* a wake.'

'Are we fashionably late enough?'

'Weren't we due at seven?'

'Yes.'

Viv consulted her watch. 'An hour and twenty-five minutes ago. Then we're just right.'

It was a fine evening in South London, warm and mellow. Had the occasion not been so solemn, a barbecue in the Johansson back garden might have been considered. But given that the hostess had recently popped her clogs, and that the invitations said, 'Armband optional', a more formal style of dinner had seemed appropriate.

'I'm dreading this,' said Viv under her breath, as Stefan opened the door. 'Belinda was bad enough when she was alive. Oh hi, Stefan!'

'Hello,' said Stefan. 'Come in. Jago, *hej!*'

'*Hej!*' said Jago. 'Did you hear I'd lost my job?'

As these first guests went inside, the door shutting behind them, a large bush in the front garden quivered in telltale fashion, betraying the fact that two Swedish women and a psychotherapist were hiding inadequately behind it. Midsummer was a terrible time for hiding outdoors, the threesome were discovering. Their only consolation was that at least this wasn't Sweden, where in the month of June it never gets dark at all.

'Lucky George! That was Lucky George! I want to kill him, too!' exclaimed the bush now, in excited tones. 'Shh, Ingrid,' it also reminded itself, in a male voice. 'Look, your friend isn't mad, is she?' it whispered, a bit worried. 'Certainly not,' it replied.

'Did you see anything odd out there?' asked Stefan quietly, as he accepted Jago's bottle of wine.

'No. Why?'

Viv had gone to find Linda.

'Ingrid's been here,' Stefan whispered. He crouched to

236

peer through the letter-box, then straightened up. 'Linda doesn't know.'

'Jesus!' said Jago. 'She escaped?'

'I've got a terrible feeling about tonight, Jago.'

'I'm not surprised. Let's go out. In fact, let's run away to Tashkent.'

'Did you see that bush move?' asked Maggie. Half-way up the garden path, she had stopped and shuddered.

Leon looked around the garden. 'No.'

'I'm sure it did.'

Leon had another look, and obligingly, the bush shivered, bounced and rocked. Since Noel was physically wrestling with a highly agitated Ingrid at the time, however, the movement in the bush was relatively modest.

'You're right,' said Leon. 'Sorry.'

He approached the bush, which shook violently and commenced shouting words like 'Bitch!' and 'Why, you—!', then abruptly became still. He returned to Maggie. 'Do you want the good news or the bad news?' he asked.

'The good news.'

'The good news is, there's a perfectly rational explanation. The bad news is that my brother has just punched Ingrid Johansson on the jaw, and knocked her cold. It was a right upper cut, if you're interested.'

Looking back on it later, Stefan always regretted carrying the unconscious (and armed) Ingrid into the house and leaving her in the Johansson master bedroom with just Birgit and the assiduous Leon for company. It was such an obvious mistake if you didn't want blood everywhere. However, persuaded by Leon, that's exactly what he did. Leon had a soft spot for Ingrid, and wanted to protect her. Meanwhile Stefan wasn't thinking straight, exactly. Because at the time he made that fateful decision, his primary concern was for Linda's worrying

237

state of mind. 'She's in the attic with a syringe,' reported Viv, breathlessly. 'She's got a syringe, and she's threatening to use it.'

So Stefan climbed to the attic, and sat down with Linda. Obviously he was neglecting other, noisier matters. But while downstairs Maggie shrieked, 'You!' at Noel in the dining room, and Jago physically slugged the despicable Tanner ('You!') on his arrival at the house, and Belinda and Viv hugged each other in forgiveness ('You!' 'You!') in the kitchen, and Ingrid stirred with an animal groan on the comfy double bed ('*Du?*'), Stefan begged Linda not to hurt herself; not to abandon him; not to abandon Belinda.

'You're too close to this,' she said, determinedly swabbing her arm. 'You don't understand. I've got to go. You've got to let me go. To other people it will always look as though I've exploited you and entrapped you, stolen your lives from you. Look how ecstatic Belinda is now I've stopped making her successful and popular and well paid. It's as though I've released her from a hundred years' sleep. I gave her exactly what I thought she wanted, did everything for her, and she turned out like *Whatever Happened to Baby Jane?*.'

'There's got to be a way forward for all of us. Belinda appreciates everything you did. We both do. You're such a good person.'

'But now it's over, isn't it?'

'It can't be. What about the baby?'

'I know.' Linda sighed. Tears came to her eyes as she put down the syringe.

'This isn't what should have happened,' she said. 'This isn't how it should have turned out. I'll get my things from our room and go.' And those were her last words before she ran to the loft-ladder, and disappeared from view.

Stefan was stunned with sadness as he heard her make her way downstairs. 'Linda, please. I love you,' he said to himself. 'I love Belinda too.' And then he remembered something rather important, concerning the master bedroom. 'Linda! Oh, my God. Don't go down there! Ingrid—' he yelled.

At which point, as Stefan always remembered it, a blood-curdling cry interrupted him from the floor below.

'AAAAAAghhhh!' came the female shriek.

'AAAAArrgh!' it shrieked again, and then came a loud thump as a person (or persons) hit the floor.

'My God,' said Stefan, sinking to his knees. 'My God. Ingrid's got her!'

As Stefan descended the ladder at speed, the other men raced upstairs, so that all converged on the landing. It was easy to spot the cinéastes among them, incidentally: those who remembered details from *Psycho* took care not to place themselves at the top of the stairs.

'Ingrid?' said Stefan, to the closed bedroom door. 'What have you done?' He tried to push open the door with his foot. Either Belinda or Linda could be hurt or dead in there! Possibly both! His wives! His darling wives!

But Leon stepped out, and solemnly closed the door behind him. He looked shaken. 'Don't go in there,' he said, running a hand through his hair.

'I must!'

'Don't go in, Stefan. Your wife—'

Everyone drew a sharp breath and looked at Leon expectantly, rather keen for more details. *Come on, Leon. Come on.* Nearly all the women in the house were Stefan's wife, in one way or another.

Leon did not understand, however. 'I'm ever so sorry, Stefan,' he said, with a gulp. 'I tried to stop her. But the truth is, I think your wife's dead.'

Jago lost patience. 'For God's sake,' he yelled, leaping up to seize Leon by the throat. 'Which one?'

'What?' Leon fought him off, confused.

'Which. Fucking. Wife?'

'Oh. Sorry,' said Leon. 'Ingrid.'

At which Birgit opened the door to reveal the lifeless Ingrid on the carpet. She was wearing Stefan's moose-hat and – strange to relate – she was smiling.

Ingrid. Ingrid was dead. Stefan sank to the floor and, for the first time in his five-year ordeal, started to cry. How strange to see her there. No longer unhappy! And in fact, if there is any justice in the spiritual cosmos, already reunited in the vivisectionist quarter of paradise with her own dear Stefan, to experiment on unwilling living tissue for the rest of all eternity.

'How did it happen?' asked Stefan. 'She didn't kill herself?' Belinda and Linda had now arrived at the scene, and between them held him tightly.

Birgit pulled a face of horror. 'I did it. I had to do it. She tried to kill this nice man who helped her in Malmö!' she said. 'Yust because his nasty brother hit her on face!' She put down the knife that she'd wrested from her friend. To her credit, she seemed pretty glum about committing murder. 'You told me she was mad, but I did not believe. Everyone tells me. But she was mad, *ja*. I had to do it. She was mad, this Ingrid, after all.'

In the ensuing month, many of the Johanssons' problems sorted themselves out pretty neatly. For a start, Ingrid was cremated at Belinda's funeral, to everyone's immense relief. Both Linda and Belinda watched from the attic as the cars drew up at the house, took the coffin and left. It was quite thrilling, in a macabre sort of way. It was also rather a privilege. Between the two of them, Belinda and Linda calculated they added up to nobody, yet all sorts of famous people came to bid them a joint farewell.

It was true that Belinda no longer wanted to work on literary doubles. She'd had more than enough of all that. But while the funeral was in progress, Belinda read aloud Hans Christian

Andersen's 'The Shadow', and both Belindas enjoyed it while agreeing it was a bit simplistic. At the end of 'The Shadow', the poor scholar doesn't hear the sound of the shadow's wedding, because by then the shadow has 'taken his life' — a nicely ambiguous phrase. Belinda said the story might have turned out better if the shadow and the scholar had become friends and enjoyed their own *faux* funeral together, laughing and making cups of tea. Linda said it might lack dramatic force that way. Belinda just said, 'Mm.'

Linda, of course, could not appear at the funeral tea. So she prepared it beautifully and then retired upstairs so that Belinda could serve it, in the guise of the new cleaning lady. She took the name 'Mrs Golyadkin' for the occasion, and pretended to be Russian, on the grounds that if you can't have a laugh at your own funeral, when *can* you have a laugh? Eavesdropping at your own funeral offers certain emotional risks, of course, but as she mingled with plates of finger food, Belinda mostly had a marvellous time, hearing herself described in glowing posthumous terms. She gave extra bits of cake to people who said nice things, and was particularly overwhelmed to meet a couple from *EastEnders*, who appeared to have gatecrashed.

Meanwhile Stefan carried off the whole event extremely well, and looked fabulous in black. He told the Archbishop of Canterbury (another fan of 'Up the Duff') that he would never grieve in a morbid way for Belinda, because in a very real sense she was still with him; he assured his guests in general that, much as they might have admired Belinda, she was in fact twice the person they knew. And then, when everyone had gone home, they sat together, all three, on the sofa and watched *The Return of Martin Guerre*, laughing hysterically.

Stefan never mentioned Malmö again. He made a little bonfire of his moose-hat and his books of English idiom, then took Belinda and Linda on a tour of Kent in the Ferrari, revisiting the scenes of his childhood. Birgit offered to nurse the baby when it was born, but the Johanssons declined. Somehow it did not seem entirely fitting to have her back in the house, despite the good deed she had done them. Anyone who could misjudge Ingrid so badly, or call herself Anni-Frid for the purpose of disguise when she looked like a Smurf, might be more trouble than she was worth. Besides, it was time for the Johanssons to cope alone with their domestic affairs, without outside help. Surely three jobless, officially dead people ought to be able to manage with one little baby? Especially three jobless, officially dead people whose lives could now never be extricated from one another's, as long as they all still lived.

Their friends were relatively content, too. Viv ditched the ghastly Dermot, but not before getting him to find Jago a better job. Maggie decided Stefan was a bit too weird for her tastes, removed his picture from her fairy-light frame, and settled at last for the wholehearted devotions of Leon. Her experience with Noel had taught her many things, but mainly it taught her to marvel at what a nice chap Leon was. Sometimes their divergence of interests caused a problem, as when they argued whether Zola was better known as a footballer or a novelist, and Leon got confused thinking that he did both. Or as when Maggie bought him a modern classic American novel called *The Sportswriter* and Leon chucked it away in disgust because it was so unclear how the protagonist filed his copy. 'Does he have a laptop or what?' he asked, quite reasonably. Six months into their relationship, however, Leon discovered independently that Rembrandt was a rather good painter as well as a toothpaste, which brought him closer to his beloved, in a small but important way.

Professionally, things were pretty straightforward. Tanner did not prosper long at the *Effort* but was picked up, of course, by the *Telegraph*. Jago, in his new job as deputy editor of the *Effort*, re-employed Leon to 'ghost' Jericho Jones's weekly column, which led to a commission to ghost his autobiography too. Maggie's success in *Three Sisters* was marred only by the subsequent approach from the Royal Shakespeare Company – the offer of a role in *The Comedy of Errors*, which she was obliged to refuse on emotional grounds, because of all the twins.

Meanwhile Viv started making curtains as a business, and Mrs Holdsworth (what a dark horse) wrote books. She sent a copy of the first one – *I Am a Vacuum Cleaner* – to her ex-employers, who were very impressed. Mrs Holdsworth turned out to have a robust style of writing and a gritty carpet's-eye view of the world, which elicited comparisons universally with Irvine Welsh.

Linda found it hard to put her feet up, so the others allowed her to do the majority of stuff around the house. As Stefan explained from his rudimentary genetic knowledge, Linda was predisposed to housework while he and Belinda were predisposed to admiring it and enjoying its benefits. Belinda finally admitted that she loathed fish, which caused less consternation than she had feared. In fact, the Burial of the Fish Kettle was a stupendous moment, which they decided to mark annually with songs and a maypole. It turned out that Stefan didn't like fish much either. In Sweden, fish had been the bane of his life for twenty years.

Against this background of domestic harmony, Belinda and Linda sometimes discussed doubles literature and professed themselves amazed by the amounts of contention and murder to be found there – so much mutual turfing of rivals out of the nest. So much winner-takes-it-all; so much uncomplicated 'him or me'.

'Written by men,' Linda surmised, controversially. 'They are so insecure, aren't they? I mean, the life-or-death tussle on the loft-ladder – who needs it?'

As for Belinda, she continued to dream about the washing-machine for a while, but it was like the last few revolves of the drum after the spin has finished. Finally there was the faintest of clicks and the cycle was over, the door lock was released.

Every day, she woke up in a house with Stefan and Linda – and she loved it. Her days as a Super Trouper were over. She had finally discovered the answer to the problem of work and life, which was to give up the former and share the latter with as many people as possible.

Neville was back, of course, but this was a good thing. Because turning her attention fully to her furry friend, she discovered that she had in fact been pregnant since Christmas. Los Rodentos had been a cunning biological disguise for foetal gestation! Within three months of the death of Ingrid, the household welcomed identical twin boys, whom they named Benny and Björn without a moment's hesitation.

No one was more surprised than Belinda. She was astonished. All that time she'd been imagining spotlights and spangles and adoring crowds, and it was not acrobatic rats at all.

It was Abba.